WILLIAM MANN

The Rancher

For the Blackfeet and Lakota peoples.
In memory of what was taken, and in honor of what survived.

"I wish it to be remembered that I was the
last man of my tribe to surrender my rifle."

— Sitting Bull, Fort Buford, 1881

Contents

Author's Note

The Rancher is a work of fiction. Elias Harlan never existed. But the winter that nearly killed him did. The people he lived among did. The dispossession he witnessed did.

The Starvation Winter of 1883-84 killed approximately one quarter of the Blackfeet people on the Montana reservation. It was not a natural disaster. It was the predictable result of deliberate policy, the destruction of the buffalo, the cutting of promised rations, the confinement of a people who had no other means of survival.

These are documented historical facts. They are not comfortable facts. But they are true, and they matter.

Elias's role in this novel is not to be a savior. It is to see clearly, and to write down what he sees. That act, witnessing and recording truth, is the novel's central argument. Memory is not passive. In the face of erasure, remembering is resistance.

The Blackfeet Nation endures. The Lakota nations endure. Their descendants are still here, still fighting for sovereignty, still refusing to sell the Black Hills. The historical notes and sources in the appendix are offered for readers who want to follow this story beyond the final page.

This novel is my attempt, imperfect as it is, to contribute to the work of honest remembering.

William Mann, 2026

1

Dawn

Dawn broke cold over the hills, gray light sliding across the frozen lake. It brought no warmth. A woman pressed her hand to the bottom of an empty parfleche. The horses stood close, ribs sharp, breath hanging white. Across the camp, the men readied their thin ponies. There was nothing left to say.

Makóyi's hands were stiff with the cold, the scars across his knuckles pale in the gray light. He stirred the coals with a short stick, coaxing a little heat from the night's ashes. The fire breathed once, then settled back into smoke. Frost clung to the lodge poles behind him.

A pony stamped in the snow. Makóyi looked up.

The young men were tightening their cinches, pulling blankets from the backs of thin ponies, checking the fletching on their arrows. The only sound was the shifting of hooves in the frozen dirt.

Makóyi watched them for a long moment, the stick still in his hand. He had ridden out like that once, before the winters grew harder, before the game grew scarce. Now he only watched, knowing what waited beyond the hills and what the young men carried on their shoulders. The fire cracked softly behind him. He turned back to it, though his eyes lingered on the warriors as they gathered in the half-light.

Two winters past, the buffalo had still come in ragged herds, enough for a few good hunts if the snow held off. Then the white hide hunters arrived in greater numbers, shooting from wagons, stripping robes, leaving carcasses to rot under the sun. The agents at the fort spoke of rations, flour, beef, coffee, but the wagons came late, or not at all. The meat rotten when it arrived at all. Last winter the cough had taken Makóyi's sister first, then her youngest boy, their bodies wasting like the ponies. Makóyi had held him until the breathing stopped, then carried him out to the burial scaffolds where the wind took the scent.

The camp had shrunk since then. Fewer lodges stood against the wind, fewer children ran between them. The women stretched the pemmican farther. The ponies grew thinner still, their coats dull. Raids had become the only way to bring in horses, trade for blankets, knives, whatever the traders would give. Horses meant movement, meat if luck turned, life for the children. The young men rode for honor once; now they rode for the camp.

Nitááhkii, his nephew, barely past his first raid, approached, leading a gray pony with a wolf pelt draped over its withers. The boy's face was painted with red ochre lines for speed and protection, his hair braided tight. "Uncle," he said softly, voice low so the women would not hear worry in it. "Will you speak a word for us?"

Makóyi rose slowly, joints protesting the cold. He took a pinch of sweetgrass from the pouch at his belt, held it to the coals until it smoldered. The smoke curled thin and sweet, carrying the prayer upward. He waved it over the pony, then over Nitááhkii, murmuring to Naatosi, the Sun, who watched all things. "Naatosi sees the thin bellies, the empty parfleches. Give these young ones the wolf's cunning. Let them bring back what the camp needs. Let them return whole."

Nitááhkii touched his forehead in thanks, then mounted. The others gathered, five in all, faces painted, blankets wrapped against the wind. One carried a rifle traded years ago, another a lance with eagle feathers tied near the tip. They moved quietly, no songs today. The women watched from lodge doors, children clinging to skirts. One young wife pressed a small bundle of dried meat into her husband's hand; he nodded once, then turned his pony south.

Makóyi stood until the riders were small against the horizon, shadows swallowed by the gray. His wife, Ísstaakii, came to stand beside him. Her hands were rough from tanning, her eyes lined from the same hard winters. She slipped her fingers into his.

"They will bring horses," she said finally. Not a question. A hope spoken aloud.

Makóyi felt the old scar on his knuckles throb. He stared at the coals, watching them wink out one by one.

"The parfleche stays empty," he said.

She nodded once. No need for more.

Ísstaakii's fingers tightened in his, cold against scarred skin.

The wind rose, rattling the lodge poles like bones. He stood a moment longer, watching the gray horizon where the young men had vanished, then ducked into the lodge.

* * *

Far to the south, under that same gray sky, Elias Harlan woke before first light, the cabin cold as a grave. He lay still for a moment, listening to the quiet. No cough from the next room, no soft breathing beside him. Only the wind under the eaves and the faint creak of timbers settling.

He rose, pulled on boots stiff with frost, and lit the lamp. The flame flickered yellow across the rough walls, catching on the few things left: a tin plate, a worn Bible, Clara's shawl draped over the chair like she might step back through the door any minute. Three months since the consumption took her. Three months of nights like this.

He stepped outside. The prairie stretched flat and gray under the coming dawn, corrals empty except for the last string of horses, eight good ones he'd raised from foals. He'd planned to drive them to Fort Benton, next week, sell enough to buy seed and a new plow. Clara had always liked the idea of a garden come spring.

Scout waited by the door, tail low, ears up. The dog, her dog, had been Clara's shadow since they'd claimed this land four years back. A scrappy cur mix, brown and white, with a bark that carried half a mile. She'd found him half-starved near the river, nursed him back, and named him for the way he scouted ahead on walks. When the cough started, Scout never left her side. Curled at the foot of the bed, head on paws, watching her waste away. Nights Elias came in from the corrals, he'd find the dog pressed against her, as if his warmth could hold back the fever.

Clara had lingered through the fall. The cough turned wet, then bloody. She'd smile through it, say the dog kept her company when Elias was out trading. "He's my guard," she'd whisper, fingers in Scout's fur. "Won't let anything get me." Elias had ridden for the doctor once, twenty miles in rain, but the man only shook his head. "Consumption. Nothing to do but wait."

She went quiet at the end, eyes on the window where the prairie met sky. Scout lay beside her until the breathing stopped. Elias buried her under the cottonwood by the creek, the one she'd liked for shade. He carved her name on a board, simple: Clara Harlan, 1852–1883. Scout stayed at the grave all night, whining low. Elias had to carry him back to the cabin.

Now the dog followed him everywhere. Ate what Elias ate, slept by the fire, watched the horizon like he expected her to walk back over it. Elias talked to him sometimes, low words about the horses, the weather, how the claim felt too big without her. Scout listened, head tilted, as if he understood.

Elias checked the corrals, fed the horses the last of the hay. Scout trotted ahead, sniffing the fence line. Elias watched him, chest tight. The dog was all that remained of her, warm, alive, loyal.

He saddled his horse, packed a bedroll in case he'd be gone overnight. Scout bounded ahead, but Elias stopped him. "Stay. Watch the ranch, boy."

Scout sat at the cabin door, tail thumping once.

He returned at dusk, smoke from the chimney thin and wrong. No bark greeted him. The corrals stood open, gates swung wide. Horses gone, all but one lame mare in the far pen. Tracks in the snow: unshod ponies, heading north.

Scout lay near the corral fence, skull caved where they'd struck him. The dog had fought. Blood on his muzzle, claw marks in the frozen dirt where he'd charged. His body was cold, stiff. They'd killed him and kept moving.

Elias knelt, hand on the rough fur. Scout's eyes were half-open, fixed on nothing. He'd died defending the place, just like Elias had told him to.

Inside, the cabin was rifled: blankets gone, tin cups, the sack of coffee. But the silence was the real theft. No bark. No tail thump when the door opened. Just empty rooms and the cold.

Elias came back out and stood over the dog for a long moment. Then he lifted the body, lighter than he expected, all bone and loyalty, and carried it to the cottonwood. He dug beside Clara's grave with numb hands, the shovel scraping frozen ground. When the hole was deep enough, he wrapped Scout in her shawl and laid him down. The dog had been hers. He belonged here.

No words. Just the wind and the scrape of dirt filling the grave.

He went back to the cabin, packed what he could: bedroll, ammunition, jerky, canteen. Loaded the lame mare with light gear, she'd follow slow. At dawn, he'd track north, follow the prints into the hills.

The men who did this would pay. They'd taken his livelihood. His future. And Clara's dog, the last piece of her that was warm and alive.

He blew out the lamp. In the dark, the wind carried nothing. Only silence. Empty corrals. Two graves under the cottonwood.

2

Clara

He had met her in Philadelphia.

That was not the kind of thing Elias Harlan told people, because people in Montana Territory did not want to hear about Philadelphia. They wanted to hear about the land, the cattle, the winters. Not the city. Not a stable hand from Ohio who'd ridden east looking for work and found himself mucking stalls for a man named Aldridge whose daughter had opinions about everything.

She had opinions about horses first. That was how he knew she was different.

Most of the women who came through Aldridge's stables treated the horses the way they treated furniture, things to be admired from a distance and occasionally used. Clara walked straight to the nearest stall, held out her hand without hesitation, and let the mare sniff her for a full minute before she tried to touch her. Then she scratched the mare's jaw in exactly the right place, and the mare leaned into it like she'd been waiting all day.

Elias watched from across the aisle, pitchfork in his hands.

She was not beautiful the way women in Aldridge's world were supposed to be beautiful. She was small and dark-haired, with ink on her fingers and a habit of squinting when she was thinking, which was most of the time. She wore her hair pinned up in a way that suggested she'd done it herself and didn't especially care if it stayed. When she laughed, she laughed too loudly for her father's parlor, and she knew it. But she laughed anyway.

Elias was twenty-six years old and had never met anyone like her.

He asked her to walk with him three weeks later. She said yes before he finished the sentence.

Her father, William Aldridge, did not approve. Not of Elias specifically, though a stable hand from Ohio was not what the man had in mind for his daughter, but of the whole direction Clara's life kept moving in. She read too much. She argued with his business associates. She had notions about going somewhere, doing something, being something other than a wife in a drawing room.

And then there was the other thing. The thing that had settled over the Aldridge house like a weather system that never quite passed.

Clara could not have children.

The doctors had told her gently, in that careful tone people use when they know the news will undo someone. She told Elias before he asked her to marry him, sitting with her hands folded in her lap, her voice steady from the long work of learning how to speak of it.

He had said it didn't matter.

She had looked at him then and said, "It matters to my father."

She was right. Aldridge wanted grandchildren. He wanted the continuation of something. A name, a line, a legacy. Clara had failed at the one thing daughters were supposed to provide, and no amount of reading, arguing, or opinions about horses changed that. She felt it at every dinner. In every long silence after she and Elias announced their engagement. In the way her father shook Elias's hand at the wedding as though handing over damaged goods.

She never said any of this plainly. Elias understood it from the way she breathed easier once they were west of the Mississippi.

They settled in Montana Territory in the spring of 1881. Elias broke the land, built the cabin, and ran the horses. Clara planted things. A kitchen garden, a row of cottonwoods along the creek, a life that was hers. She wrote long letters to a cousin back east who always answered, and she read whatever she could find, and she learned the land the way she'd learned horses, by watching, by listening, by wanting to understand what it asked of her.

In the second summer, Dooley rode in with a half-starved pup in his saddlebag. Found it by the river, couldn't keep it. Elias said no. Clara said yes.

She called him Scout for the way he ranged ahead and returned, always making sure the world was safe before she stepped into it.

* * *

He was digging again.

Elias heard the sound from the corral, that particular combination of excited panting and wet dirt flying, and he knew before he rounded the corner of the cabin what he would find.

Scout had located the soft ground beside the kitchen garden and was working it with the focused dedication of an animal who had found his life's calling. He was muddy from nose to tail, spectacular in his filth, entirely satisfied with himself.

"Scout," Elias said it flat and hard, the way you said a dog's name when you meant business.

Scout's head snapped up. Mud flew. His ears, floppy, oversized, never quite in proportion to the rest of him, bounced with the motion. He looked at Elias with an expression of complete seriousness, as though he had been engaged in important work and resented the interruption, which would have been more convincing if he had not been covered head to toe in wet black earth.

Elias started toward him.

Scout bolted.

Not away, toward the cabin door, which was the wrong direction entirely, where Clara was standing in the doorway with her arms crossed and her mouth doing the thing it did when she was trying not to laugh.

"Don't you let him—" Elias said.

Scout hit the step at full speed, skidded, recovered, and launched himself at Clara with the confidence of an animal who had never once been turned away.

She caught him. Somehow. Both arms full of muddy ecstatic dog, his paws on her shoulders, his tongue on her cheek, mud transferring to her dress in enthusiastic quantities.

"Clara—"

She was laughing now, the too-loud laugh, her face turned away from the worst of the licking. "Leave him be," she said. "I'll clean him up."

"You always say that."

"And I always do." She pulled Scout back enough to look at him, his muddy face level with hers, his tail going hard enough to spray mud on the doorframe. She said his name softly, the way she said it, like a question she already knew the answer to. Scout stopped thrashing and looked at her with sudden gravity, as if he understood that a shift in register had occurred.

"Look at you," she said. *Look at you.*

Like it was the best thing she'd seen all week.

Elias stood in the yard, hands on his hips, trying to hold onto his irritation and losing. "You're going to spend an hour on that dog."

"Probably." She was already carrying Scout inside, one hand under his muddy chest, the other holding the door. "Put the kettle on when you come in."

She didn't look back.

Scout looked back. Once, over her shoulder, straight at Elias, tail still going.

Elias stood in the yard a moment longer.

Then he went in and put the kettle on.

* * *

That was Clara.

That was what the cabin meant when it was full. What it meant when the shawl hung over the chair and the lamp burned in the window and the dog's nails clicked on the floorboards.

What it meant before the cough started.

Elias did not think about Philadelphia anymore. Did not think about Aldridge and his silence and his careful handshake. Did not think about the thing Clara could not give her father, the grandchildren that never came, the line that would not continue.

He only thought about the mud on the doorframe that he'd never quite scraped clean.

And the way she'd said, *look at you* like it was the best thing she'd seen all week.

3

Nitááhkii

They rode south at first light, five men on thin ponies, breath hanging white in the cold. Nitááhkii felt the weight of Makóyi's blessing still on him. The sweetgrass smoke, the words about empty bellies, and the wolf's cunning. He gripped the pony's mane tighter, the wolf pelt shifting beneath him.

He wanted to bring something back. Something that mattered.

The land stretched gray and endless, broken only by low hills and frozen creeks. They rode in silence, saving breath, watching the horizon. Nitááhkii studied the older warriors, how they sat their ponies, how their eyes moved across the land, reading tracks and wind. He wanted to move like that. Certain. Unafraid.

He thought of his mother, of the winter she died, of Makóyi taking him in after. He thought of the camp: the empty parfleches, the children's coughs, the ponies too weak to carry much weight. He thought of Makóyi's scarred hands, the way his uncle had looked at him this morning, not with words, but with a nod that said: *Come back whole.*

The wolf pelt warmed his legs. Cunning. Speed. Survival.

* * *

They saw the ranch at midday: smoke rising thin from a chimney, corrals visible against the flat land, horses moving inside the fence. Eight, maybe more. Good stock.

Nitááhkii's heart hammered against his ribs.

One of the men, Apiistoomska, the eldest, gestured with his chin. They spread out, moving low along a shallow draw. No songs. No shouts. Hunger had stripped the ceremony from it. This was work now, not honor.

Apiistoomska's voice came low: "Nitááhkii, the far corral. Cut the rope. Oksksin, watch the ridge. The rest, drive them north when the gates open."

Nitááhkii nodded. His hands were steady. He was ready.

* * *

They moved fast when the moment came.

Nitááhkii slid from his pony, knife in hand, and ran to the corral fence. The rope was thick, stiff with frost. He sawed through it, the fibers parting one by one. The gate swung open. Horses snorted, stamped, ready to bolt.

He felt it then, the surge of pride, the thrill of doing what needed to be done. He was part of something. He was helping the camp. He was proving himself.

He mounted his pony again, ready to bring the horses north.

* * *

Then the dog came.

It appeared from nowhere. A brown and white blur, barking,

charging straight at the horses. Nitááhkii's pony shied hard, rearing. The dog planted itself between the horses and the open gate, teeth bared, hackles up. Not wild. Not mad. Just doing what it knew.

Nitááhkii pulled his pony up hard, watching the dog for one suspended moment.

It was not attacking. It was defending.

He understood that. In his chest, in the place below words, he understood it completely. This animal knew nothing of treaties or hunger or children with hollow eyes. It knew only that something belonging to its people was being taken, and it would stand against that taking with everything it had.

Just like us, Nitááhkii thought. *Exactly like us.*

He tried to drive around it. Kicked his pony left, then right. The dog countered both moves, fast and fearless, cutting back to block the horses.

Nitááhkii pulled up. Looked at the dog. The dog looked back.

"Let them go, little brother," he said quietly. "We both go home."

The dog's hackles rose. A low sound came from deep in its chest.

Then it lunged.

His pony screamed, rearing. The dog leaped, teeth finding the pony's nose, and the world collapsed into noise and motion and blood.

He struck down hard with the heavy quirt, leather and wood, meant for driving horses.

The blow caught the dog across the skull.

A yelp.

Then silence.

The dog crumpled, legs folding slowly, like something leaving it. Blood pooled dark on the frozen ground. Its eyes stayed open. Still defending. Still certain it was right.

Nitááhkii sat motionless on his dancing pony, the quirt hanging from his hand.

Just like us.

Apiistoomska was already driving the horses from the corral. Nitááhkii kicked his pony forward, the blood on its muzzle bright against the white breath.

* * *

They rode hard, the stolen horses streaming ahead. Nitááhkii kept glancing at the wound on his pony's nose, a clean slash, not deep, but bleeding. He kept hearing the dog's last sound. The yelp. The silence after.

He didn't tell the others.

He didn't know how to put the feeling into words.

The land opened up before them, gray and vast. The cold bit through his blanket. The wolf pelt no longer felt warm.

* * *

The camp saw them coming from a distance.

Women gathered at the edge, children clinging to skirts. When the men drove the horses into the open space near the lodges, relief rippled through the camp like wind through grass. Horses meant life. Horses meant trade. Horses meant the children might eat.

One woman touched the nearest horse's flank, whispered thanks. Another called to her husband, tears on her lined face. The children stared wide-eyed, pointing.

Nitááhkii dismounted, legs stiff from the cold and the ride. His pony stood with its head low, blood dried black on its nose.

Makóyi approached slowly, eyes moving over the horses, then to Nitááhkii's pony. He saw the wound. His gaze lifted to Nitááhkii's face.

He said nothing.

Nitááhkii looked away.

Makóyi nodded once, then turned to help with the horses.

* * *

That night, Nitááhkii sat by the fire in Makóyi's lodge, the flames casting shadows on the hide walls. Ísstaakii had given him soup, thin, but warm. He drank it slowly.

Makóyi sat across from him, tending the fire with the same short stick from that morning. The camp outside was louder than it had been in weeks. Voices, movement, the sound of children playing near the new horses.

Makóyi spoke without looking up. "Your pony fought well."

Nitááhkii stared into the fire. "It was just a dog."

"Yes."

Silence stretched between them. The fire cracked.

"But you will remember it," Makóyi said finally.

Nitááhkii nodded. He would.

Makóyi set the stick aside. "That is what it means to ride for the camp. You bring back what we need. And you carry what it cost."

Nitááhkii felt something in his chest loosen, just slightly. Not relief. Not forgiveness. Just understanding.

He was older now. Not in a proud way. In a way that carried weight, the kind that gathers and stays.

Outside, the wind rose. The lodge poles creaked. The camp settled into sleep, bellies a little less empty, hope a little less thin.

But Nitááhkii lay awake, staring at the smoke hole, seeing the dog's eyes in the darkness.

Just a dog.

But he would remember.

4

Camp Life

Morning came slow over the camp, pale light catching on the frost that rimed the lodge poles. Smoke drifted thin from a few fires, not enough to warm much, just enough to keep the cold from settling too deep in the bones. Women moved between the lodges with scraped hides over their arms, children trailing behind them, breath white in the air. The new horses stood in a gaunt cluster near the edge of camp, heads low, steam rising from their backs.

Makóyi walked among them, hand on a flank here, a muzzle there, feeling the ribs under the winter coats. Good horses. Not enough to change the road ahead, but enough to buy time. Enough to keep the camp moving when the snow softened.

Ksisstaki spotted him from across the trampled snow and hurried over, a pot of water balanced against her hip. She was young, not yet married, her braids tied with scraps of red cloth. She had a way of watching things, people, horses, the direction of smoke, that made her seem older than her years. Her smile came quick, even in the cold.

"You saw them come in last night," she said. "The whole camp heard the horses."

Makóyi nodded. "They rode well."

She glanced toward Nitááhkii's lodge, where the boy still slept. "He rode well," she said, softer.

Makóyi didn't answer. He watched the steam rise from the horses, watched the children edging closer, curious and hungry. The camp felt different this morning, lighter in some places, heavier in others. That was the way of raids. Something always came back. Something always stayed behind.

Ksisstaki shifted the pot in her hands. "The elders say we should give thanks today," she said. "For the horses. For the riders returning whole."

Makóyi looked out over the camp, the thin smoke, the frost, the faces lined by too many hard winters. "Yes," he said. "Give thanks."

But his eyes lingered on Nitááhkii's lodge, and on the pony with the dried blood on its nose.

Something had come back with the boy.

Something he hadn't spoken of yet.

* * *

The camp woke slowly. Women scraped hides outside their lodges, breath white in the cold. Children circled the new horses, careful not to spook them. One boy reached out to touch a gray mare's flank, then pulled back, grinning.

Makóyi stirred the coals, watching. The horses were strong. They'd trade two for blankets at the fort, another for flour if the agent would deal. The rest they'd keep, breeding stock, maybe, or meat if the winter turned harder.

Ísstaakii came out with a bowl of thin soup and handed it to him without speaking. He drank. It was warm. That was enough.

Across the camp, Nitááhkii worked on his pony's wound, cleaning it with snow. The boy hadn't said much since they'd returned yesterday.

Hadn't looked up when the camp celebrated. Just tended his pony, shoulders carrying something new.

Makóyi flexed his hands, feeling the old ache in the knuckles. The scar there, pale, raised, was from a knife fight years back, when the buffalo still came in numbers. A Crow raider had come at him in the dark. Makóyi had been faster. The Crow hadn't gotten up.

He'd been proud then. Young. Thought scars made you a man.

Now he just thought they made you old.

His sister had laughed at him once, touching that scar. "You'll collect these," she'd said. "One for every season you survive." She'd been right. But she hadn't collected enough of her own.

* * *

Ksisstaki appeared at the edge of the fire circle, water skins slung over her shoulder. Quick-footed, quick-tongued. She set the skins down, eyes on Nitááhkii where he worked across the camp.

"The great raider tends his horse," she said, voice light with teasing.

Makóyi grunted. "He brought back horses. That's enough."

She looked at him sideways. "Uncle, did you ever bring back so many?"

"More."

"How many?"

"Enough to feed the camp."

She smiled. "And did your pony come back bleeding?"

Makóyi studied her. A smile met his lips before he turned away again. "All ponies bleed when they work."

She nodded, satisfied, then looked back at Nitááhkii. "He looks different."

"He is."

She waited for more, but Makóyi offered nothing. After a moment, she picked up the water skins and moved on, bare feet quick across the frozen ground.

* * *

Nitááhkii sat by his pony, working carefully. The gash on the pony's nose had stopped bleeding but looked angry. He didn't look up when the children passed. Didn't call out to the other young men when they gathered to divide the horses.

Makóyi watched from across the camp.

Ísstaakii saw it too. "He will carry that dog a long time," she said quietly.

"Yes."

"Was it necessary?"

"The dog was necessary. The pony lived. That's all."

She nodded, but her eyes stayed on Nitááhkii. "He's young to carry such things."

"We all carry what we must."

The wind picked up, rattling the lodge poles. Makóyi turned back to the fire. The coals were dying. He added a few sticks, watched the flames catch.

An old woman passed, carrying a hide bundle. She nodded to him. He nodded back. No words. She'd lost her son to the cough last winter. Her daughter the winter before. She still scraped hides, still tended fires, still moved through the camp like the wind, quiet, persistent, unstoppable.

That was survival. Not glory. Just the daily work of staying alive.

* * *

Ksisstaki returned at midday, something bundled in her arms. She approached Makóyi's fire, eyes bright.

"Uncle, look."

She opened the bundle. A pup. Dark along the spine, tawny at the chest, ribs showing under thin fur. It whimpered once, then pressed against her warmth.

"Where?" Makóyi asked.

"By the old lodge poles. There was a litter, but the others…" She didn't finish.

Makóyi looked at the pup. It was starving. They all were. "It will take food we don't have."

"It's small. It won't eat much."

"It will eat."

She held the pup closer. "Please, Uncle. I'll share my portion."

Makóyi sighed. Looked at Ísstaakii. She said nothing, but her mouth softened slightly.

"Keep it warm," he said finally. "If it lives, we'll see."

Ksisstaki's face lit. She turned and ran over to show Nitááhkii, who was still working on his pony across the camp. He glanced at her, at the pup, then back to his work.

But Makóyi saw the flicker in the boy's eyes.

Just a dog.

* * *

The afternoon passed in the rhythm of camp life. Women stretched hides. Men checked the new horses, discussed which to trade, which to keep. Children played near the fires, their laughter thin but real.

Ksisstaki kept the pup tucked inside her blanket, feeding it drops of broth from her own bowl. The pup's eyes were barely open, but it lapped at the liquid, swallowing weakly.

Nitááhkii watched her from across the camp. Makóyi watched them both.

An elder approached, gray-haired, bent with age. He sat by Makóyi's fire without asking. That was his right.

"The horses are good," the old man said.

"Yes."

"The young men did well."

"They did what was needed."

The old man nodded. "But Nitááhkii carries something."

Makóyi poked the fire. "A man always carries something after a raid."

"This is different."

"Yes."

They sat in silence. The old man knew not to ask. Makóyi knew not to explain. Some things were carried alone.

After a while, the elder rose. "The camp is grateful," he said. Then he walked away, back bent, steps slow but steady.

* * *

That night, Makóyi sat by the fire, watching Ksisstaki curl the pup against her side in her sleeping robes. The pup's breathing was thin but steady. She stroked its head, whispering words Makóyi couldn't hear.

Nitááhkii sat across from him, staring into the flames.

"She'll try to save it," Makóyi said.

Nitááhkii said nothing.

"It won't make it through winter."

Still nothing.

Makóyi poked the fire with his short stick. "That depends on her."

Nitááhkii looked up then. Met his eyes. They understood each other well enough.

The wind rose outside, colder than before. The camp settled into sleep. Somewhere in the dark, a coyote called, the sound carrying across the frozen land.

Makóyi thought of the white man's ranch to the south. Of the tracks heading north. Of what would come when the man followed those tracks.

But that was tomorrow's problem.

Tonight, the camp had horses. The children had played. A girl was trying to save a pup.

Outside, the wind carried the scent of snow. Another storm coming. Another test.

Makóyi added one more stick to the fire, watched the flames rise, then banked the coals for the night.

He lay down beside Ísstaakii, her warmth a comfort against the cold. He closed his eyes.

But sleep came slowly.

In the darkness, he saw the tracks heading north. Saw the white man's ranch. Saw the empty corrals and the dog lying still.

He knew what came next.

5

The Storm

Elias rode north at first light, the lame mare trailing behind. The tracks were clear in the snow. Five ponies, unshod, moving fast. He followed them with his jaw set tight, the cold biting through his coat. Scout's grave was still fresh under the cottonwood. He could feel the weight of that dirt on his hands.

The land was open, empty. Nothing moved but the wind.

He kept riding.

By midmorning, the sky had gone darker, a hard gray that meant weather coming. Snow started to fall, thin flakes at first, drifting sideways. The tracks blurred at the edges. The lame mare stumbled once, caught herself, kept going.

Elias leaned forward in the saddle, eyes on the ground. He could still see the prints. Still see the direction. North, always north.

He rode harder.

* * *

The storm hit without warning.

Wind slammed into him, driving the snow sideways. The world

vanished in white. The tracks disappeared under fresh drifts. His horse tossed its head, fighting the gusts. The mare lagged behind, blowing hard.

Elias pulled up, blinking against the snow. He couldn't see ten feet. The cold cut through him like a blade.

He thought of Clara's last winter. The way the cold had settled in her chest, the way she'd tried to smile through it. He thought of Scout lying by the corral fence, blood frozen on his muzzle.

He looked north, but there was nothing there. Just the storm.

He sat in the saddle a long moment, snow piling on his coat, breath freezing in his beard. The horse shivered beneath him.

He knew what waited if he kept going.

He turned west.

* * *

The fort lay somewhere beyond the storm. Two days, maybe three. He'd been there once, a few years back. Soldiers, scouts, men who knew the tribes and the country. Men who might help. Or not. But it was a direction that didn't end with him frozen stiff in a drift.

He rode with his head down, reins stiff in his hands. The wind howled across the open land, carrying the smell of more snow.

Behind him, the ranch sat empty. Two graves under the cottonwood. A dog that had died doing what he'd been told.

Elias kept riding.

He wasn't done.

Just not this way.

Not today.

* * *

The storm reached the camp by late afternoon.

Makóyi saw it coming from the south, a wall of white moving across the prairie like smoke. He called to the women, who hurried to secure the lodge poles, weight them with stones, bring in what they could.

The wind hit hard. Snow drove sideways through the camp. The new horses huddled together in the lee of the lodges, heads down, tails to the wind.

Ksisstaki ducked into Makóyi's lodge, the pup tucked inside her blanket. Its eyes were barely open, but it was breathing. She curled by the fire, holding it close.

"It will die in this cold," Ísstaakii said quietly.

"Maybe," Ksisstaki said. "But not tonight."

Nitááhkii sat across the fire, watching the storm through the lodge opening. His pony was outside, tied with the others. The wound on its nose had scabbed over, but it still looked angry.

"Close the flap," Makóyi said.

Nitááhkii tied it shut. The wind screamed outside, rattling the poles.

They sat in silence. The fire crackled. The pup whimpered once, then settled.

Makóyi listened to the storm. Beneath the wind, he felt something else. Not a sign, not a warning, just a familiar pressure in the chest. He had known it before, in other winters, when men with rifles had ridden too close to their camps. Trouble had a way of moving through the world with its own kind of weather.

He looked at Nitááhkii. The boy wasn't looking at the fire anymore. His shoulders were tight, his eyes fixed on the flap.

"You feel it," Makóyi said.

Nitááhkii nodded once. "Someone's out there."

"Maybe," Makóyi said. "Or maybe it's only the storm making everything sound like footsteps."

Nitááhkii didn't answer.

Makóyi added, "If he's out there, this cold will slow him. It slows everyone."

Nitááhkii looked down at his hands. "The dog—"

"Was necessary," Makóyi said. "But a man who's lost something doesn't think about what's necessary."

Outside, the wind howled. The lodge poles creaked. Somewhere in the camp, a child cried, then quieted.

Ksisstaki held the pup closer. "Will he come?"

Makóyi shook his head. "Not tonight. No one rides in this."

He didn't say more. He didn't need to. Men who had been wronged, or believed they had, often came back. Not because of fate. Because that was how men were.

The fire burned low. Makóyi added a stick, watched the flames rise.

Tomorrow the storm would pass. Tomorrow, they would see what the world looked like.

Tonight, they waited.

6

The Bear

Winter carried warnings on the wind, and the horses caught them first.

A sharp whinny cut through the cold, close and urgent, the kind of sound animals make when something on the wind is wrong. Makóyi reined his pony and listened. Nitááhkii pulled up beside him, silent. The ridge ahead held its breath.

Makóyi turned his pony toward the treeline and climbed slowly, keeping to the shadows. At the top, he saw the creek below: a man on foot, two horses at the water's edge. And beyond him, rising from the willows.

The bear was already up on its hind legs.

Makóyi pulled his rifle.

The man's horse saw the bear and bolted, the second stumbling after. The man spun, reached for his saddle, gone. The bear dropped to all fours.

The man ran.

Makóyi shot.

The bear lurched, roared, turned. He levered and fired again. The bear went down hard, skidding through the snow before it lay still.

* * *

He rode down the ridge. Nitááhkii followed.

The man stood catching his breath, not shaking, just spent from the run. He stared at the bear, then at Makóyi.

Makóyi nudged the carcass with his rifle barrel. Dead.

He looked at the man. "You run from grizzly," he said. "Bear is always faster."

The man nodded once, still breathing hard. "I know." A beat. "You dropped it clean."

Makóyi studied him. A rancher, trail-worn, alone. He gestured to Nitááhkii and said in Blackfoot, "Find his horses." Nitááhkii rode off without a word.

Makóyi knelt by the bear and drew his knife.

The man watched him work. Silent at first. Then, not looking at Makóyi, he said, "Didn't expect anyone out here."

Makóyi didn't look up. "Storm drove us south."

A moment passed.

The man shifted his weight. "Most folks would've let it take me."

Makóyi made his cut, clean and long. "Most folks haven't seen what a bear leaves behind."

He worked in silence. The man held his place, not interfering, not wandering. He simply stood back and let Makóyi work.

After a time, the man said, "Elias Harlan. Sun River."

Makóyi wiped his blade. "Makóyi."

Elias nodded. Nothing more.

When Makóyi had made the first cuts, he looked up. "You take half. I take half."

Harlan frowned. "I didn't kill it."

"You brought it to this place. I killed it. We share." Makóyi returned to his work. "That is fair."

Harlan crouched across from him and helped without being asked, holding the hide back, steadying the meat. He knew what he was doing.

They worked.

* * *

Cold settled around them. The creek moved under its ice, slow and quiet.

Hoofbeats behind them. Nitááhkii returned leading two horses, a riding horse and a lame mare, both skittish, both blowing hard. He tied them to a low branch and dismounted.

Makóyi saw the man's eyes go to Nitááhkii's pony.

To the nose.

The wound had scabbed over dark, the line of it clean and straight across the bridge.

Harlan looked at it the way a man looks at something that answers a question he hadn't finished asking yet.

"Your pony," he said. "What happened there?"

Nitááhkii glanced at Makóyi.

Makóyi set down his knife. "Wolf. Three nights past. The pony fought back."

Harlan studied the wound a moment longer. "Wolves usually go for the legs to bring an animal down."

"Must have spooked him." Makóyi picked up his knife. "Wolves spook just like men."

Harlan nodded. He didn't say anything else about it.

They finished wrapping the meat in hides Makóyi provided. They tied half the meat behind Harlan's saddle. Makóyi tied his own portion to his.

He mounted. Nitááhkii mounted.

"You ride to the fort," Makóyi said.

Harlan looked up. "Yes."

"The soldiers there do not help my people."

"I know."

Makóyi held his gaze. He thought of the wound on Nitááhkii's pony.

"You have bear meat to dry," Makóyi said. "The tale will stay fresh. The meat will not."

Harlan understood what lay beneath the words.

"A few days," he said.

Makóyi nodded once.

* * *

Elias stood by his horses and watched them go. Two figures moving north without hurry, shrinking against the white land until they were only shapes, and then not even that.

His thoughts kept returning to that wound. The placement. A dog would go for the nose if it were defending something. A corral. A home.

His home.

The thought settled cold in his chest, but he pushed it down.

He mounted. The sun was still high enough. He could make ten miles before dark, maybe more. The fort was two days out.

He sat in the saddle and didn't move.

The bear meat was tied behind him. That was true enough. A man riding with fresh meat in winter needed to make camp, start a fire, and do it right.

He turned his horse east, toward a stand of cottonwoods where the wind would break.

But the wound on that pony stayed with him. The way the young man had looked at the older one before answering.

The way the older one had looked back.
A wolf, he'd said.
Elias rode slowly.
He didn't believe it.
But he'd said a few days.
And he meant it.

* * *

Nitááhkii rode beside Makóyi, silent.

"That was the rancher," Nitááhkii said quietly. "The one with the dog."

Makóyi nodded. A rancher missing horses in winter had only one place to go.

"We could have let the bear kill him."

"Yes."

"No one would have known. The soldiers would find him in the spring. Another dead white man in the cold."

Makóyi wrapped the remaining meat. "Yes."

Nitááhkii was quiet for a moment. Then: "Why did you shoot the bear?"

Makóyi tied the hide bundle to his saddle. "Because a man was about to die, and we need the meat."

"He will bring soldiers. He knows it was us. He saw the wound on my pony."

"He suspects. He does not know."

"He will tell them anyway."

"Maybe. Maybe not."

Nitááhkii's pony moved close to Makóyi's. "Uncle, I do not understand. That man, his dog died because of me. His horses are in our camp. And you save his life?"

Makóyi rode in silence for a time. Snow muffled the ponies' steps. The sky was pale and cold.

"The raid was for horses," Makóyi said finally. "Not for killing. The dog attacked you. Your pony would have died. That was necessary."

"And the man?"

"The man was walking. He did nothing to us. The bear would have killed him, and we would have watched." Makóyi looked at his nephew. "I have watched too many people die. I will not stand by and watch another when I can stop it."

"Even if he is white? Even if he brings trouble?"

"Even then."

"The elders say the whites take everything. They kill the buffalo, break their promises, and let us starve. Why should we save one of them?"

Makóyi reined across Nitááhkii's path, stopping them both. He waited until the boy looked up.

"Because we are not them," Makóyi said. His voice was harder now. "We do not become what we hate."

Nitááhkii opened his mouth.

"Enough," Makóyi said. "What is done is done."

* * *

They rode north through the snow. Neither spoke again until camp came into view.

Ísstaakii stood outside their lodge, scraping a hide. She looked up, saw the bundles of meat, and came forward.

"Bear?" she asked.

"Yes." Makóyi dismounted and set the meat down.

She knelt, unwrapped the hide, and examined the cuts. Good meat. But not enough. Not for a whole bear.

She looked up. "Where is the rest?"

"I gave half to a white man."

Her hands stilled. "You gave our meat to a white man?"

"A grizzly attacked him. I shot the bear. We shared it."

"We need this meat. The camp needs it."

"The camp has it. Half a bear will feed many."

Ísstaakii stood, wiping her hands on her dress. Her face was tight. "And the white man? Where was he going?"

"West. To the fort."

"He will tell the soldiers he saw us."

"I asked him not to."

"And you believe he will listen?"

Makóyi said nothing.

She looked at Nitááhkii, then back at Makóyi. "Mercy is a warm thing," she said. "Winter is not."

She picked up the meat and carried it toward the lodge.

* * *

Makóyi watched her go. She was right. He knew she was right.

But he could not have stood there and watched the bear kill the man. Even knowing who he was. Even knowing what might come.

That night, Makóyi sat by the fire, tending the coals. The camp was quiet. Children slept. The new horses stood in a line near the lodges, dark shapes in the night.

Ísstaakii lay in their robes, back to him. Angry still. Or worried. Maybe both.

Nitááhkii sat across the fire, whittling a stick, silent.

Makóyi stared into the flames. He thought of the white man's face when he saw the wound on Nitááhkii's pony. The way his eyes had narrowed. He had not believed the story about the wolf.

The man knew. Or suspected. And soon he would know for certain.

Makóyi had asked him to wait. To let the meat keep him for a few days before he rode to the soldiers. But would he honor that? Would he remember that Makóyi had saved his life?

Or would he remember his dog, his horses, his losses?

Makóyi did not know.

He only knew their paths would cross again. The white man would come back. Maybe with soldiers. Maybe alone. But he would come.

And when he did, there would be no bear to decide things. Only men. And choices.

Makóyi added another stick to the fire. The flames rose, then settled.

Outside, the wind picked up. The lodge poles creaked. Somewhere in the distance, a coyote called.

Makóyi looked south, toward where the white man had ridden. Toward the fort. Toward whatever came next.

He had saved the man's life today.

He did not know if that was mercy or a mistake.

He only knew he could not have done otherwise.

The fire burned low. He banked the coals and lay down beside Ísstaakii. She did not turn toward him. He closed his eyes.

But sleep was slow to come.

In the darkness, he saw the white man's face. Saw the way he had looked at the wound on the pony. Saw the suspicion in his eyes.

Remembering was dangerous.

And the white man would remember.

7

The Fort

Four days later, Elias rode into Fort Shaw. The fort sat on a rise above the Sun River, its log walls dark against white fields. Elias had been here once before, three years back, trading horses with the quartermaster. He remembered the smell, wood smoke, manure, and something sour that never went away.

The flag hung limp in the cold. No wind.

He rode through the open gate. Two soldiers on watch looked up from their fire. One nodded. The other stared at the bundle tied to Elias's saddle, the bear meat, wrapped in tanned hide.

Blackfeet hide.

Elias dismounted at the hitching post outside the headquarters building. His legs were stiff. Three days in the saddle. The cold had settled into his bones.

Behind him, he heard voices. Low. Not trying to hide, but not speaking to him either.

"That hide is Blackfeet work."

"Where'd a rancher get that?"

"Killed 'em, maybe."

"Or trading with 'em."

"Either way, Captain'll want to know."

Elias tied his horse, pulled his coat tighter, and walked toward the door. He didn't look back. But he felt their eyes on him.

* * *

The headquarters building was warmer than outside, but not by much. A clerk sat at a desk near a small stove, writing in a ledger. He looked up when Elias entered.

"Help you?"

"Need to see the commanding officer."

"Captain Thornton's busy."

"It's about stolen horses. Blackfeet raid."

The clerk set down his pen. "Wait here."

He disappeared through a door at the back. Elias stood by the stove, holding his hands near the heat. The room smelled of ink and old paper.

The clerk returned. "Captain'll see you."

* * *

Captain Thornton's office was larger and better-heated. A map of Montana Territory hung on one wall, marked with forts, rivers, and shaded areas labeled "Blackfeet Range," "Assiniboine," "Gros Ventre." A rifle leaned in the corner. Papers covered the desk.

Thornton stood when Elias entered. Mid-forties, clean-shaven, uniform pressed despite the frontier cold. He extended a hand.

"Captain Charles Thornton. You are?"

"Elias Harlan. I have a ranch on the Sun River, about 40 miles west of here." "Sun River country." Thornton gestured to a chair. "Sit. What brings you to Fort Shaw?"

Elias sat. "Blackfeet raided my place four days ago. Took eight horses. Killed my dog."

Thornton leaned back, fingers steepled. "How many raiders?"

"Five. Maybe six."

"Which direction?"

Makóyi's face. The bear. *A few days is all he asked.*

"Tracks headed north," Elias said. "Unshod ponies."

"You follow them?"

"Started to. Storm hit. Lost the trail."

Thornton nodded. "Smart. A man alone against a Blackfeet raiding party rarely comes back." He pulled a sheet of paper from his desk and dipped a pen in ink. "Describe the horses."

Elias did. Thornton wrote it down, methodical, thorough. When Elias finished, Thornton set the pen aside.

"We'll get them back."

Elias felt something loosen in his chest. "What do you mean?"

"We patrol that region regularly. It's our responsibility to maintain order, protect settlers." Thornton's voice was calm, matter-of-fact. "The Blackfeet have been raiding more frequently this winter. Desperation, probably. Their rations haven't arrived on schedule."

"Can't you just—"

"We distribute what we're sent," Thornton said. "The Indian Bureau handles that. We handle security." He stood, walked to the map, and tapped a spot north of the Marias. "They're wintering somewhere in here. We'll find them."

"And my horses?"

"We'll recover what we can." Thornton turned back to him. "But more importantly, we'll make it clear that raiding white property has consequences. Can't let them think they can act with impunity."

Elias nodded slowly. "Listen, I just want my horses."

"Of course." Thornton smiled. "But we need to send a message. A show of force. Make them understand that the Army protects its settlers."

Something in the way he said it made Elias uneasy. "You're going to ride out there?"

"With a full patrol. Twenty men, maybe more. Enough to be... persuasive."

"I didn't—don't want—"

"Violence?" Thornton sat back down. "Neither do we, Mr. Harlan. But sometimes it's necessary. Last time we conducted operations against the Blackfeet in this region, we settled things quite decisively."

The word hung in the air. 'Decisively.'

Elias remembered.

* * *

January, 1870. Thirteen years ago. He'd read about it in a newspaper back east. One of those stories that stays with a man whether he wants it to or not.

Fort Shaw cavalry. Led by Colonel Eugene Baker. Two hundred soldiers. Rode out in winter to punish a Blackfeet band for killing a white trader.

They'd attacked the wrong band.

Heavy Runner's people. Peaceful. Camped on the Marias River. Many sick with smallpox. Heavy Runner had held up his safe-conduct paper, proof the government promised he'd be left alone.

They shot him anyway.

Then they shot everyone else.

One hundred seventy-three dead. Mostly women, children, and old men. The soldiers burned the lodges, took the horses, and left the survivors in thirty-below cold with no shelter.

The newspapers back East had called it a massacre. The Army called it a victory.

Elias looked at Thornton. "That was… a long time ago."

"Different commander," Thornton said. "But the principle stands. When we respond, we respond decisively. The Blackfeet respect strength. Nothing else."

Elias's throat felt tight. "Look, I just want my horses back."

"And you'll have them. But we'll do this properly. By the book." Thornton stood again, signaling the meeting was ending. "I'll organize a patrol. Should be ready to move in two days. You're welcome to ride with us, help identify your property."

"I…" Elias hesitated. "I'll think about it."

"Of course. You're tired. Long ride. The sutler can find you a bunk for the night." Thornton extended his hand again. "We'll take care of this, Mr. Harlan. That's what we're here for."

Elias shook his hand. It was firm, confident. The hand of a man who believed he was doing right.

Elias left the office, walked back through the outer room, and stepped into the cold.

His horse stood at the post, the dried bear meat tied to the saddle. The hide visible. Blackfeet work.

He thought of Makóyi. The way he'd saved him from the bear. The way he'd shared the meat. The way he'd asked, quietly, with dignity, for a few days. Just a few days.

Elias had waited. He'd kept his word.

But it didn't matter. Thornton had maps, scouts, and patrols. He'd find them soon enough. And Elias had given him the justification to look.

He stood there, breath steaming in the cold air, and felt the weight settle on him.

One hundred seventy-three dead. Women. Children. Smallpox victims shot in their beds.

'Decisively.'

Thornton hadn't said it outright. But Elias heard it anyway.

The captain wasn't planning to recover horses. He was planning to make an example.

And Elias had just given him the justification.

* * *

A voice spoke behind him. "You met them, didn't you?"

Elias turned. A man stood in the shadow of the headquarters building. Older than the soldiers. Maybe fifty. He wore buckskin and wool, a mix that marked him as neither Army nor settler. His face was weathered, his eyes sharp.

"Met who?" Elias asked.

"The Blackfeet. The ones who took your horses." The man nodded toward the hide on Elias's saddle. "That's not trader hide. That's fresh. Someone gave it to you."

Elias said nothing.

The man stepped closer. "I'm Jonas Bridger. Scout. The captain'll want me to guide the patrol." He looked at Elias for a long moment. "You should know what you've started."

"I just want my horses."

"I know. But that's not what he wants." Bridger glanced back at headquarters. "He wants something to put in his reports. Something that shows he's winning, and the Blackfeet are starving, which makes them easy targets."

Elias exhaled once, slowly. "I didn't think—"

"Yes," Bridger's voice stayed quiet. "But it doesn't matter. You told him. He'll ride out. And people will die."

Something tightened in Elias's chest. Not surprise, just the weight of understanding settling where it belonged.

"Can you do anything?" he said.

Bridger shook his head. "Me? No. I'm the scout. I point. They shoot. That's the arrangement." He started to turn away, then stopped. "But you might. Ride with us. A witness changes things sometimes. Not much. But sometimes."

He walked off, boots crunching in the snow.

Elias stood alone.

He thought of Clara. How she'd nursed that dog back from starvation, how she'd loved him, how she would have grieved when Scout died defending their home. She'd been kind in ways that embarrassed people who weren't. Fed travelers. Left water out for coyotes in summer. Scraps in winter.

She wouldn't have wanted this. Soldiers riding north to "settle things decisively." A starving camp caught in the middle. Women and children in the line of fire.

Scout was dead. But Clara would have been ashamed of what he'd set in motion.

The fort moved around him, soldiers crossing the yard, smoke rising from chimneys, horses stamping in the stables. All of it preparing. All of it pointing north.

Toward Makóyi. Toward the young man with the wolf pelt. Toward the camp with thin children and empty packs.

Toward the people who had saved his life three days ago.

Elias untied his horse and led it toward the stables.

He didn't know what he was going to do.

Only that he wasn't riding away.

Not yet.

8

The Ride

The patrol assembled at dawn, twenty soldiers saddling horses in the cold. Their breath steamed. Metal clinked. Horses stamped and snorted, impatient.

Elias stood near the stables, watching.

A young soldier, couldn't have been more than nineteen, checked his rifle, worked the lever action, grinned at his companion. "Finally get to do something besides freeze my ass off."

"About time," the other said. "Been here four months. Haven't shot at anything but targets."

"You ever kill a redskin before?"

"Nope. You?"

"Nope. Guess we'll both find out."

They laughed. Easy. Like they were talking about hunting deer.

An older soldier nearby, thirty, maybe, with a beard going gray, glanced at them but said nothing. He tightened his saddle cinch, face expressionless.

Elias felt something cold settle in his stomach.

A sergeant walked past, barking orders. "Check your ammunition. Two days' rations. We're riding light and fast."

"How many hostiles we expecting, Sarge?" someone called.

"Don't know. Don't care. However many there are, there'll be fewer when we're done."

Laughter rippled through the group.

"Only good Indian's a dead Indian," another soldier muttered.

* * *

Elias looked away. His horse stood tied nearby, already saddled. He'd slept poorly, if at all. The barracks had been cold, the thin mattress hard, and every time he closed his eyes he saw Makóyi's face. The way he'd saved him from the bear. The way he'd asked for a few days. Just a few days.

He'd waited. He'd kept his word.

But it hadn't mattered.

Captain Thornton emerged from the headquarters building, adjusting his gloves. His uniform was clean, pressed despite the cold. He walked to his horse, mounted smoothly, and surveyed the assembled men.

"Gentlemen," he said. His voice carried across the yard. "We ride north to recover stolen property and restore order. The Blackfeet have been raiding with increasing frequency. This ends today. We will locate their camp, recover Mr. Harlan's horses, and make it clear that attacks on settlers carry consequences."

He paused. "I expect discipline. Follow orders. Stay alert. These are not soldiers we're facing, they're savages. Desperate, hungry, and dangerous. Do not underestimate them. We've handled situations like this before."

A few soldiers nodded. Others grinned.

"Mount up."

Private Henderson was already mounted, his horse standing square, equipment properly stowed. Thornton noticed, without looking, the way a good officer notices without making a production of it.

"Henderson."

"Sir."

"You're on the remuda tonight. Pick your relief man before we stop."

"Yes, sir."

Thornton moved on down the line without another word. That was all. But Henderson sat a little straighter in the saddle.

Twenty soldiers, one captain, one scout, mounted and ready. And Elias.

Jonas Bridger sat his horse near the gate, waiting. He wore buckskin and wool, a rifle across his saddle. His face was unreadable.

The gate swung open. Thornton led them out onto the frozen plain.

Elias followed, heart heavy.

Behind him, he heard the young soldier whisper to his companion: "Think we'll take scalps?"

"Heard the hostiles do. Maybe we should too."

"Fair's fair."

More laughter.

Elias rode on. He didn't look back.

* * *

They rode north through snow and cold, following the Sun River valley before angling toward the Marias. The land was open, empty, white under a pale sky. No wind. Just the crunch of hooves, the creak of leather, the occasional cough from a soldier.

Bridger ranged ahead, reading the land, then fell back to ride near the middle of the column.

Near Elias.

They rode in silence for a while. Snow squeaked under the horses' hooves. The air was sharp enough to sting.

Bridger spoke first, voice low. "Get any sleep?"

Elias shook his head. "Not much."

Bridger nodded, eyes on the horizon. "Hard to sleep when you know the day's headed somewhere bad."

Elias didn't answer.

After a long stretch, Bridger said, "My mother was Crow. Father was a French trapper. I grew up between camps. Crow and Blackfeet fought each other for generations. Took horses, counted coup. That was war." He gestured toward the column ahead. "This isn't that."

Elias kept his eyes forward.

"Thornton wants a result," Bridger said. "Something he can write down. Something that makes him look like he's fixing the frontier."

Elias exhaled. "And the horses?"

Bridger's mouth tightened. "If we find them, good. If not, he'll take something else and call it even."

They rode on. The sun climbed, pale and cold. The soldiers ahead laughed at something Elias couldn't hear.

After a while, Elias said, "Why stay with them? If you know what they're doing."

Bridger was quiet for a long time. "Because a man needs to eat. Because there aren't many places for someone like me to stand. Because I thought I could make things less bad." He shrugged once. "Turns out I was wrong."

Elias didn't speak.

Bridger went on, softer now. "When I was a boy, buffalo covered the prairie. Days to ride past a herd. Haven't seen one in years. Not a wild one." He didn't look at Elias. "That wasn't an accident."

Elias felt something settle in him. Not surprise, recognition.

"My wife died three months ago," he said. "Consumption."

Bridger nodded. "I'm sorry."

"She wasted away. Nothing I did mattered."

Bridger's voice stayed low. "Up there, sickness is taking whole families. Hunger makes it worse. Government promised medicine. Sent nothing."

Elias didn't answer. He didn't need to. He understood what it meant to watch someone fade.

They rode on. The wind picked up. The column ahead tightened its formation.

Elias thought of Makóyi's steady hands. Of the young man who'd ridden off to find his horses without complaint. Of the way they'd stood between him and a grizzly without asking anything in return.

He didn't know what waited north of here. A camp, a family, a handful of lodges, or nothing at all. But he knew the Army wasn't riding toward warriors. They were riding toward people trying to survive winter.

They kept riding north.

* * *

Ksisstaki sat outside Makóyi's lodge, the pup in her lap. It was stronger now, eyes clear, drinking broth from her fingers. Its coat was filling in where the cold had tried to take it.

She murmured to it, words only the pup could hear. Promises that spring would come. That the camp would survive. That everything would be all right.

She wasn't sure, but the pup seemed to believe it.

Across the camp, Nitááhkii worked on his gear. Checking straps, mending tears, and sharpening his knife. His face was set, serious. He hadn't smiled in days.

She wanted to go to him. Ask what was wrong. Make him laugh the way he used to when they were younger.

But she knew what he'd say. *You're too young to understand.*

So she stayed where she was, holding the pup, watching him.

He looked up once, saw her, and nodded. Then went back to his work.

Her chest felt tight.

The pup licked her fingers. She stroked its head, felt its heart beating against her palm.

At least something was getting stronger this winter.

Ísstaakii emerged from the lodge, a hide bundle in her arms. She saw Ksisstaki, saw the pup, shook her head, but said nothing. She'd stopped arguing about the pup days ago.

"Where's Makóyi?" Ksisstaki asked.

"With the scouts." Ísstaakii's voice was tight. "They saw something. Riders."

Ksisstaki's hand stilled on the pup. "From where?"

"South."

The word hung in the air like smoke.

Ksisstaki looked toward the southern horizon. The camp horses were restless, shifting in their lines, ears pricked south.

She thought of the raid. The horses they'd brought back. The way Nitááhkii's pony had come home bleeding. The way he'd been different ever since.

She held the pup closer.

Makóyi appeared from between two lodges, walking with purpose. Nitááhkii saw him, set down his work, stood.

Other young men gathered. Five of them. The ones who'd ridden on the raid.

Ksisstaki watched, heart pounding.

Makóyi spoke quietly. She couldn't hear the words. But she saw the way the young men's faces changed. The way their hands moved to their weapons.

The way Nitááhkii's jaw tightened.

The scouts had seen riders. Many of them. Coming north.

The white man from the bear. The one Makóyi had saved.

He'd brought soldiers.

Ksisstaki stood, still holding the pup. She walked toward Makóyi's group, slow, careful not to intrude.

Makóyi saw her, gestured her closer.

"Go inside," he said gently. "Stay warm. Stay quiet."

"What's happening?"

"Soldiers. Maybe a day's ride south."

"Will they come here?"

Makóyi looked at her for a long moment. Then: "Yes."

She felt cold spread through her chest. "What will we do?"

"We will talk. Offer to return the horses. Hope they accept."

"And if they don't?"

Makóyi's face was unreadable. "Then we will see."

Nitááhkii stood nearby, watching the southern horizon. His hand rested on his knife.

Ksisstaki wanted to say something. Wanted to tell him to be careful. To not do anything foolish. To remember that he was important to the camp. To her.

But the words wouldn't come.

She turned and walked back to the lodge, the pup warm against her chest.

Inside, she sat by the fire, holding the pup, staring at the flames.

Outside, she heard voices. Low. Urgent. Preparing.

She closed her eyes and whispered a prayer to Naatosi.

Let them talk. Let them find peace. Let no one die.

But in her heart, she knew.

Men with guns rarely came to talk.

They came to take.

And when taking didn't work, they came to kill.
She held the pup tighter.
Its heartbeat was steady against her palm.
Small. Fragile. Alive.
For now.

9

The Accusation

They stopped within sight of the camp at dusk.

Thornton raised his hand. The patrol halted on a low rise, twenty soldiers silhouetted against the darkening sky. Below, maybe a mile north, thin smoke rose from lodges scattered along a frozen creek.

"We camp here," Thornton said. "Post guards. No fires. We move at first light."

The soldiers dismounted and began unpacking. Quiet, efficient. They knew what came next.

Elias stood holding his horse's reins, staring at the distant camp. Smoke. Lodges. People moving between fires. From here, they looked small. Fragile.

He felt sick.

Bridger appeared beside him. "Help me with the horses."

They led the animals to a stand of cottonwoods and tied them on a long line. The soldiers were settling in, laying out bedrolls, checking weapons, and eating cold rations. No talking. Just the sound of leather and metal in the cold air.

Bridger worked in silence. Then, low: "I'm getting your horses back tonight."

Elias looked at him. "How?"

"Thornton posts one man on the remuda. Midnight he rotates the watch. Ten minutes where nobody's looking at anything." He checked a knot, moved to the next horse. "I know his rotations."

"If they catch you—"

"They won't." Bridger checked a knot, moved to the next horse. "Thornton attacks at dawn. You should be gone before then."

Elias said nothing.

"Get some sleep," Bridger said. "Long day tomorrow."

He walked away.

Elias stood alone in the darkness, listening to the wind.

* * *

Something woke him.

Not a sound. A presence.

Elias opened his eyes. Bridger crouched beside him, barely visible in the starlight.

"Your horses," Bridger whispered. "Tied past that cottonwood stand. Fifty yards south."

Elias sat up. "You got them?"

"All eight. The big ones, easy to spot among their ponies."

"Did anyone see you?"

"No." Bridger glanced toward where Thornton slept. "Leave before he wakes. He won't let you go if you wait."

Elias felt his chest tighten. "What about you?"

"What I did wasn't a crime. Just took back stolen property." Bridger stood. "But if you're here when he attacks, you become part of it. Witness. Complicit. Leave now."

He disappeared into the darkness.

Elias lay there, heart pounding. Then he rose, gathered his gear as quietly as he could, and moved toward the horses.

***

The sky was just beginning to lighten when Elias rode away.

His eight horses followed on a line, moving quietly through the snow. Behind him, the patrol camp was still dark, soldiers sleeping except for the guards at the perimeter. He waited until they had walked past, then he slipped through.

Elias rode south. Toward home. Toward the empty ranch, the two graves under the cottonwood, the cabin that echoed with Clara's absence.

He had his horses. His future. His way forward.

He rode a mile. Then two.

The sun broke the horizon, pale and cold.

He stopped.

Sat in the saddle, breathing hard, though he hadn't been riding fast.

Behind him, north, Thornton would be waking. Mounting up. Leading twenty soldiers toward the camp for a dawn attack.

Makóyi, who had saved his life.

The young man with the wolf pelt, who'd been there when it happened.

The girl he'd glimpsed holding a pup, thin and scared.

Clara's voice in his head: *What kind of man lets that happen when he could stop it?*

Scout's body in the snow. The grave under the cottonwood.

But also, the bear meat, shared fairly. The few days he'd waited. The word he'd kept, and the soldiers who came anyway.

The life-debt, unpaid.

Elias closed his eyes.

Then he turned his horse.

* * *

He tied his eight horses to a cluster of pines a quarter-mile from the camp. If things went wrong, he didn't want them caught in it. Then he rode toward the lodges, alone, unarmed except for the Winchester in his saddle scabbard.

The sun was up now. The camp was waking, smoke rising, voices carrying across the cold air.

He rode to the edge, stopped, and called out: "Makóyi! Elias Harlan! We need to talk!"

Silence. Then movement.

Warriors appeared from between lodges, rifles raised. Five of them. The young man with the wolf pelt was among them, face hard, weapon pointed at Elias's chest.

Elias raised his hands. "I'm not here to fight. I need to talk to Makóyi."

The warriors didn't move.

Then Makóyi emerged from a lodge, walking slowly, studying Elias with sharp eyes.

"Why are you here?" His voice was calm but wary.

"The soldiers," Elias said. His breath came short. "They're camped south of here. They're not far. Could be hours. Could be less. You need to leave. Now."

Makóyi's face didn't change. "You came to warn us?"

"Yes."

"Why?"

Elias reached slowly for his saddle scabbard and pulled out the Winchester. Held it by the barrel, stock toward Makóyi.

"For the bear meat," he said. "And this warning for my life. We're even now."

Makóyi walked forward and took the rifle. Examined it. A good weapon. Well-maintained. Worth more than bear meat.

He looked at Elias. "You will be in great danger for this."

"I know."

"Then why?"

Elias's jaw tightened. "Because it's mine to fix."

Makóyi studied him for a long moment, then nodded once.

"Go," he said. "Quickly. They will look for you."

He turned, barking orders in Blackfoot. The camp erupted into motion. Women grabbing children, men taking down lodges, everyone moving fast.

Elias wheeled his horse, rode hard back toward where he'd left his string.

Behind him, he heard the camp dissolving as people fled north. He'd given them some time. Maybe it would be enough.

* * *

Elias reached the pines where he'd tied his horses.

He should have mounted up. Should have ridden hard, put miles between himself and the patrol before Thornton woke.

But he stood at the edge of the trees, looking out at the frozen creek, the low bank, the open ground beyond.

He knew this place. Not from memory. From ink on paper. A newspaper account he'd read years ago in Ohio, the kind of story that stays with a man whether he wants it to or not.

Heavy Runner's camp had been here. Or close enough to here that it made no difference.

He stood there and let himself see it. Dawn light on snow. Lodges. Fires just starting. People waking. A man walking out to meet soldiers, holding up a paper that was supposed to mean something.

A breath of cold air hit his face, and for a moment, he saw Clara at the kitchen table, reading that same story beside him.

He stood there a long time, staring at nothing, breath rising in pale clouds. He could have left. He could have vanished into the hills. But he didn't move.

The land held him.

Hoofbeats broke the silence.

He didn't turn.

Thornton rode up with six soldiers, horses blowing steam in the cold. The captain pulled his mount to a stop beside Elias.

"Harlan," Thornton said. "What are you doing?"

Elias didn't answer. He kept looking at the ground.

Thornton frowned. "I asked you a question."

Elias finally spoke, voice low.

"This is where it happened, isn't it?"

Thornton stiffened.

"What are you talking about?"

"The massacre," Elias said. "Heavy Runner's people. Women. Children. Sick with smallpox. Shot in their lodges. Burned. Left to freeze." He looked at Thornton now. "Right here."

Thornton's jaw tightened. "That was thirteen years ago."

Elias nodded. "And you're about to do it again."

Thornton's face hardened. "Get back on your horse."

Elias didn't move.

Thornton hissed, "You warned them."

Elias said nothing.

"You warned them," Thornton repeated, louder now. "You aided hostiles. You interfered with a military operation. You forfeited your property and your freedom."

He turned to his men. "Arrest him."

Two soldiers dismounted, grabbed Elias by the arms, and bound his wrists. He didn't resist. He just kept looking at the ground.

Thornton wheeled his mount. "Mount him on that spare. We're going to that camp."

They dragged Elias to an Army horse, tied his hands to the saddle horn. The patrol formed up and rode north.

They crested the rise overlooking the Blackfeet camp.

It was empty.

Lodges half-collapsed. Fires still smoking. Tracks everywhere, heading north. Women, children, ponies, all fleeing fast.

Thornton sat rigid in the saddle.

He turned to Elias. "You cost me this."

"They're just people trying to survive."

"They're hostiles," Thornton snapped. "And you protected them. That's treason. You'll hang for it."

A shout came from behind. "Captain! Rider coming!"

Bridger approached at a trot, face unreadable.

Thornton glared at him. "Convenient timing, scout."

Bridger looked at the empty camp, then at Elias bound to the saddle.

"They ran," he said.

"Because someone warned them." Thornton's eyes stayed on Bridger. "You wouldn't know anything about that, would you?"

"No, sir."

"Or about how Harlan got his horses back in the middle of the night?"

"No, sir."

Thornton stared at him a long moment.

"We're returning to Fort Shaw. Harlan will be tried. You'll be questioned."

"Yes, sir."

They mounted up. Began the ride south.

Elias rode with his hands bound, the empty camp shrinking behind them.

* * *

They camped that night in a ravine, sheltered from the wind.

Elias was tied to a cottonwood tree at the edge of camp, hands bound, feet hobbled. A guard sat fifteen feet away, rifle across his knees, half-asleep.

The camp was quiet. Soldiers exhausted.

Thornton's tent glowed faintly with lamplight. Through the canvas, Elias could see his silhouette, bent over a field desk, writing. The careful posture of a man who still believed in the forms. The reports, the records, the chain of command that stretched from this frozen ravine all the way back to Washington.

A man who still thought this was going to go the way he'd planned.

Footsteps approached. Bridger, carrying two tin cups.

"Coffee," he said to the guard. "Go get some supper. I'll watch him."

The guard took the cup and walked toward the mess tent.

Bridger knelt and cut the ropes at Elias's wrists. Then the hobbles.

"Two horses tied past that ridge," he said quietly. "One to ride, one with gear. Enough to get you clear."

Elias rubbed his wrists. "My horses—"

"Gone," Bridger said. "Forget them."

He glanced back toward the camp, then handed Elias the knife.

"They'll come looking," Elias said.

Bridger shrugged. "Let them."

Elias stood. His legs were stiff. "You sure about this?"

Bridger's jaw tightened. "I'm done here. That's all you need to know."

Elias nodded. "Thank you."

"Don't waste it," Bridger said. "Now go."

Elias moved toward the ridge. Found two horses tied there, a sturdy roan and a smaller pack horse loaded with gear. Not his horses. Army horses. Bridger had taken them from the patrol's own string.

He mounted the roan, took the pack horse's lead rope, and rode southwest into the darkness.

* * *

Makóyi led the camp north through the day and into the night.

They moved fast, abandoning what they couldn't carry. The children cried. The old people struggled. The ponies were thin, weak. But they moved.

Nitááhkii rode beside him. "The white man, why did he warn us?"

"Because not all white men are the same."

"He brought the soldiers."

"He also saved us from them." Makóyi touched the Winchester slung across his back. "That matters."

"Will they come again?"

Makóyi looked north, toward the invisible line where the medicine land began. Canada. Safety, maybe.

"Yes," he said. "They'll come again."

"Then why run?"

"Because we're still alive. And while we live, we can fight, run and survive." He looked at his nephew. "When we're dead, we can do nothing."

They rode on.

Behind them, the abandoned camp grew smaller. Ahead, the land stretched white and frozen.

The wind rose, carrying snow. Another storm coming.

They rode into it, heading north.

Heading anywhere the soldiers weren't.

10

On the Run

Elias rode southwest through the night.

The roan was steady beneath him, the pack horse following on the lead rope. Behind them, the Army camp disappeared into darkness. Ahead, the land stretched empty and white under a sky full of stars.

Bridger had said southwest. Away from Montana. Toward Wyoming, Colorado, somewhere Thornton's authority didn't reach.

Elias rode.

The cold bit through his coat. His hands ached inside his gloves. The horses' breath came in white clouds, their hooves crunching through crusted snow.

He didn't look back.

* * *

Dawn broke pale and gray.

Elias stopped in a shallow draw, dismounted, let the horses drink from a creek where the ice had broken. He pulled jerky from the pack, chewed it slowly. It was frozen, hard. He ate anyway.

He assessed his supplies: bedroll, more jerky, coffee he couldn't brew without a fire, ammunition for a rifle he no longer had, a knife. Enough for maybe a week if he rationed. Less if the cold kept stealing his energy.

The roan stood with its head low, breathing hard. They'd ridden eight hours, maybe more. The horse needed rest.

Elias studied the land. Open prairie. Flat. Visible for miles in every direction.

He thought of Thornton. Of the patrols that would come looking.

They'd expect him to go southwest. It's what Bridger had told him. It's what made sense, escape south, get out of Montana Territory, disappear into Wyoming or Colorado where the Army couldn't follow.

Which meant Thornton would send patrols southwest.

Which meant riding this direction made him easy to find.

Elias looked north. The opposite direction. Deeper into Montana. Toward colder country, harder terrain, the Canadian border.

Toward where Makóyi's camp had fled.

He stood there a long time, thinking.

Then he swung back into the saddle and turned the horses north.

* * *

The temperature dropped as he rode.

The wind picked up, constant, pushing against him. The sky stayed gray, heavy with snow that didn't quite fall. Just hung there, waiting.

Elias pulled his coat tighter. His face was already raw from the wind, his hands stiff inside his gloves.

The roan's gait was steady but slower now. The pack horse followed without complaint.

He rode through the day, stopping only to rest the horses briefly. No fires. Smoke would be visible for miles. He ate jerky frozen solid, drank snow melted in his mouth.

By evening, he'd covered maybe twenty miles north. Not enough. Never enough.

He made camp in a stand of cottonwoods, tied the horses, wrapped himself in the bedroll. Sleep came in fits, too cold, too exposed, too aware of every sound.

When dawn came, he was already moving.

***

Day two.

The land changed as he rode north. Less open, more broken. Low hills, frozen creeks, clusters of pine and cottonwood. Better cover. Harder to spot from a distance.

But also harder to see what was coming.

The roan's breathing was louder now. Labored. Elias checked the horse at midday. No obvious injury, just exhaustion. Pushed too hard, too long.

He eased the pace. But not much. Couldn't afford to.

That afternoon, he saw them.

Riders on the horizon. Maybe a mile east. Moving in a line, searching.

Elias pulled into a draw, dismounted, held the horses still. Waited.

The patrol passed north of him. Six soldiers, maybe more. Moving in a grid pattern, systematic, thorough.

Thornton had sent multiple patrols. Organized. Serious.

Elias waited until they were gone, then rode on.

But slower now. Watching. Always watching.

***

Day three.

The jerky was half gone. He was rationing now, eating less than his body needed. The cold stole energy faster than the food replaced it.

His hands were numb most of the time. His face felt tight, skin cracked from the wind. His toes, he couldn't feel them anymore inside his boots.

The roan was limping.

Elias had noticed it that morning. A slight favoring of the left foreleg. By midday, it was worse. By evening, the horse could barely walk.

He made camp early, examined the leg. The tendon above the fetlock was swollen and hot to the touch. Strained. Maybe torn.

The horse couldn't continue.

Elias sat in the snow, staring at the roan. Good horse. Bridger's gift. His way out.

Now useless.

He couldn't leave it to starve. Couldn't leave it for wolves.

He stood, pulled the knife from his belt.

The roan watched him with dark, tired eyes.

"I'm sorry," Elias said.

He did it quick. One cut, deep, across the throat. The horse went down fast, legs folding, blood dark on white snow.

Elias stood over it until the breathing stopped. Then he stripped the saddle, the bridle, took what he could carry. Left the rest.

The pack horse stood nearby, watching.

Elias mounted. The pack horse wasn't built for riding long distances. Smaller, broader, meant for carrying gear not men. But it was all he had.

He rode north.

Behind him, the roan lay in the snow. Already freezing.

* * *

Day five.

Or maybe six. He'd lost count.

The pack horse struggled under his weight and the remaining gear. Moved slower. Stumbled more.

Elias couldn't feel his feet. His hands were white, fingers swollen. His face was a mask of pain—cracked skin, frostbitten nose, and cheeks.

He couldn't think straight anymore. Thoughts came slow, fragmented.

Keep moving. North. Don't stop.

That was all.

He saw another patrol. Or thought he did. Riders in the distance. Or maybe just trees. He wasn't sure anymore.

He hid anyway. Waited. Rode on.

The snow started falling. Light at first, then heavier. The wind picked up.

A storm coming.

Elias hunched in the saddle and pulled his coat over his face. The pack horse walked on its own now, following some instinct.

North. Always north.

* * *

Day seven.

Or eight.

Time had stopped meaning anything.

Elias saw things.

Clara, standing on a ridge ahead. Her shawl wrapped around her shoulders. Smiling. Waiting.

She was gone.

Scout, running ahead through the snow. Looking back. Tail

wagging. Leading the way.

Nothing there.

Makóyi, riding toward him. Waving. Calling out.

Empty land.

Soldiers behind him. Close. Rifles raised.

He turned. Nothing.

He didn't know what was real anymore.

The pack horse kept walking. Elias slumped forward, hands frozen to the reins. He couldn't sit up. Couldn't feel anything. Just cold. Just emptiness.

Clara, standing ahead. Her shawl around her shoulders. Smiling.

He wanted to stop. Lie down in the snow. Sleep.

But the horse kept walking. The horse walked because horses walk. Because stopping meant dying.

North.

Always north.

* * *

The pack horse stopped.

Elias tried to kick it forward. His legs didn't respond. He tried to lift his head. It was too heavy.

He looked up. Barely. Through narrowed vision.

Smoke?

Lodges?

Or just more snow?

He couldn't tell.

His hands slipped from the reins. He slid sideways, slow, inevitable. Hit the ground. Hard.

He lay there, staring at the gray sky. Snow falling on his face. Melting. Freezing.

Voices.

Distant. Muffled. Or maybe just the wind.

Faces above him.

Dark. Moving. Speaking words he didn't understand.

Hands grabbing him. Lifting.

He tried to say something. Nothing came out.

Darkness closed in from the edges. He didn't fight it.

He thought of Clara. Of Scout. Of Makóyi.

We're even.

The darkness took him.

* * *

Somewhere far to the south, Thornton sat in his tent at Fort Shaw, reading reports.

Three patrols deployed. Grid search pattern. Southwest quadrant covered. No sign of the fugitive.

He set the papers down, stared at the map on his desk.

"Where are you, Harlan?" he muttered.

A knock at the tent flap. A sergeant entered.

"Sir. Patrol Three reports no contact. They're requesting permission to expand search north."

Thornton looked at the map. North. Deeper into Montana. Toward the Blackfeet range. Toward the border.

"No," he said. "He's not stupid enough to go north. Keep searching southwest."

"Yes, sir."

The sergeant left.

Thornton turned back to his paperwork.

He was wrong.

But he wouldn't know that for weeks.

11

Suffering

They moved north through the night, a long line of people and ponies stretched thin across the frozen prairie. The storm had eased, but the cold had not. It clung to them, slowed them, made every breath a small pain.

Makóyi rode at the front, scanning the land ahead. Behind him, the camp followed in fits and starts, elders slumped over saddles, children bundled in robes, women leading ponies loaded with what little they could carry. The wind pushed against them, steady and merciless.

They were not moving fast enough.

By midmorning, the first pony went down.

A small bay mare, ribs sharp under her hide, legs trembling. She stumbled once, twice, then folded into the snow. The woman leading her cried out, tried to lift the mare's head, but the animal was done. It lay still, breath shallow, eyes dull.

Makóyi rode back, knelt beside the woman. "Take what you can," he said softly. "Leave the rest."

She nodded, wiping her face with the back of her hand. She pulled the packs from the mare's back, slung them over her own shoulders. The children with her watched in silence.

They moved on.

* * *

By noon, the old ones were falling behind.

Ísstaakii rode beside an elder whose cough had worsened in the cold. Each breath rattled. His eyes were half-closed, his hands shaking on the reins. She tried to steady him, but he swayed, nearly fell.

"Stop," she said.

Makóyi circled back again. He saw the elder's face, gray, hollow, the look of a man whose body had nothing left to give.

"We rest," Ísstaakii said.

"We can't," Makóyi answered. "Not here."

Natosapi lifted his head. His voice was thin but steady. "I will stay."

"No," Ísstaakii said. "Natosapi. We don't leave our people."

Natosapi pushed her hand away. He tried to stand, legs shaking, but he forced himself upright. "I am not a child to be dragged like meat on a travois." He steadied himself, breath coming hard. "Give me a rifle."

Makóyi stared at him. "You cannot fight."

"I can die standing," the elder said. "That is enough."

The wind cut through them. Snow drifted around their feet. The camp moved ahead in a slow, struggling line.

Makóyi dismounted. "If you stay, they will kill you."

The elder nodded. "Better by a bullet than by breath failing in the snow. Better here than slowing the children." He looked north, where the camp was disappearing into white. "Go. Protect them. That is your work now."

Makóyi's throat tightened. He took the elder's hand, pressed it once. Then he placed a rifle in the man's grip.

Natosapi held it with both hands, steadying himself. "Tell my daughter I walked into the wind. Tell her I was not afraid."

Makóyi bowed his head. "I will."

The elder turned south, facing the storm, facing whatever came. He stood straight, as straight as his body allowed.

Makóyi mounted. Ísstaakii wiped her eyes with the back of her hand. Nitááhkii watched in silence.

They rode on.

Behind them, the elder became a dark shape in the snow.

Then a smaller shape.

Then nothing at all.

* * *

The children cried from hunger. The cold made their voices thin, weak. A woman carried a baby wrapped in two robes, but the baby's face was pale, lips blue. She held it close, whispering prayers.

Nitááhkii rode beside her. "Give him to me," he said.

She hesitated, then handed the baby over. Nitááhkii tucked the child inside his own coat, against his chest. The baby's breath was faint, barely there.

He rode on, jaw tight.

* * *

By late afternoon, the storm returned.

Snow swept across the prairie in long, white sheets. The wind rose, cutting through robes and hides. The ponies lowered their heads, pushing forward step by step.

Makóyi looked back at his people. A line of shadows in the blowing snow. Too slow. Too exposed. Too many weak, too many sick.

They would not outrun soldiers like this.

He rode to Nitááhkii. "We need shelter."

"There is none," Nitááhkii said.

"There must be."

Nitááhkii looked north, squinting through the storm. "There is a coulee ahead. Maybe trees. Maybe a place to hide."

"Show me."

They rode ahead together, the wind pushing against them, the land disappearing into white.

Behind them, the camp struggled on. Elders coughing, children crying, ponies stumbling, women carrying more than their bodies could bear.

They were alive.

But not fast enough.

* * *

The storm thickened as they rode. Snow swept sideways, stinging their faces, clinging to robes and hair. The wind howled across the prairie, drowning out voices, turning the world into white and shadow.

Nitááhkii led the way, head low, eyes narrowed against the blowing snow. "There," he said, pointing with his chin.

Makóyi saw it, a dark line in the land, barely visible through the storm. A coulee, shallow but deep enough to break the wind. Trees clustered along its edge, black shapes swaying in the gale.

"Go," Makóyi said.

They descended the slope one by one. The wind eased as they dropped below the ridge. The snow still fell, but the air was calmer, the cold less sharp.

The people collapsed into the shelter like animals fleeing fire.

Women lowered children from ponies. Men pulled down packs. The sick were laid against the lee side of a cottonwood, wrapped in robes. The ponies stood with heads low, sides heaving.

Ksisstaki stumbled down the slope, the pup tucked inside her coat. Its small body trembled against her chest. She pressed her hand over it, whispering to calm it, or herself.

Ísstaakii moved among the people, checking the old ones, the coughing ones, the ones too weak to stand. Her face was tight, jaw clenched against fear.

Nitááhkii paced the coulee's edge, scanning the white horizon. "They'll find us," he said. "Tracks lead straight here."

"Not in this storm," Makóyi said.

Nitááhkii shook his head. "Storm won't last."

Makóyi didn't answer. He knew the boy was right. The storm was a gift, but a short one.

He walked the length of the coulee, checking each family, each child. The baby Nitááhkii carried earlier was breathing shallowly, but breathing. The mother sat beside him, hands shaking as she held a robe around them both.

Ksisstaki approached Makóyi. Snow clung to her braids, her cheeks red with cold. "We can't stay long," she said.

"No."

"The old ones... some won't make another day."

"I know."

She swallowed. "What will we do?"

Makóyi looked north. The storm hid everything, but he knew what lay beyond it. More cold, more hunger, more miles. And soldiers behind them.

"We move when the storm breaks," he said. "Even if it kills us."

Ksisstaki nodded, though her eyes shone with fear.

Makóyi turned to Nitááhkii. "No fires," he said. "Not even small ones."

Nitááhkii scowled. "The children—"

"Will die if the soldiers see smoke."

Nitááhkii looked away, jaw tight.

The storm raged above them, wind screaming over the ridge. In the coulee, the people huddled together, sharing what warmth they had. The ponies stood close, steam rising from their bodies.

Makóyi sat alone for a moment, back against a cottonwood, snow settling on his shoulders. He thought of the elder standing in the storm behind them. He wondered how long the man had lasted. He wondered if the soldiers had found him.

He closed his eyes.

12

The Turn

The storm had passed by the time Thornton stepped out of his tent. The air was sharp, the sky pale, the parade ground covered in a thin crust of new snow. Soldiers moved between the barracks and the stables, breath rising in white clouds.

Thornton watched them for a moment, jaw tight.

"Harlan," he muttered. "Where are you."

A lieutenant approached, saluted. "Sir. Patrols One and Two returned. No sign of him."

Thornton didn't look at him. "And Three?"

"Still out, sir."

Thornton nodded once. "Have the officers meet me in the command tent."

"Yes, sir."

Thornton crossed the yard, boots crunching in the snow. His face was calm, but his eyes were hard. He passed a group of soldiers cleaning rifles. They straightened as he approached.

"You men," Thornton said. "Mount up. Full kit. We ride soon."

They exchanged glances but obeyed.

Inside the command tent, the map lay open across the table, corners held down by stones. Thornton stood over it, tracing lines north with a gloved finger.

A lieutenant entered, stamping snow from his boots. "Sir. Report from Patrol Four. They've picked up the hostiles' trail. Moving north. Slow."

Thornton nodded. "Good."

"Sir… they're only fifteen men. If they make contact—"

"They won't," Thornton said.

"But if they do—"

"They won't," Thornton repeated, sharper now. "They're there to track, not engage."

The lieutenant swallowed. "Sir, respectfully… if the hostiles turn on them, they'll be wiped out."

Thornton finally looked at him. His eyes were flat, cold. "Then they should ride faster."

Bridger stood near the tent flap, arms crossed, face unreadable.

Thornton tapped the map again. "The hostiles are not my concern. Harlan is."

He turned to Bridger. "You. Take a fresh horse. Ride north. Recall Patrol Four."

Bridger didn't move. "Sir… if we pull them off the hostiles, the trail goes cold."

"I don't care about the trail."

Bridger's jaw tightened. "Sir, that patrol is too small. If the hostiles double back—"

"They won't," Thornton snapped.

Bridger kept his voice level. "Sir, I've seen winter fights. A small patrol in deep snow—"

"I said recall them."

Bridger stared at him. "Sir… this is a mistake."

Thornton stepped closer, voice low and dangerous. "You think I don't know what I'm doing."

Bridger didn't answer.

Thornton's breath came hard through his nose. "The hostiles raided a ranch. Fine. That's what they do. But Harlan—" He jabbed a finger at the map. "Harlan warned them. Harlan defied me. Harlan made a fool of me in front of my men."

He leaned in. "This is not about Indians. This is about a traitor."

Bridger looked at the map, then at Thornton. "Sir... you're chasing one man and leaving a whole camp to run free. That's not strategy."

Thornton's eyes narrowed. "That sounded like criticism."

"It's experience," Bridger said quietly. "You pull that patrol, they'll vanish. And if they don't vanish, they'll kill the patrol. Either way, it comes back on me."

Thornton's voice dropped to a growl. "Bring them back. Or I'll have you in irons before sundown."

Bridger held his gaze for a long moment. Then he nodded once. "Yes, sir."

He stepped out into the cold.

Outside, the soldiers were mounting up. Fifty men. Full kit. Extra ammunition. The kind of force meant for a campaign, not a manhunt.

Bridger swung into the saddle, the cold biting through his coat. He looked north, toward the deep country where the tribe fled and where Elias had vanished.

He knew what this was now.

Not pursuit.

Not justice.

Not even revenge.

Obsession.

And it would get men killed.

He touched his heels to the horse and rode north into the gray morning.

* * *

The storm had blown itself out, but the cold behind it was worse. The fifteen men of Patrol Four rode single file across the white prairie, horses blowing steam, hooves sinking into drifts crusted with ice.

Corporal Hayes led them, scarf frozen stiff across his face. He kept glancing north, where the land dipped and rose in long, empty waves.

"Tracks are fresh," one of the privates said, leaning from his saddle to study the snow. "Maybe an hour."

Hayes nodded. "They're close."

No one looked eager about it.

Another man rode up beside him. "Corporal… if they turn on us—"

"They won't," Hayes said. "They're running."

"Running can turn fast," the man muttered.

Hayes didn't argue. He'd seen winter fights. He'd seen what happened when a small patrol pushed too far into deep country. Snow made men slow. Hunger made them stupid. Fear made them dead.

He looked at the tracks again. Dozens of ponies, moving unevenly. Some dragging. Some stumbling. A line that wavered like a drunk man's walk.

"They're hurting," Hayes said quietly.

"Hurting people fight harder," the private said.

Hayes didn't answer.

The wind picked up, blowing loose snow across the ground in thin, ghostly sheets. The men hunched deeper into their coats.

"Corporal," another soldier said, voice tight. "What if they're waiting for us in one of these coulees?"

Hayes scanned the land. Too many dips. Too many shadows. Too many places to die.

"We keep our distance," he said. "We're not here to fight."

"Then why are we here?"

Hayes didn't know how to answer that. Orders were orders. But he'd seen the look in Thornton's eyes before they rode out. It wasn't strategy. It wasn't duty.

A rider appeared on the horizon behind them, a dark shape moving fast.

Hayes stiffened. "Who the hell—"

The rider drew closer. A scout's coat. A familiar seat in the saddle. Bridger.

Hayes felt his stomach drop.

"Goddamn it," he muttered. "This won't be good."

The patrol slowed, turning toward the approaching rider. Bridger reined in hard, breath steaming, horse lathered.

"Orders," he said.

Hayes swallowed. "What kind."

"Recall," Bridger said. "We're pulling back."

The men looked at each other, relief, confusion, fear.

Hayes stared north, toward the faint line of the land where the tribe had vanished.

"Sir," he said quietly, "we're close."

Bridger's jaw tightened. "Too close."

Hayes nodded once. He understood.

"Form up!" he called. "We're heading back!"

The men turned their horses south.

Behind them, the wind swept across the prairie, erasing their tracks.

* * *

The sun was low by the time the soldiers finished loading supplies. The sky had gone the color of old iron, the cold settling in hard. Thornton raised a hand and waved the sergeant over.

"We'll stay here tonight," Thornton said.

The sergeant blinked. "Sir? I thought—"

"We lost half the day laying in supplies," Thornton said. "No point riding blind into the dark. We move at first light."

The men didn't argue. They were tired, cold, and the thought of a roof, even a rough one, was enough.

Thornton pushed through the trading post door. The warmth inside was thin, but it was warmth. The trader looked up, startled again.

"Captain."

Thornton scanned the room. Nothing had changed since the morning. Shelves of flour and salt. A few pelts. A lantern guttering in the draft.

"We'll be staying the night," Thornton said. "My men will need space in the barn."

"Yes, sir. Plenty of room."

Thornton nodded once and stepped back outside. The men were already leading horses toward the barn, stamping their feet, rubbing their hands. A few laughed quietly, the first sound of ease all day.

"Let them have their night," Thornton said to the sergeant. "No whiskey. No trouble. I want them sharp at dawn."

"Yes, sir."

Thornton walked to the edge of the yard, looking southwest. The land stretched out in long, dark waves, disappearing into the coming night.

He stood there a long time, breath rising in slow clouds.

"Harlan," he muttered. "You're not clever. You're predictable. You went where any man would go."

He turned back toward the trading post, the lantern light flickering in the windows.

Inside, the men settled in. Boots off. Coats steaming. Quiet talk. Cards. The soft clatter of tin cups.

Thornton didn't join them. He sat alone near the door, coat still on, hat pulled low, eyes fixed on nothing.

Outside, the wind picked up, rattling the shutters.

Somewhere out in the dark, a horse whinnied. Distant, faint.

Thornton didn't look up.

13

Life

He came back slowly.

First, the heat: a dull, heavy warmth pressing against his face. Then the smell of smoke. Then the ache in his hands, his feet, his ribs. His eyes fluttered, closed again, then opened for real.

He was propped against a log, wrapped in hides that smelled of smoke and old blood. A fire crackled a few feet away, throwing orange light across the snow. Two men crouched beside it, one stirring a tin pot, the other pouring coffee from a blackened kettle.

Both turned when they saw him move.

"Well now," the one with the longer beard said. "Look who's decided to join the living."

The other grinned through a tangle of hair. "Thought we'd lost you, friend."

Elias blinked, trying to make sense of the shapes, the voices. His throat was raw. "Where...?"

"Where're you?" the long-bearded one said. "Right where we found you, more or less. Half buried in snow, stiff as a fence post. Lucky we come along when we did."

The other man nodded. "Lucky you weren't froze solid. Another hour, maybe less…"

Elias tried to sit up. Pain shot through his legs and he sucked in a breath.

"Easy," the bearded man said. "You ain't goin' nowhere tonight."

Elias looked at them properly now. Hard men. Weathered. Faces half lost behind beards and dirt. Coats patched with whatever cloth they'd had on hand. Their boots were crusted with ice. Their hair hung long and wild. They looked like they'd been out here for months, maybe longer.

Behind them, three mules stood tied to a scrub pine, two of them piled high with furs. Wolf, fox, beaver, mink, whatever the land had given up. A pair of horses stamped in the snow nearby, steam rising from their backs.

Trappers.

Of course.

The long-bearded one poured a cup of coffee and held it out. "Here. Warm you up."

Elias took it with shaking hands. The heat bit into his fingers, painful and good. He drank, the bitter taste cutting through the fog in his head.

"You're lucky we were headin' south," the other man said. "Got a load of hides to sell at the post. Figured we'd make camp early when we saw somethin' lyin' in the snow that didn't look like a rock."

The long-bearded one chuckled. "Didn't look like much of a man neither."

Elias managed a faint smile. "Thank you."

"Don't thank us yet," the man said. "We ain't sure you're gonna live till morning."

Elias closed his eyes for a moment. The fire popped. The wind moved through the trees above them, a low, cold whisper.

He was alive.

He didn't know how.

But he was alive.

The long-bearded trapper nudged the pot with a stick. "We'll get some food in you. Warm you up proper. Then you can tell us what in God's name you were doin' out here alone."

Elias opened his eyes again, staring into the fire.

He didn't know where to begin.

* * *

By midday of the second day, Elias could stand without the world tilting under him. His hands still burned when he flexed them, and his feet felt like blocks of wood, but he was alive. The trappers had fed him coffee, thin stew, and strips of dried meat until the color crept back into his face.

He stepped away from the fire, testing his legs, scanning the tree line and the open snow beyond. Something tugged at him. A memory, a shape, a weight that should have been there.

"My horse," he said quietly. "Did you see a horse when you found me."

The long-bearded trapper shook his head. "Ain't no horse around here."

"I had one," Elias said. "When I went down."

"Then he's gone," the trapper said. "Storm like that, they don't stick around. They drift with the wind, lookin' for shelter. Might be ten miles from here. Might be twenty. Might be in Canada by now."

The other man snorted. "If the wolves didn't get him."

Elias looked at the snow, jaw tight. The cold pressed in around him, sharp and indifferent.

The long-bearded trapper shrugged. "Ain't nothin' you could've done. You were near froze solid. Horse did what horses do."

Elias nodded once, though the loss hit him harder than he expected. Another piece gone. Another subtraction. The land taking what it wanted.

He stepped back toward the fire, the hides around his shoulders heavy with smoke.

The trapper watched him for a moment, then said, "You'll need somethin' to take its place."

He turned to a canvas roll tied to one of the mules, rummaged through it, and came up with an old Springfield Model 1873. The stock was scarred, the bluing worn thin, the trapdoor hinge a little loose, but it was clean, oiled, cared for.

"Here," the trapper said, holding it out. "A man won't last long out here with no rifle."

Elias stared at it. "I can't take that."

"You can," the trapper said. "And you will. Ain't charity. It's common sense. You go wanderin' around out here unarmed, you'll be dead before the week's out."

He reached into a saddlebag and tossed Elias two small cloth pouches. Ammunition.

"Couple handfuls of .45-70. Enough to keep you fed, if you know what you're doin'."

The other trapper spat into the snow. "Don't know why he's still lugging that old junk around anyway. Heavy as sin. Slow. He's got himself a new Winchester repeater."

The long-bearded one patted the lever-action rifle slung over his shoulder. "This here's just takin' up space."

Elias took the Springfield, feeling the weight settle into his hands. Solid. Real. A lifeline.

"Thank you," he said.

The trapper waved it off. "Don't thank us. Just try not to die."

* * *

The light faded early. By the time the trappers finished tending the animals and stacking more wood on the fire, the sky had gone the color of bruised steel. The cold settled in again, sharp and dry, the kind that made a man's breath feel like it froze in his chest.

Elias sat wrapped in the hides they'd given him, the old Springfield across his knees. His hands still shook when he held the tin cup, but the coffee helped.

The long-bearded trapper poked at the fire with a stick. Sparks drifted up, caught in the wind, and vanished.

"Storm's movin' off," he said. "Be clear tonight. Cold as hell, though."

The other man grunted. "Clear skies just mean you freeze slower."

They both chuckled at that, the kind of humor men earned by surviving too many winters.

For a while, no one spoke. The fire cracked. The mules shifted in the dark. Somewhere far off, a coyote yipped once and fell silent.

The long-bearded trapper finally said, "You never did tell us what you were doin' out here alone."

Elias stared into the flames. "Got turned around."

The trapper snorted. "Everybody gets turned around. Not every-body ends up half-dead in a snowdrift."

Elias didn't answer.

The other trapper leaned back against his saddle. "We been up along the St. Mary for near two months. Good country for beaver. Cold enough to freeze your piss mid-stream, but the pelts are thick."

"Too thick," the long-bearded one said. "Means the winter's meaner than usual."

He took a drink of coffee, wiped his mouth with the back of his hand.

"On our way down," he said, "we crossed sign. Big sign."

Elias looked up. "What kind."

"Blackfeet," the trapper said. "Whole damn village movin' north. Ponies, dogs, the works. Trail wide as a road."

The other man nodded. "Too early for 'em to be headin' to their summer grounds. Way too early."

The long-bearded trapper tossed another stick on the fire. "Somethin' spooked 'em. Somethin' bad."

Elias felt his chest tighten. He kept his voice steady. "How far north."

"Couple days from here," the trapper said. "Maybe less, if you're ridin' hard. But you ain't ridin' hard. Hell, you ain't ridin' at all."

Elias looked down at the rifle across his knees.

The trapper watched him for a moment. "You fixin' to follow 'em."

Elias didn't answer.

The trapper shook his head. "You're touched, friend. North in winter? Alone? After a village that's runnin' from somethin'?"

The other man spat into the snow. "Ain't our business. Ain't yours neither."

Elias stared into the fire. "It is."

The trappers exchanged a look. Not understanding, not agreeing, but recognizing something in him. A kind of stubbornness. A kind of grief.

The long-bearded trapper sighed. "Well. You got a rifle now. And enough cartridges to keep you fed if you don't miss."

He pointed north with his chin. "But you best keep your eyes open. Folks movin' that fast, that early… somethin' put fear in 'em."

The fire popped. The wind shifted. The cold pressed in around them.

Elias didn't speak again that night.

Neither did the trappers.

The land did all the talking.

* * *

The next morning broke clear and bitter. The sky was a hard, pale blue, the kind that promised cold all day. Frost clung to the mules' backs, their breath rising in slow white plumes. The trappers moved through camp with the easy rhythm of men who'd done this too many times to think about it.

Elias tightened the strap on the Springfield, the weight of it settling across his shoulder. His hands still shook when he cinched the blanket roll to the borrowed saddle, but he could stand, walk, lift. That was enough.

The long-bearded trapper watched him for a moment, then nodded. "You're lookin' less like a corpse today."

The other man grinned. "Still walkin' like one."

Elias managed a faint smile. "I'll get better."

"Maybe," the long-bearded one said. "If the cold don't take you first."

They finished packing in silence. The trappers checked their loads, tightened cinches, slung their rifles. Elias adjusted the hides around his shoulders, feeling the cold bite through them anyway.

The long-bearded trapper stepped closer. "We're headin' south. Fort Benton, maybe Fort Shaw if the weather turns. You oughta come with us. Warm bed. Real food. Doctor, if you need one."

Elias shook his head. "I'm going north."

The trapper stared at him like he was trying to see the sense of it. "North? In this weather? Alone?"

Elias didn't look away. "I have business there."

The other trapper spat into the snow. "Ain't nothin' north but cold and Indians."

Elias didn't answer.

The long-bearded trapper sighed, the sound heavy in the cold air. "Well. You got a rifle now. And enough cartridges to keep you fed if you don't miss."

Elias nodded once. "Thank you. For everything."

The trapper waved it off. "Don't thank us. Just try not to die. Be a shame to waste all that coffee."

They mounted up. The mules shifted, the horses stamped, the leather creaked in the cold.

The long-bearded trapper tipped his hat. "Good luck to you, friend."

The other man added, "You'll need it."

They turned south, riding in a slow line across the white land, the mules trailing behind them like shadows.

Elias watched until they were small shapes against the snow.

Then he turned north.

The wind cut across the prairie, sharp and clean. The land stretched out before him, empty and waiting.

He started walking.

14

The Elder's Last Stand

By midday, the camp at the St. Mary was taking shape. Fires burned low under the trees. Women boiled snow for water. Children gathered sticks. The ponies stood with their heads low, steam rising from their backs.

Makóyi sent three young men south to read the land, Nitááhkii among them. He watched them ride out, their silhouettes small against the white plain, and felt the familiar ache in his chest. Nitááhkii rode like a man twice his age, quiet in the saddle, eyes always moving.

The scouting party returned near dusk. Nitááhkii rode ahead of the others, his face tight, his jaw set. He dismounted before his horse had fully stopped and walked toward Makóyi with that same slow, deliberate step Makóyi had seen once before, thirteen years ago.

Makóyi felt the memory rise before the boy even spoke.

Nitááhkii stopped in front of him. "We found him," he said.

Makóyi didn't ask who.

"Show me," he said.

***

They rode out at first light. The storm had smoothed the land, leaving only faint depressions where the soldiers' horses had passed. The sun was low when they reached the rise.

The elder sat where they had left him, or where he had chosen to die. Snow had drifted around his legs, covering him to the waist. His rifle lay across his lap. Three spent cartridges glinted in the frost.

Twenty paces away, a cavalry horse lay on its side, stiff, its blood frozen in a dark pool. Another pool of blood lay farther off, with drag marks leading away. The soldiers had taken their dead.

Nitááhkii stood over the elder for a long time, breathing hard, his hands clenched at his sides. His face was not angry, not exactly. It was something older. Something carved into him long before this day.

Makóyi knew that look. He had seen it once before, thirteen years ago, on a burned plain along the Marias River. The memory came back with the clarity of a wound reopening.

* * *

Makóyi had been wintering with his own band that year, far to the west. His sister had married into another band, a peaceful group, mostly elders, women, and children, camped along the Marias River.

He hadn't seen her in weeks.

When word reached him that soldiers had been seen riding north, he saddled his horse and rode hard toward her camp. The snow was deep, the cold bitter, and the land silent.

By the time he arrived, the killing was done.

The lodges were burned. Bodies lay in the snow, women, old men, children. The air stank of gunpowder and blood. The soldiers were gone. Only the crows remained.

He walked through the ruins calling names, but no one answered.

And then, across the plain, he saw a small figure walking toward him.

A child. Alone. Moving slowly, as if each step cost him something.

Nitááhkii.

His sister's son.

His face was streaked with dirt and tears, but his eyes were dry. Empty. Older than they should have been. He did not run to Makóyi. He simply stopped in front of him and looked up.

Makóyi asked him where his mother was.

Nitááhkii pointed back toward the smoke.

Later, Makóyi learned the rest.

The boy had been out on the plain, hunting prairie dogs with a stick. He heard the whooping, the gunfire, the screams. He ran toward the camp, toward his mother, his father, his little sister, and saw the soldiers firing into lodges, cutting down people as they fled.

He saw his mother fall.

He saw his father fall.

He saw children he played with lying still in the snow.

He knew, even at six, that if he ran to them, he would die too.

So he crawled into a badger hole and waited until the soldiers left.

When he emerged, the world he knew was gone.

He walked toward Makóyi because there was nowhere else to go.

Makóyi took him in.

Raised him.

Trained him.

But the look in the boy's eyes that day had never fully left.

* * *

They buried Natosapi on a rise above the river, where the cottonwoods leaned toward the water and the wind carried the smell of ice and willow bark. The ground was frozen, but the young men worked with axes and fire-heated stones until the earth softened enough to take him.

Nitááhkii placed the elder's rifle beside him.

Makóyi placed a small pouch of tobacco.

The women sang a low, steady song that carried across the valley.

Ksisstaki stood among them, quiet, the pup tucked inside her robe. She didn't step forward. She didn't speak. But her eyes stayed on Nitááhkii the entire time. Not with childish longing, but with the kind of pride and fear a young woman feels for someone she admires more than she can say.

When the burial was done, the people drifted back to camp. Nitááhkii lingered a moment longer, staring at the mound of earth. Ksisstaki watched him go, her breath fogging in the cold.

* * *

The camp settled into the St. Mary valley with the weary relief of animals finding shelter. Children chased each other between the willows, their laughter thin but real.

Nitááhkii helped mend a torn lodge cover, his hands steady despite the cold. A small boy hovered nearby, watching him. Nitááhkii handed him a bone awl.

"Hold this," he said.

The boy's face lit up. He held the awl with both hands, proud, serious. Nitááhkii tied the last knot and ruffled the boy's hair. The child grinned and ran off, shouting to his friends.

Ksisstaki saw it from across the camp. She didn't approach. She only watched him for a moment. The way he moved, the way the children trusted him, the way he carried himself like someone older than his years, then turned back to her work, cheeks warm despite the cold.

Makóyi noticed.

He said nothing.

Later, Nitááhkii joined a small hunting party. They moved quietly through the cottonwoods, following the tracks of a lone deer. They didn't find it, but they found sign, fresh droppings, a broken branch, a warm patch of snow where it had bedded down.

"Tomorrow," Nitááhkii said. "We will find it tomorrow."

Ksisstaki heard him from where she was gathering wood. She didn't speak to him. She only murmured, almost to herself:

"He will."

* * *

That night, as the fires burned low and the people slept, Makóyi stood at the edge of camp, looking north. The sky was clear, the stars sharp. The cold bit at his face.

Something was coming.

He didn't know what.

But the land felt watchful.

Nitááhkii approached, silent as a shadow.

Ksisstaki was nearby, trying to coax the pup into settling on a folded robe. He kept tumbling off, rolling in the snow, then scrambling back up with stubborn determination. She sighed, scooped him up, and held him against her chest.

She looked up when she saw the two men standing together, their silhouettes dark against the snow. She didn't join them. She only watched, her face half-lit by the flames.

"You feel it too," Makóyi said.

Nitááhkii nodded. "Someone is out there."

Makóyi looked north again, toward the dark line of the foothills.

Whoever it was, they were moving through the same cold, the same wind, the same white emptiness that had nearly killed them all.

And they were coming closer.

Ksisstaki held the pup tighter, her eyes on Nitááhkii.

Makóyi saw that too.

He said nothing.

But he knew the peace they'd found in the St. Mary valley would not last.

15

The Man in the Snow

The morning broke cold and brittle. Frost clung to the cottonwoods along the St. Mary, and the air held that sharp stillness that comes after a storm. Nitááhkii moved through the trees with two young warriors, following the faint trail of the deer they had tracked the day before. The snow was crusted now, the prints shallow but clear.

He knelt, touched the edge of a hoof mark, and nodded. "Not far."

The others trusted him. They always had.

They moved north, single file, breath rising in thin plumes. The land was quiet. Too quiet. Even the birds were still.

Then Nitááhkii stopped.

A different track cut across the deer's trail, deeper, longer, the stride uneven. A man's track. Alone. Heading north.

He crouched, studying the print. The heel dug deep, the toe dragged. Whoever made it was tired. Hurt. Or both.

He looked at the others and motioned forward.

They followed.

* * *

Three days north of where the trappers had left him the cold had settled into his bones like a debt he couldn't pay, the borrowed rifle heavy across his shoulder. He didn't know where he was going anymore, only that he had to keep moving north. Away from Thornton. Away from the soldiers. Away from everything.

His breath burned in his chest. His hands shook. The world felt too bright, too sharp.

Then he heard it.

Snow crunching.

Soft voices.

Close.

He froze.

He turned slowly, scanning the trees. Nothing. But the sound was there, faint, steady, coming closer.

Indians.

His heart slammed against his ribs. He stumbled toward a fallen log, dropped behind it, and fumbled with the Springfield. His fingers were stiff, clumsy. He pulled the hammer back, sighted down the barrel, breath shaking.

A shadow moved between the trees.

He fired.

The shot cracked across the valley, echoing off the ridges. The recoil slammed into his shoulder. The smoke drifted in a thin gray ribbon.

He didn't wait to see if he'd hit anything. He dropped to one knee, trying to reload, but the cartridge slipped from his fingers and fell into the snow. He cursed, grabbed another, tried again.

Too slow.

Too cold.

Too scared.

By the time he got the round halfway in, they were on him.

* * *

Nitááhkii burst through the trees first, the bullet having kicked up snow inches from his foot. He didn't hesitate. He hit Elias hard, knocking the rifle from his hands. The other two warriors were on him a heartbeat later, dragging him out from behind the log, pinning him to the ground.

Elias fought like a trapped animal, wild, desperate, terrified. He swung an elbow, caught one of the young men in the jaw, tried to twist free. But he was weak, half-frozen, and outnumbered.

A blow to the side of his head sent stars across his vision. The world tilted. Snow filled his mouth. Hands grabbed his wrists, twisting them behind his back. A rope cinched tight.

He lay gasping, face pressed into the cold earth.

Nitááhkii stood over him, chest rising and falling, eyes hard.

"Enough," he said.

The others hauled Elias to his feet. His legs barely held him. Blood trickled from his temple. His breath came in ragged bursts.

Nitááhkii retrieved the Springfield, checked the chamber, and slung it over his shoulder. He looked at Elias, really looked at him, and something flickered across his face. Not pity. Not anger. Something older. Something wary.

"Come," he said.

They led Elias south, toward the valley.

* * *

The camp was quiet when they emerged from the trees. Smoke drifted from the lodge fires. Children played near the riverbank, their laughter sharp in the cold air.

Ksisstaki was carrying wood toward her family's lodge, the pup trotting at her heels. He kept darting in front of her, tugging at her skirt, tripping her. She stumbled, caught herself, and hissed, "Stop that," but the pup only wagged his tail and pounced on her bootlace.

She looked up when she heard the voices.

Nitááhkii.

The other young men.

And a white man between them, hands bound, stumbling in the snow.

Her breath caught. The pup barked once, startled, then hid behind her leg.

Makóyi stepped out from between the lodges, drawn by the noise. He stopped when he saw the group approaching.

Nitááhkii pushed Elias forward. The man nearly fell.

Makóyi studied him, the torn coat, the blood on his temple, then his eyes narrowed. "I know you," he said. Elias looked up. Makoyi looked at the rifle slung over Nitááhkii's shoulder. He looked at the tracks in the snow behind them.

Then he looked at Nitááhkii.

"What happened?"

Nitááhkii's jaw tightened. "He shot at us."

Makóyi's gaze returned to Elias. He looked like a man with nothing left.

Makóyi stepped closer, his voice low, steady.

"Why are you here?"

Elias swallowed hard. His lips were cracked. His voice came out rough.

"I… I'm just trying to stay alive."

Makóyi held his gaze for a long moment.

The wind shifted. The pup whimpered. Ksisstaki watched from a distance, her eyes moving between Nitááhkii and the stranger.

Makóyi finally spoke.

"Bring him inside."

* * *

They pushed Elias into Makóyi's lodge and forced him down onto a buffalo robe near the fire. His hands were still bound. His head throbbed where the blow had landed. The heat inside the lodge hit him hard after the cold outside, making his vision swim.

Makóyi sat across from him, silent, steady, watching him with the patience of a man who had lived long enough to see every kind of trouble.

Elias tried to sit straighter, but the rope bit into his wrists. His breath came sharp through his nose. He kept his eyes on Makóyi, refusing to look at the others.

Nitááhkii stood near the doorway, arms crossed, shoulders tight, eyes fixed on Elias with a cold, controlled fury. The other two young warriors hovered behind him, whispering low.

Makóyi finally spoke.

"Why are you here?"

Elias lifted his head. His jaw tightened. A muscle jumped in his cheek. He stared at Makóyi as if the question itself were an insult.

"Because I didn't die," he said.

His voice was raw, scraped thin by cold and anger. He didn't look away.

Makóyi studied him, unreadable.

Elias's breath hitched once in his chest. "I didn't ask for any of this."

Nitááhkii shifted, the firelight catching the hard line of his jaw.

Elias's bound hands flexed uselessly against the rope. "I'm alive. That's all."

The lodge went still.

Nitááhkii stepped forward. "He shot at us," he said. "He would have killed us if he could."

Elias snapped, "You killed my dog."

The words tore out of him, sharp and ragged. His voice cracked on the last word. He hated that. Hated the weakness in it. Hated the way the grief rose up in him like a hand around his throat.

Nitááhkii's expression didn't change. "Your dog attacked me."

Elias's jaw clenched. "He was protecting my wife."

Nitááhkii didn't look away. "I know."

Nothing more.

Elias felt the heat rise in his face. Rage, grief, humiliation, all of it twisting together until he couldn't tell one from the other.

Makóyi spoke quietly. "You are alive because we chose not to kill you."

Elias looked away, breathing hard.

* * *

Ksisstaki hovered near the doorway, pretending to sort firewood. The pup kept tugging at her skirt, tripping her, chewing the fringe. She nudged him away with her foot, but he kept coming back, tail wagging, determined to be part of whatever was happening.

She could hear the voices inside, low, tense, sharp.

She heard Elias's anger.

She heard Nitááhkii's cold replies.

She heard Makóyi's calm, steady tone.

The pup barked once at a raised voice. Ksisstaki scooped him up, pressing him against her chest. His little heart thumped fast against her palm.

She looked toward the lodge flap again, worry tightening her throat.

* * *

Makóyi motioned for the others to leave. Nitááhkii hesitated, eyes still locked on Elias, but Makóyi gave him a look that ended the argument before it began.

When they were alone, Makóyi spoke.

"You will stay here tonight," he said. "You will not be harmed."

Elias let out a bitter breath. "Forgive me if I don't believe that."

Makóyi ignored the tone. "You are cold. You are hungry. You are wounded. Rest."

"I don't want your help."

"You are in no position to refuse it."

Elias looked away, jaw clenched, eyes burning.

Makóyi set a small bowl of broth near his bound hands. "Eat."

Elias stared at it.

He didn't move.

But the smell hit him, warm, rich, alive, and his stomach twisted painfully.

Makóyi waited.

Finally, Elias leaned forward and drank awkwardly from the bowl, his hands still tied. The broth burned his throat in a good way. He hated how good it tasted.

Makóyi watched him without judgment.

When Elias finished, Makóyi spoke again.

"You are not our enemy," he said. "Not unless you choose to be."

Elias closed his eyes.

He didn't know what he was anymore.

* * *

Nitááhkii stood outside the lodge, staring into the darkness. His breath rose in thin clouds. His hands were fists at his sides.

Ksisstaki approached quietly, the pup wriggling in her arms.

"He is afraid," she said softly.

Nitááhkii didn't look at her. "He is dangerous."

"He is alone."

Nitááhkii's jaw tightened. "So was I once."

Ksisstaki looked at him, something tender and painful in her eyes.

The pup squirmed, trying to lick Nitááhkii's hand. He ignored it.

Ksisstaki whispered, "Be careful."

Nitááhkii didn't answer.

* * *

Makóyi banked the fire and stepped outside, leaving Elias alone in the dim light.

The lodge felt too quiet.

Too warm.

Too close.

Elias stared at the shadows on the hide walls, his breath uneven.

He thought of Clara.

He thought of Scout.

He thought of the snow, the blood, the screams.

He thought of the man outside, the one who had killed his dog.

He hated him.

He hated all of them.

He hated himself for being here.

But beneath the hatred, something else stirred, something he didn't want to name.

He lay down on the buffalo robe, hands still bound, and closed his eyes.

Sleep took him like a blow.

* * *

Elias woke to the sound of voices outside the lodge, low, curious, rising and falling like the murmur of a river. The fire had burned down to coals. His hands were still bound. His head throbbed.

When Makóyi lifted the flap and stepped inside, the cold rushed in with him.

"You will come out," Makóyi said.

Elias pushed himself upright, stiff and sore. Makóyi cut the rope at his wrists but left the ends tied, a warning more than a restraint.

Makóyi led Elias toward the woodpile at the edge of camp. The morning was bright, the snow hard underfoot, the air sharp enough to sting the lungs. Elias walked stiffly, every muscle sore, every stare burning into him.

Children followed at a distance, whispering, daring each other to get closer. One boy crept up behind Elias and poked the back of his coat, then sprinted away shrieking with laughter. Elias flinched, teeth clenched.

Women watched from their fires, some nodding politely, others simply observing him the way one might observe a strange animal brought into camp. A few offered small smiles, cautious, curious, not unkind.

The braves stood farther back, arms crossed, eyes hard. Their stares were colder than the wind. Elias felt them like stones against his ribs.

Nitááhkii stood among them, silent, unreadable. The gray pony behind him stamped the snow, the pale scar across its nose catching the light. Elias's stomach twisted at the sight.

Makóyi stopped near a stack of split logs. "You will carry these," he said.

Elias didn't move.

Makóyi's voice stayed calm. "You will work. Or you will not eat."

Elias's jaw tightened. He reached for a log.

The pup barreled into Elias's leg, teeth sunk into his pant cuff, growling with all the ferocity his tiny body could muster. His tail wagged wildly, betraying his courage.

Elias jerked back, startled.

Makóyi nudged the pup away with the side of his foot, gentle, firm. "Enough."

The pup skidded in the snow, shook himself, and lunged again.

Ksisstaki hurried forward, breath fogging in the cold. "No, come here," she whispered, scooping the pup into her arms before he could make another charge.

The pup wriggled, paws flailing, still trying to get at Elias's boot. She held him tighter, murmuring something soft into his fur.

Then she looked up.

Her eyes met Elias's.

Not long.

Not deep.

Just long enough.

He saw something move across her face. The pup still straining in her arms, still fighting, still certain it could win.

His breath caught.

Ksisstaki's grip tightened on the pup.

For a moment, the cold between them thinned.

Then Elias looked away.

Ksisstaki turned, carrying the pup back toward her family's lodge. The pup twisted in her arms to keep his eyes on Elias, tail still wagging.

Nitááhkii watched all of it, jaw tight.

Makóyi handed Elias a log. "Work."

Elias took it.

The camp watched.

Elias carried wood until his arms shook. The children watched until they got bored. The pup slept in Ksisstaki's arms, dreaming of enemies to fight.

16

The Machinery Turns

The trappers reached the trading post after nearly two weeks on the trail. The snow had begun to rot in the afternoons, turning the ground to mud, and the river ice cracked and groaned under its own weight. Their horses were thin. Their faces were wind-burned. Their packs were heavy with winter furs.

The trading post sat low against the gray sky, smoke drifting from its chimney, the smell of wet hides and woodsmoke hanging in the air. A few soldiers lounged near the gate, rifles propped against the wall, boots muddy to the ankles.

They rode in slow, stiff in their saddles, and the story they carried, the story of a half-dead white man wandering the northern foothills, spread through the post like smoke.

By the next morning, a message was on its way to Fort Shaw.

* * *

It took the messenger days to find Thornton.

Thornton had scattered his patrols across the southwest, sending men into every coulee and draw, convinced Elias was hiding somewhere in the broken country. The messenger rode through sleet, mud, and wind, asking at every campfire, every picket line, every lonely outpost.

When he finally found him, Thornton was standing over a map spread across a saddle blanket, barking orders at two lieutenants. His face was gaunt from lack of sleep. His eyes were sharp with frustration.

The messenger saluted. "Sir. Message from Fort Shaw."

Thornton tore it open.

A white man.

Found alive.

Heading north.

His jaw tightened. His breath came slow and dangerous.

"Pack up," he said. "We're going back."

* * *

Thornton rode into Fort Shaw three days later, mud up to his stirrups, temper coiled tight. He expected to stride into his office, slam the door, and begin issuing orders.

Instead, he found a colonel sitting behind his desk.

Colonel Harrington.

Former aide to General Terry.

A man who had ridden with Custer's staff in the weeks before the Little Bighorn, and survived only because he'd been sent east on a supply errand.

Thornton had been a junior officer then.

He had been sent away too, a courier assignment, routine, forgettable.

He'd ridden back into a world that had already changed.

The bodies.

The horses.

The silence.

The shame.

He had missed the battle.

Missed the chance to prove himself.

Missed the chance to make his name.

And he had never forgiven the tribes for it.

"Captain Thornton," Harrington said without standing. "We need to talk."

Thornton stopped in the doorway, rain dripping from his coat. "Sir."

Harrington folded his hands. "You've spent the winter chasing one man."

Thornton's jaw flexed. "A dangerous man."

"A rancher," Harrington said. "One rancher. Meanwhile, the tribes are moving freely. Our objectives are not being met. Washington wants the tribes on the reservations by spring. They are not making it a suggestion."

Thornton's face darkened.

Harrington continued. "Your patrols are scattered. Your supplies are depleted. Your men are exhausted. And now I hear you intend to march north."

Thornton didn't answer.

Harrington leaned back. "You will recall your patrols. You will resupply. You will reorganize. And then you will resume your duties."

Thornton's voice was low. "My duties are to bring that man in."

Harrington's eyes hardened. "Your duties are what I say they are."

Silence.

Thornton's hands curled into fists at his sides.

Harrington stood. "Get your house in order, Captain. Then we'll discuss your... priorities."

He walked past Thornton without another word.

Thornton stared at the empty desk. He sat down in his own chair. Slowly. Like a man taking back something that had been taken from him.

* * *

The room smelled of damp wool and old paper.

Maps curled at the edges.

A lantern hissed softly.

Thornton rubbed his temples.

He had carried it for seven years.

He had told himself for years that he was serving justice.

Serving order.

Serving the country.

But the truth was simpler.

He hated them.

All of them.

Every tribe.

Every camp.

Every warrior.

And Elias, Elias had run north.

Elias had escaped him.

Elias had humiliated him.

Thornton leaned over the map, tracing a line north with one finger.

The tribe his scouts had been following before the storm had gone that way too.

He didn't know if Elias was with them.

He didn't know if Elias had crossed their path.

He didn't know anything for certain.

But he didn't need certainty.

He needed a reason.

A justification.

A story Harrington would believe.

"Raiders," he murmured. "I'll call them raiders."

It was the perfect excuse.

Washington wanted the tribes pushed back.

The Army wanted results.

Harrington wanted order.

Thornton wanted Elias.

And now he had a way to get all three.

* * *

It took weeks.

Riders were sent to recall the scattered patrols.

Men straggled in, tired and irritated.

Supplies were inventoried.

Horses were shod.

Ammunition was counted.

Wagons repaired.

Orders rewritten.

Maps redrawn.

Thornton oversaw every detail, jaw clenched, eyes hollow with purpose.

He told his officers they were pursuing a band of raiders.

He told Harrington he was fulfilling federal policy.

He told his men they were avenging a rancher's loss.

He told himself he was going after Elias.

And somewhere in that slow grind, Thornton found Bridger.

The scout looked older than he had a month ago. More tired. More wary.

Thornton didn't ask if he would come.

He told him.

Bridger didn't argue.

But something in his eyes dimmed.

* * *

By the time the last patrol limped back into Fort Shaw, the snow was melting fast. The river ran high with runoff. The prairie smelled of wet earth and new grass.

Thornton stood on the parade ground, watching the men assemble.

He felt the old fire rising in him, the one he had carried since the Little Bighorn, the one that had never gone out.

"North," he said.

The officers nodded.

The men mounted.

The wagons creaked.

And the Army began to move.

Slowly.

Inevitably.

Toward the valley where Elias lived, though Thornton did not yet know it, among the people he hated most.

17

Early Spring

Elias waited until the camp had gone quiet.

The fires burned low.

The dogs curled near the lodges.

The wind had died to a whisper.

He lay still on the buffalo robe, listening.

A man learns to hear patterns in captivity, footsteps, voices, the rhythm of a guard's boredom.

Tonight, the rhythm was loose.

Complacent.

He eased himself up, careful not to disturb the hide flap. His ribs ached. His head still throbbed from the blow days earlier. But he moved quietly, slowly, the way a man moves who has spent years working cattle in the dark.

He slipped out into the cold.

The moon was thin, the snow crusted hard.

He kept to the shadows between lodges, breath held tight in his chest.

He was almost past the last row of lodges when he saw it.

A small shape sitting in the snow.

Watching him.

The pup.

Its ears perked.

Its tail thumped once.

Then it let out a soft, questioning whine.

Elias froze. "No," he whispered. "Not now."

The pup tilted its head.

Then it barked.

Loud.

Sharp.

Elias flinched. "Shh—"

The pup barked again, louder this time, tail wagging like this was the best game in the world.

Elias hissed, "Go on, get," and made a half-hearted swipe with his boot.

The pup dodged easily, he'd grown up around boots, and barked again, delighted.

A lodge flap opened.

Another.

Voices rose.

A woman laughed.

A man cursed.

Elias closed his eyes.

Makóyi appeared first, hair loose around his shoulders, blanket thrown over one arm. He squinted at Elias, then at the pup, then back at Elias.

"Did you have to make water?" he asked, voice flat as a winter stone.

A ripple of laughter moved through the camp.

Elias felt heat crawl up his neck.

Ksisstaki hurried over, breath fogging in the cold, the pup now circling her legs, proud of himself. She scooped him up, murmuring to him in Blackfoot, though she was smiling.

Her eyes met Elias's.

There was no mockery in them.

Only something softer.

Something like understanding.

Makóyi stepped closer. "Next time," he said quietly, "wake me. I will walk with you."

Elias swallowed hard. "I wasn't—"

Makóyi raised a hand. "It is cold. And dark. Easy to get lost."

Another wave of laughter rolled through the camp.

Nitááhkii pushed through the small crowd, eyes sharp, jaw tight. He looked Elias over, then the pup, then Ksisstaki holding him.

For a moment, his gaze lingered on the pup's wagging tail before flicking back to Elias.

His shoulders eased, barely, and he let out a slow breath.

He didn't speak.

His hand left his knife.

Makóyi gestured toward the lodge. "Come. Sleep."

Elias nodded, defeated, humiliated.

As he turned back toward the lodge, the pup wriggled out of Ksisstaki's arms, trotted after him, and dropped a small stick at his feet.

Elias stared at it.

The pup wagged his tail.

Ksisstaki laughed softly.

Elias didn't pick up the stick.

But he didn't kick it away either.

* * *

The morning after the failed escape, Elias woke to the sound of scraping hides.

A woman knelt outside the lodge, pulling a bone scraper along a stretched deer hide, the rhythm steady as breathing. Children played in the slush near the fire pits, their voices carrying across the thawing valley. Smoke drifted low across the camp, carrying the smell of boiled meat and sweetgrass.

Makóyi appeared at the lodge entrance, ducking inside without ceremony.

"You work today," he said.

Elias pushed himself upright. "Doing what?"

Makóyi shrugged. "Whatever needs doing."

He led Elias out into the camp. The sun was just clearing the ridge, turning the frost on the lodge poles to silver. Women were already at their tasks, scraping hides, pounding chokecherries, tending fires. Men checked the horses, tightening rawhide bindings, rubbing warmth into stiff legs.

Elias watched them move with a quiet efficiency he hadn't expected. No shouting. No wasted motion. Everyone knew their place, their task, their rhythm.

Makóyi handed him a bundle of firewood. "Carry this to Aakíiwa's lodge."

Elias hesitated. "Who?"

Makóyi pointed with his chin. "There."

Aakíiwa saw him coming and smiled, a small, polite smile, nothing more. She took the wood from him and thanked him in Blackfoot. Elias didn't understand the words, but he understood the tone.

When he turned, the pup was sitting behind him, tail sweeping the snow.

Elias sighed. "Not you again."

The pup barked once, sharp and pleased with himself.

Makóyi chuckled. "He likes you."

"I kicked at him last night."

"He has been kicked before," Makóyi said. "He knows the difference."

Elias didn't answer.

* * *

Later, Makóyi sat with him near the horse line, showing him simple words.

"This," Makóyi said, touching his chest, "ni'tá."

Me.

He pointed at Elias. "Kitsíks."

You.

Elias repeated it, stumbling over the sounds.

Makóyi corrected him gently, never impatient.

Children gathered nearby, whispering and giggling as Elias tried again. One boy mimicked him, exaggerating the sounds until the others burst into laughter. Elias felt his face heat, but Makóyi only smiled.

"They laugh because you try," he said. "Not because you fail."

Elias wasn't sure he believed that.

But he tried again.

* * *

Ksisstaki passed by with a basket of dried meat, the pup trotting at her heels. She paused when she saw Elias repeating the words, her expression unreadable.

Makóyi nodded to her. She nodded back.

Her eyes lingered on Elias for a moment, unreadable, neither warm nor cold, before she moved on.

Nitááhkii stood a few paces behind her, arms crossed. He watched

Elias too, but without the sharpness of before. His gaze was cooler now, more measuring than hostile.

The pup broke the moment by dropping a stick at Elias's feet.

Ksisstaki laughed softly.

Nitááhkii watched.

Elias looked at the stick for a long moment.

Then he picked it up and threw it.

The pup exploded after it, a gray blur across the snow, skidding on the crust, tumbling, recovering, coming back at full speed with the stick clamped in his jaws and his tail going hard.

He dropped it at Elias's feet again.

Nitááhkii turned and walked away.

* * *

The sun had climbed high enough to soften the snow along the riverbank. Water trickled beneath the crust, a faint, steady sound that reminded Elias of spring back home, the kind of spring that came late and left early.

He carried a bundle of firewood across the camp, passing a group of women painting parfleche bags. They worked with quiet concentration, dipping brushes made from animal hair into small bowls of crushed ochre and blue-green clay. The geometric patterns grew under their hands, diamonds, stepped lines, the shapes of mountains and rivers. A girl no older than ten held up a finished piece to the light, proud of the symmetry she'd achieved.

Elias slowed without meaning to.

A shout rose from the riverbank. Young men racing horses along the thawing edge, hooves kicking up slush. Their laughter echoed across the valley, wild and bright. One rider leaned low over his horse's neck, urging it faster, while another whooped as he pulled ahead.

The camp felt alive in a way Elias didn't know how to name.

He set the firewood down beside a lodge and straightened, rubbing the stiffness from his hands.

That's when he felt something bump his boot.

He looked down.

The pup sat there, tail sweeping the snow, a stick clamped proudly in his mouth.

Elias sighed. "You again."

The pup dropped the stick at his feet and backed up a step, expectant.

"No," Elias said. "I'm not doing this."

The pup barked once, sharp, insistent, then nudged the stick closer with his nose.

Elias shook his head. "I said no."

The pup barked again, louder this time, tail wagging so hard his whole body wiggled.

A couple of children nearby giggled. One pointed. Another whispered something in Blackfoot that made the first laugh harder.

Elias felt heat rise in his face.

He bent down, picked up the stick, and tossed it a few feet away, mostly to shut the pup up.

The pup exploded after it, skidding across the melting snow, triumphant.

Makóyi appeared beside him, arms folded loosely. "He has chosen you," he said.

Elias snorted. "He's a nuisance."

Makóyi nodded toward the pup. "Imitaa."

Elias frowned. "What's that mean?"

"Dog," Makóyi said. "She has not given him a name yet."

"Why not?"

Makóyi watched the pup circling Elias's legs, tail sweeping the snow. "She is waiting to see what he becomes."

Elias looked down at the pup, who dropped the stick at his feet with absolute confidence.

Makóyi added, "Names come when they are earned."

This time, Elias didn't hesitate.

He threw it a little farther.

The pup tore after it, yipping with joy.

Across the camp, Ksisstaki paused in her work and watched, not smiling, not staring, just watching. Her eyes followed the arc of the stick, then the pup, then Elias's hand as he lowered it again.

Nitááhkii stood a few paces behind her, arms crossed. He didn't say anything. But he didn't look away either.

The pup returned, panting, triumphant.

Elias threw the stick again.

And again.

And again.

Until he realized he was smiling.

He stopped.

Makóyi pretended not to notice.

* * *

The next morning, the camp woke slowly under a pale sun. Snowmelt trickled along the packed paths between lodges, and the air carried the smell of damp earth and woodsmoke. Elias stepped out into the cold, rubbing sleep from his eyes, unsure where he was supposed to go or what he was supposed to do.

Ksisstaki crossed his path before he'd taken three steps. She held a small wooden bowl in both hands, steam curling from it. Without a word, she offered it to him.

Elias hesitated. "For me?"

She nodded once.

He took it carefully. The broth was rich and warm, thick with meat and something sweet he couldn't place. Ksisstaki said a short phrase in Blackfoot, then pointed to the bowl and repeated the last word.

"Aáhpo," she said.

Elias tried it. "A…aáhpo."

Her mouth twitched, almost a smile, and she moved on, the pup trotting behind her, pausing only to glance back at Elias as if making sure he understood the gift.

He watched her go, the warmth of the bowl seeping into his hands.

Makóyi found him soon after and motioned for him to follow. They walked to the edge of camp where a small fire burned low, surrounded by elders sitting in a half-circle. Sweetgrass smoldered in a clay bowl, its scent drifting on the breeze.

Makóyi didn't explain. He simply sat.

Elias stood awkwardly until one of the elders gestured for him to join them. He lowered himself to the ground, unsure if he was intruding.

The elders spoke softly, their voices weaving together like wind through dry grass. One lifted a handful of sweetgrass smoke toward the sky, then toward the earth, then toward the river. Another murmured a prayer, the cadence slow and steady.

Elias didn't understand the words.

But he understood the feeling.

It was gratitude, for the thaw, for the horses, for the food that had lasted the winter.

When the ceremony ended, Makóyi rose and brushed ash from his hands. "Spring comes," he said simply.

Elias nodded, though he wasn't sure if Makóyi meant the season or something else.

They walked back toward the center of camp. Children were chasing each other between the lodges, their laughter sharp in the cold air. A woman knelt beside a hide stretched taut on a frame, scraping it with a bone tool in long, practiced strokes. The sound, rasp, rasp, rasp, blended with the distant rush of the river.

Elias slowed without meaning to.

There was something calming about the rhythm, the way her hands moved with certainty, the way the hide brightened under her work.

He didn't know why it struck him.

Only that it did.

Makóyi noticed him watching but said nothing.

Near the river, Nitááhkii was working with a young bay colt, trying to get a halter over its head. The colt tossed nervously, whites of its eyes showing, hooves slipping in the slush.

Nitááhkii clicked his tongue, patient but firm. The colt jerked away again.

Elias stopped a few paces off. He didn't speak. Didn't want to intrude. But he couldn't help watching. The colt's fear was familiar, the way it danced sideways, the way its ears flicked back and forth.

Nitááhkii tried again. The colt reared its head, snorting.

Elias stepped forward before he could think better of it.

"Easy," he murmured, voice low, the way he used to talk to skittish yearlings back home. He kept his hands loose at his sides, shoulders relaxed. "Easy now."

Nitááhkii shot him a sharp look, but didn't tell him to leave.

Elias angled his body slightly, not facing the colt head-on. He lowered his gaze, softened his breath. The colt's ears flicked toward him.

"That's it," Elias whispered. "You're all right."

He took one slow step.

Then another.

The colt didn't bolt.

Didn't rear.

Just watched him.

Elias reached out, palm open. The colt sniffed his hand, trembling, then let him touch its cheek.

Nitááhkii stared, jaw tight, but not with anger this time.

Elias stroked the colt's neck, then nodded toward the halter. "Let him smell it first," he said quietly. "Don't rush him."

Nitááhkii hesitated, then held the halter out. The colt sniffed it, snorted, then stood still.

Together, without speaking, they slipped it over the colt's head.

Nitááhkii stepped back, studying Elias as if seeing him for the first time.

Elias stepped back too, suddenly self-conscious.

The pup barreled into his leg, stick in his mouth, tail wagging like a banner.

Nitááhkii's mouth twitched, not a smile, but close.

Elias threw the stick.

The colt watched it arc through the air, ears pricked.

Nitááhkii watched Elias.

And for the first time, there was no hatred in his eyes.

* * *

Later that day, as Elias gathered kindling near the edge of camp, he heard footsteps behind him, not hurried, not stealthy, but deliberate. He turned to see Nitááhkii walking toward him with the same focused stride he'd used with the colt earlier.

The young warrior stopped a few paces away, expression unreadable. He held something in his hand, a small bundle wrapped in softened hide.

Elias straightened, unsure whether to brace or relax.

Nitááhkii extended the bundle toward him.

Elias hesitated. "What's this?"

Nitááhkii didn't answer at first. He simply waited, arm outstretched, eyes steady. Elias took the bundle carefully. Inside were strips of dried meat, a handful of chokecherries, and a small piece of pemmican pressed into a neat square.

Food.

Not scraps.

Not leftovers.

Something prepared with intention.

Nitááhkii finally spoke, his voice low, the words accented but clear. "Eat. You work better when you are strong."

Elias blinked, caught off guard. "Thank you."

Nitááhkii's gaze flicked to the colt tied nearby, then back to Elias. "You know horses," he said. Not a question. A statement.

"I was raised around them," Elias said. "Worked with them my whole life."

Nitááhkii nodded once, slow and thoughtful. "The colt… he listened to you."

Elias shrugged. "He just needed someone to show him he wasn't in danger."

Nitááhkii's jaw tightened. Not with anger, but with something like reluctant acknowledgment. "You saw what he needed."

Elias didn't know what to say to that.

For a moment, they stood in silence, the wind carrying the distant sound of children laughing and the steady rasp of a woman scraping a hide. The pup trotted up between them, tail wagging, a stick in his mouth. He dropped it at Elias's feet, then looked up at Nitááhkii as if inviting him into the game.

Nitááhkii's mouth twitched, the faintest hint of amusement, before he masked it again.

He stepped back. "Tomorrow," he said, "you help with the horses."

Elias nodded. "All right."

Nitááhkii turned to leave, then paused, glancing over his shoulder. "Do not waste the food," he said. "It is good."

Elias looked down at the bundle in his hands. "I won't."

Nitááhkii gave a single, sharp nod, not approval, not friendship, but something in between, and walked away.

The pup barked once, as if satisfied with the exchange.

* * *

The next morning Elias was at the horse line before most of the camp was moving.

He worked quietly, checking legs, running his hands along flanks, feeling for heat or swelling. The horses had come through the winter thin but sound. A few needed their hooves looked at. He picked up a roan mare's near foreleg and bent to examine it, holding the hoof between his knees the way his father had taught him, scraping mud from the sole with a stick.

He became aware of the shadow after a few minutes.

A boy. Twelve, maybe thirteen. Standing just outside arm's reach, watching with the particular stillness of someone trying not to be noticed. Dark eyes moving from Elias's hands to the mare's hoof and back again.

Elias didn't look up. Kept working.

"She's been favoring this leg," he said quietly, not sure if the boy understood any English. "Something packed in here."

He found it. A small stone wedged near the frog, and worked it free with the stick. The mare shifted her weight, relieved.

Elias set the hoof down and straightened, rolling his shoulder.

He glanced at the boy. Nodded toward the next horse in line, a gray gelding standing with one hip cocked, head low.

"That one next," Elias said. "You want to hold him?"

The boy looked at the gelding. Then at Elias. He didn't move toward it.

Elias crossed to the gelding himself, ran a hand along its neck, then looked back at the boy and held out the lead rope without urgency. Just held it out.

The boy stepped forward and took it.

They worked down the line that way. The boy holding. Elias checking. Neither of them speaking. The camp waking up around them, smoke rising, voices starting up, children appearing between the lodges.

When they finished, the boy coiled the lead rope carefully and hung it back on the post.

He looked at Elias once, direct and brief.

Then he walked back toward the lodges without a word.

Elias watched him go.

Makóyi appeared at his shoulder, two strips of dried meat in his hand. He offered one to Elias without preamble.

"That is Apinakoi's son," he said. "His father died last winter."

Elias took the meat. Said nothing.

Makóyi looked down the line at the horses. "They look better," he said.

"They needed their feet done," Elias said.

Makóyi nodded. Ate his meat. Walked away.

18

The Raid

The morning came in quiet and pale, the sky the color of old bone. Along the riverbank, snowmelt trickled under the crust, and the air smelled of wet earth and woodsmoke. Birds moved through the cottonwoods, restless, their calls brief and scattered.

Elias was at the horse line when the pup lifted his head.

Not toward the camp.

Toward the tree line.

His ears flattened. A low sound rose in his chest, not a bark, just a vibration, a warning that came from instinct. Then he took off at a run, straight to Ksisstaki.

Elias looked up.

The horses shifted. The bay colt stamped once, twice. Elias put a hand on its neck and felt the muscles coiled tight beneath the hide.

Nitááhkii appeared beside him, already reading the same signs, already turning.

The Cree came out of the trees fast and low, riding hard, their horses' hooves barely making sound on the softened ground until they were close, too close, and then the sound was everywhere, pounding and shouting and the sharp crack of a rifle from somewhere in the trees.

The camp erupted.

Women grabbed children. Men shouted. Someone screamed. A horse broke free of the line and bolted south, mane flying.

Nitááhkii was already running toward the lodges, shouting commands. Warriors appeared from between the hides, weapons in hand.

Elias stood at the horse line, unarmed.

He looked for a rifle. A knife. Anything.

Nothing.

A Cree warrior swung toward him on horseback, leaning low, a hatchet rising.

Elias threw himself sideways. The hatchet glanced off his shoulder, not the blade, the handle, and pain burst white through his arm. He hit the ground, rolled, came up moving.

The warrior wheeled his horse for another pass.

Elias grabbed the only thing within reach.

A piece of split firewood, thick as his wrist and heavy as a maul, stacked beside the lodge at his back.

The warrior came again.

Elias swung.

The wood caught the man across the forearm with a sound like a branch breaking. The hatchet spun away. The warrior cursed, clutching his arm, and his horse shied and carried him sideways.

Elias didn't follow.

He turned toward the camp.

* * *

Ksisstaki had been gathering wood when the Cree came out of the trees.

For one breath she stood still, mind refusing what her eyes were telling her.

telling her.

Then a child screamed and she was moving, grabbing the nearest child by the arm, then another, pulling them toward the shelter of a lodge, calling to the others in the sharp, clear voice she'd learned from necessity.

The pup was at her heels, frantic, whipping back and forth. When the first riders swept through the center of camp he launched forward, snarling, a sound too big for his body, and she grabbed him by the scruff with both hands.

He twisted and lunged, fighting her, his whole body straining toward the fighting.

"No," she said.

He snarled again, paws churning at the air.

She dragged him back against her chest, both arms wrapped around him, his heart hammering against her forearm like something trying to break through.

"Not yet," she whispered. "Not yet."

She pressed her back against the lodge and held him, watching.

* * *

The camp was fighting now. Blackfeet warriors pushing back against the raiders, the Cree losing the advantage of surprise. Makóyi's voice cut through the chaos, steady and commanding, directing men left and right.

The Cree hadn't come for a battle. They'd come for horses, for food. For whatever the winter had left behind.

But the camp had more fight in it than they'd counted on.

Elias moved through the chaos with the piece of firewood, staying out of the way of the warriors, watching for openings. He was not a soldier. He was not a warrior. But he had been in enough cattle drives, enough rough country, enough desperate situations to know how to keep himself moving and his eyes open.

He saw a young woman fall, knocked aside by a horse.

He pulled her up, pushed her toward the nearest lodge.

He saw a child frozen in the open, staring.

He crossed the ground in six strides, grabbed the child, handed him off to a woman running past.

He was looking for something useful to do when he heard it.

A sound he knew.

Not a shout.

Not a scream.

The sound a man makes when the air goes out of him.

He turned.

Nitááhkii was on the ground.

* * *

He'd taken a blow from a Cree warrior's rifle butt. Elias didn't see it happen, only the aftermath. Nitááhkii on one knee, head down, trying to rise. The warrior above him, a Winchester in his hands, already lifting it.

Three steps away.

Maybe four.

Elias stopped.

One breath.

He saw Scout in the snow. Head caved in. Eyes dark.

He saw Nitááhkii's face.

Nitááhkii had looked up. He was looking at Elias. Not calling out. Not begging. Just looking, the way a man looks when he knows he's out of time and he's seeing what's in front of him clearly for the first and possibly last time.

His eyes said nothing.

They said everything.

Elias ran.

He didn't think. There was no thought in it. Just the ground under his feet and the firewood in his hand and the warrior's back filling his vision.

He hit the man from behind, shoulder into the small of his back, driving him forward and down. The Winchester flew. They hit the ground hard, Elias on top, and the warrior twisted, strong, fighting.

An elbow caught Elias across the cheekbone. His vision went white.

He swung the firewood.

Connected.

The warrior went still beneath him.

Elias hit him again.

He heard nothing.

Not the battle. Not the shouting. Not the horses or the crying or Makóyi's voice cutting through it all.

Just his own breathing.

Just the sound of the wood.

He saw Scout.

He saw Clara's face in the firelight, thin, too thin, her hand in his.

He saw the empty corral. The gate swinging open.

He saw the grave under the cottonwood.

He saw everything the winter had taken from him and everything the land had taken before that and everything he had never been able to stop or fix or hold onto.

The coppery smell of blood. His mouth dry.

His hands kept moving. Long after everything beneath them had gone still.

Long after they needed to.

A hand on his shoulder.

He stopped.

The hand didn't grab him. Didn't pull. Just rested there, steady, unmistakable.

He looked up.

Nitááhkii.

Standing over him, breathing hard, a cut above his eye leaking blood down his temple. His expression was unreadable, neither horrified nor approving. Something older than both.

The battle was over.

The Cree had pulled back into the trees. Voices moved through the camp, low, urgent, checking the wounded, securing the horses.

Elias looked down.

His hands were dark.

He stared at them.

* * *

Nitááhkii stepped away, bent, and picked something up from the trampled snow.

The Winchester.

The same rifle the Cree warrior had meant to kill him with.

Nitááhkii checked the action with a practiced flick of his thumb, then turned back to Elias. He held the rifle out, stock first, offering it the way a warrior offers another man a weapon, not lightly, not casually, but with intention.

Elias stared at it.

Nitááhkii didn't speak. His arm didn't waver.

Elias reached out and took the rifle.

It was heavier than he expected. Solid. Real. Warm from Nitááhkii's hand.

Nitááhkii gave a single, sharp nod, not gratitude, not friendship, but something older than both, and turned away, limping slightly as he walked back toward the camp.

He didn't look back.

* * *

Ksisstaki let the pup go.

He tore across the camp like something had lit him on fire, a low, flat run, ears back, legs a blur, and launched himself at Elias's chest, nearly knocking him sideways.

Elias caught him with one arm, the Winchester in the other, and the pup was everywhere at once, nose on his face, on his hands, on the dark stains, frantic, checking, whining low in his throat.

Elias held him.

Just held him.

His face pressed into the pup's fur.

He didn't make a sound.

Across the camp, Ksisstaki watched. Her arms were still wrapped around the children she'd pulled to safety. The smallest one had fallen asleep against her shoulder, exhausted.

Her eyes met Elias's over the pup's head.

She didn't smile.

She didn't need to.

She nodded once.

Then she turned back to the children.

* * *

That evening, Makóyi moved through the camp checking the wounded. Three warriors had taken arrow wounds, painful, none fatal. A woman had a broken wrist from being knocked aside. The bay colt had a gash on its flank that Elias had already cleaned and bound without being asked.

Makóyi stood outside his lodge as the stars came out, cold and sharp.

Elias sat at the edge of camp in the growing dark, the Winchester across his knees. The pup lay against his leg, already asleep. The man sat still, not staring at anything in particular. Just sitting.

Makóyi watched him for a moment.

Then he went inside.

He said nothing to Elias.

The stars burned cold overhead. Somewhere in the cottonwoods, a great horned owl called once and fell silent.

Elias sat at the edge of camp, the Winchester across his knees, the pup warm against his leg.

He looked at his hands in the dark.

He thought about what they had done.

He thought about Scout. About Clara. About the cold and the winter and all the miles and all the loss that had led him here, to this camp, to this fire, to this moment.

He thought about Nitááhkii's hand on his shoulder.

Not pulling him back in anger.

Just stopping him.

The way you stop someone you recognize.

The pup stirred in his sleep, legs twitching, chasing something in a dream.

Elias looked down at him.

He put his hand on the pup's side and felt him breathe.

In.

Out.

In.

Out.

He sat there until the fire burned low.

He did not feel like himself.

He did not feel like the man who had ridden out of Fort Shaw with revenge in his chest and nothing else.

But he was still here.

And somewhere across the dark camp, Nitááhkii sat at his own fire.

And neither man looked at the other.

The Messenger

The morning after the raid came gray and heavy, as if the sky itself were tired.

Frost clung to the trampled snow where the fighting had been, and the air held the sharp, metallic smell of blood beneath the woodsmoke. A thin mist drifted along the river, catching on the willows like torn cloth.

Elias woke stiff and sore, every bruise announcing itself as he pushed himself upright. The pup was already awake, pressed against his hip, watching him with worried eyes. When Elias moved, the pup rose too, leaning into him as if to keep him from falling.

* * *

Outside, the camp was quiet in the way places are quiet after violence, not peaceful, but subdued. Voices were low. Movements careful. The world felt thinner.

Elias stepped out into the cold.

Women were already at work, sweeping debris from the paths, gathering broken lodge poles, checking on the children who had cried themselves to sleep. A few men stood near the horse line, speaking in low tones as they examined the animals for wounds.

Nitááhkii was among them.

He glanced up when Elias approached. Just a glance. No smile. No nod. But he didn't look away immediately, and that was something.

Makóyi stood beside him, arms folded, listening to a younger warrior describe where the Cree had come through the trees. When he saw Elias, he gave a small, quiet nod, the kind a man gives another man after something has shifted between them.

Elias returned it.

He didn't know what else to do.

* * *

The camp spent the morning tending wounds.

Three warriors had taken arrows, one in the shoulder, one in the thigh, one through the soft flesh of the upper arm. None were life-threatening, but all were painful. Makóyi moved between them with calm hands, applying poultices, binding wounds, speaking softly.

A woman sat with her wrist splinted, her face pale but composed. Children hovered near her, bringing water, bringing blankets, bringing whatever they thought might help.

The bay colt stood tied near the river, flank bandaged where a Cree blade had caught him. Elias checked the wound again, smoothing the colt's neck with a steady hand. The animal leaned into him, trusting.

Nitááhkii watched from a distance.

Not suspicious.

Not hostile.

Just watching.

* * *

By midday, the camp had settled into a rhythm again, a bruised, limping rhythm, but a rhythm nonetheless.

Women boiled broth.

Men repaired damaged lodges.

Children gathered firewood, their laughter returning in small, hesitant bursts.

The pup followed Elias everywhere, refusing to leave his side.

Ksisstaki approached him once, carrying a bowl of food. She didn't speak. She simply held it out. When he took it, her fingers brushed his for the briefest moment.

She looked at him, really looked, then turned and walked away.

Elias watched her go, unsure what to do with the warmth that rose in his chest.

The afternoon passed slowly. Clouds thickened over the mountains. A cold wind came down the valley, carrying the smell of distant snow.

Elias sat near the edge of camp, mending a broken bridle strap. The pup lay across his boots, asleep. The Winchester rested beside him, its walnut stock catching the dull light.

He still wasn't used to the weight of it.

He wasn't used to the weight of anything.

It was near sunset when the rider appeared.

A lone figure on a dun-colored horse, coming from the south, moving at a steady, unhurried pace. Not Cree. Not Blackfeet. Not Army.

But not a stranger.

Warriors rose from their fires. Nitááhkii stepped forward, hand on the knife at his belt. The pup lifted his head and growled low in his throat.

Elias stood.

The rider slowed as he approached the camp, raising one hand in greeting. He stopped a good distance away, waiting.

Makóyi walked out to meet him.

Elias felt his breath catch.

Jonas Bridger swung down from his horse.

He looked older than Elias remembered, thinner, dust-covered, eyes shadowed from too many miles and too little sleep. But he stood straight, respectful, hands visible, the way a man does when he knows he's on someone else's ground.

Makóyi spoke first. Bridger answered in Blackfoot, halting, but understandable. Makóyi's expression didn't change, but he stepped aside and let Bridger walk into the camp.

Nitááhkii watched him like a hawk.

Ksisstaki stood near the fires, children behind her, eyes narrowed.

Elias felt the pup press against his leg.

Bridger stopped a few paces from him.

For a long moment, neither man spoke.

Then Bridger said, "I heard a story."

Elias didn't answer.

"You going to ask how I found you?" Bridger said.

"I figured you'd tell me whether I asked or not."

Bridger almost smiled. "A man running from something always ends up somewhere worth running to. I just had to think about what that looked like for you." He glanced at the camp. "Wasn't hard."

Bridger's eyes moved back over the camp. The wounded, the thin horses, the patched lodges, then back to Elias.

"I heard a story of a man who shouldn't be alive," he said. "I heard he was living with the Blackfeet."

He let that settle.

The wind shifted.

Somewhere behind them, a child cried once and fell silent.

"And I heard this man will bring hell."

Silence stretched between them.

Bridger looked at Elias for a long moment.

"I don't see him," he said finally. "Must just be a story."

He stepped back then, giving the camp space to react.

Nitááhkii's jaw tightened.

Ksisstaki's breath caught.

Makóyi's face went still.

The pup pressed harder against Elias's leg.

And Elias felt the truth settle in his chest like a stone.

He was the danger.

He was the storm.

And he had brought it here.

20

The Promises

Elias had worked with Biter every morning since Bridger left.

The horse was coming along. Took the saddle without flinching now. Let Elias mount from either side. Walked when asked, stopped when asked. The trust was building slow but it was building.

The camp stayed watchful. Eyes turned more often toward the tree line. Sentries doubled at night. Makóyi said nothing about the warning, but the question hung in the air like smoke.

When would the soldiers come?

The pup stayed close. At night pressed against Elias's ribs, warm and solid. Sometimes Elias woke to find the dog watching him in the darkness, pale eyes catching the starlight.

Nitááhkii still nodded when they passed. The Winchester still leaned against Elias's blankets. But something had shifted in how people looked at Elias. Not hostility. Not fear. Just awareness. The camp knew what he'd brought with him, even if he hadn't meant to.

That evening, Elias sat with Makóyi and Nitááhkii by the fire. The day's work was done. The night was cold. Clear. Stars thick overhead.

The fire had burned down to coals. Most of the camp had gone to their lodges. Only a few men remained, talking quietly, passing a pipe.

The pup lay at Elias's feet, head on paws, half asleep.

Footsteps approached from the darkness. Two people.

Ksisstaki walked into the firelight, leading an old man by the arm. She moved slow, matching his pace. Patient.

The old man leaned on a walking stick. Maybe seventy winters. Gray hair in two long braids. His face deeply lined, weathered like old leather. He wore a buffalo robe over his shoulders despite the season. His eyes were dark and sharp.

Makóyi stood immediately. Nitááhkii stood. The others around the fire stood.

Elias stood too, following their lead.

Ksisstaki helped the old man sit near the fire. He nodded to her. She touched his shoulder briefly, then stepped back into the shadows. Sat down outside the circle of light. Watching.

Makóyi spoke in Blackfoot. Gestured to Elias.

The old man looked at Elias. Studied him in the firelight. His gaze steady, appraising. Not hostile. Just looking.

Makóyi looked at Elias. "Mountain Chief," he said in English. Then added, "He was there when the treaty was made. At Fort Benton."

Mountain Chief spoke. His voice was rough, quiet.

Makóyi translated. "He says you warned us the soldiers were coming."

"Yes," Elias said.

Mountain Chief spoke again.

"He asks why," Makóyi said.

Elias thought about the question. About the real answer.

"Because I know what happens when they come," he said.

Makóyi translated.

Mountain Chief nodded slowly. Said something.

"He says he knows it too," Makóyi said. "Has seen it many times."

The old man looked into the fire. Was quiet for a long time. Then he began to speak. Slow. Deliberate. Makóyi translated as he went, keeping his voice low, matching the old man's rhythm.

"I was young when the white chiefs came to Fort Benton. Summer. Hot. Many bands came together. We thought it was good the white chiefs wanted to talk. Wanted to make peace.

"They brought papers. Maps. They drew lines on the maps and said this is where you can live. This is where you can hunt. They promised us the land from the mountains to the Milk River. All of it. They said it would be ours forever. They said no white men would come onto our land.

"They promised us goods every year. Cattle when the buffalo got scarce. Flour. Coffee. Blankets. They said this was payment. For letting them build roads through our hunting grounds. For peace.

"They promised to protect us. From enemies. From bad white men.

"We signed their paper. Lame Bull signed it. Others signed it. We thought their promises were real. We thought when white men wrote words on paper, the words had power.

"That was the year they call eighteen fifty-five. I had maybe fifteen winters then."

Mountain Chief paused. Stared into the fire. The coals glowed red.

"For a few winters, they sent what they promised. Not always what they said. Not always good. Rotten blankets. Spoiled flour. But something came.

"Then men came into the mountains. Looking for the yellow metal. Gold. Hundreds of them. Then more. They were not supposed to be there. The treaty said our land. But they came anyway.

"Tearing up the earth. Killing the game. Leaving their trash everywhere.

"We told the agent. He said he would stop them. He did nothing.

"Then the buffalo hunters came. White men with big rifles. Killing buffalo just for the hides. Leaving the meat to rot. Hundreds killed.

Thousands. On our land where the treaty said they could not hunt.

"We told the agent. He said the buffalo belonged to everyone. Said we could not stop white men from hunting.

"The goods they sent got smaller. Less every year. The agent said the white chiefs in the East had no money. He said we should learn to farm. But the land where they wanted us to farm was bad. Rocky. Nothing grew.

"We started to go hungry.

"Some young men took horses. Took cattle. Their families were starving. The white men called us thieves. Called us savages. Sent soldiers.

"It was always the same. They broke their word. We went hungry. We took what we needed to live. They sent soldiers to punish us."

Mountain Chief was quiet. The fire popped. Sparks drifted up.

When he spoke again, his voice was harder.

"In the winter they call eighteen seventy, the soldiers came. Colonel Baker. They said they were hunting for Mountain Chief's band. Hunting for me. Because young men from my band had taken horses to feed their families.

"But they did not find my band.

"They found Heavy Runner's band. Peaceful people. Camped on the Marias River. Women. Children. Old people. Many sick with the spotted sickness.

"Heavy Runner had a paper from the agent. A safe paper. It said his band was peaceful. Protected. Friends.

"When the soldiers came at dawn, Heavy Runner walked out to meet them. He held up the paper. Showed it to them. Called out that his people were friendly.

"They shot him.

"Then they shot into the lodges. Women ran with children. The soldiers shot them. Old people too sick to run. The soldiers shot them.

They set fire to the lodges. People burned inside.

"One hundred seventy-three killed. My son was there. Visiting his mother's relatives. He had sixteen winters. They killed him too.

"The soldiers said later it was a mistake. They attacked the wrong camp. They said they were sorry.

"But the colonel was not punished. The soldiers were not punished. No one paid for the dead. No one gave anything to the families.

"That was when I understood. The papers mean nothing. The treaties mean nothing. The promises mean nothing.

"When white men want a thing, they take it. If we stand in the way, they kill us. Then they say it was our fault."

The old man looked at Elias. Held his gaze.

Mountain Chief spoke. Makóyi translated.

"He asks if you understand this."

"Yes," Elias said quietly. "I understand."

Mountain Chief nodded. Spoke again.

"After the killings on the Marias, we were careful. We did not fight. We stayed peaceful. We thought if we showed we were not dangerous, they would leave us alone.

"But the buffalo kept disappearing. Every year, fewer. The white hunters killed them all. On purpose. To make us weak. To make us come to the reservation.

"By the year they call eighteen eighty, the buffalo were almost gone. A few small herds far north in the Grandmother's land. That was all.

"The agent said we had to come to the reservation. Said there would be food there. We went. We had no choice. Our children were hungry.

"The food they gave us was bad. Rotten meat. Wormy flour. Not enough for everyone. People got sick. Children died. Old people died.

"We told the agent. He said the white chiefs had not sent enough. He said we should be grateful for what we got.

"This winter—" Mountain Chief gestured around at the camp. "This winter they cut what they give us again. Said we were getting too much. Said we needed to work for food like white men work.

"But there is no work. No buffalo to hunt. No crops in winter. Nothing. Just hunger.

"That is why some people left the reservation. Why we are here. Not to fight. Just to live."

The old man was quiet. The fire burned low.

Then he spoke again. Softer.

"You warned us the soldiers were coming. That was good. That was right.

"But doing right does not stop soldiers. Does not feed hungry children. Does not bring back the dead. Does not make white men keep their promises."

He paused.

"But it matters anyway."

Mountain Chief looked at Elias again. Those old eyes. Tired. Eyes that had seen too much.

Then he spoke once more. Makóyi's voice stayed quiet, translating.

"The white men will take everything. They have already decided. The papers they write, the promises they make, these are just words. Words to make themselves feel better about what they will do anyway.

"They will take the land. They will scatter us. They will say it is good for us. They will write in their books that we were savages. That we needed their help to become civilized.

"When our grandchildren's grandchildren are old, they will read those books. They will not know the truth. They will not know about the promises we were given. About the treaties. About the killings. They will only know what the white men wrote down.

"Unless someone remembers. Unless someone tells what really happened."

He looked at Makóyi. Spoke in Blackfoot. Makóyi nodded.

Mountain Chief stood. Slow. Using the walking stick.

Everyone stood.

Ksisstaki came out of the shadows. Took his arm again. Helped him.

The old man said something to her. She nodded.

They walked back into the darkness together. The sound of their footsteps fading. The tap of the walking stick on hard earth.

Elias sat down. Stared into the fire.

Makóyi sat. Nitááhkii sat. The others drifted away to their lodges.

The fire burned lower.

Elias thought about the ranch. About the men who'd come and taken his horses. About riding to Fort Shaw to report it. About the Army column riding north.

It had seemed simple then. Thieves. Soldiers. Justice.

Makóyi spoke. "Mountain Chief does not talk much anymore. When he does, people listen."

Elias nodded.

He thought about treaties. Promises written on paper that meant nothing when one side decided they meant nothing.

He thought about Heavy Runner on the Marias. Walking out with his safe-conduct paper. Being shot anyway.

He thought about what Mountain Chief had said.

It was always the same. They broke their word. We went hungry. We took what we needed. They sent soldiers.

And the last thing.

Unless someone remembers. Unless someone tells what really happened.

Makóyi stood. Walked to his lodge.

Elias stayed by the fire. Pup's head on his feet. The dog's warmth.

He sat there until the coals went dark.

Then he went to his blankets and lay down.

But sleep was a long time coming.

21

Bridger's Return

Bridger rode into Fort Shaw at dusk, a muddy trail behind him like a long, tired ribbon. The sun was low, a red smear along the horizon, and the air carried the cold bite of a night that would freeze hard before morning.

Soldiers moved through the yard with the slow, automatic rhythm of men who had done the same tasks too many times, hauling water, stacking wood, checking tack. A few glanced up as Bridger passed.

He swung down stiffly, tied his horse, and stood for a moment with his hands on the saddle horn, letting the ache settle through his bones. He'd ridden too far, too fast. He felt every mile.

Inside the headquarters building, lamplight flickered against the windows.

He went in.

First Lieutenant Hargreaves sat behind a desk cluttered with papers and half-finished reports. He looked up when Bridger entered, relief flickering across his face.

"Jonas," he said. "Thought you'd frozen out there."

"Not yet," Bridger said.

Hargreaves gestured to a chair. "Report."

Bridger sat. He kept his hat in his hands, turning it slowly. He spoke in the same way he always did, sparse, factual, giving just enough to satisfy a man who didn't know what questions to ask.

"Trails are open," he said. "Snow's thinning. Game's scarce. Tribes are moving early."

Hargreaves nodded, making notes.

"Any sign of trouble?"

Bridger shrugged. "Cree raided a Blackfeet camp. Took some horses. Nothing new."

Hargreaves sighed. "Damn shame."

Bridger didn't answer.

The door banged open, cold air rushed in swirling the papers on Hargreaves' desk.

Thornton stepped inside. Hargreaves stood at attention and saluted, "Captain." Thorton waved the gesture away and stepped past him.

He looked like a man who hadn't slept in days, jaw tight, eyes sharp, coat still buttoned as if he'd never taken it off. He stopped when he saw Bridger, and something cold flickered across his face.

"Bridger," he said. "You're back."

Bridger nodded once.

Thornton moved closer, boots loud on the floorboards. "Where'd you ride?"

"North," Bridger said.

"Where north?"

"Where the trails took me."

Thornton smiled without warmth. "You always were a poet."

Hargreaves cleared his throat. "Captain, Bridger was giving his report…"

Thornton didn't look away from Bridger. "I'll hear it."

Bridger kept his voice even. "Snow's melting. Tribes are hungry. Nothing you don't already know."

Thornton stepped around the desk, slow, deliberate. "You hear anything else?"

Bridger didn't blink. "Plenty of things."

"Anything useful?"

"Depends who's asking."

Hargreaves shifted uncomfortably. Thornton ignored him.

"There's talk," Thornton said. "Rumors. A white man running with the tribes."

Bridger didn't move. "There's always talk, always stories."

"Stories start somewhere."

"So does trouble."

For a moment, the room felt too small.

Thornton's eyes narrowed, searching Bridger's face.

"You were seen," Thornton said quietly. "Rider coming south reported a scout matching your description two days north of here. Near a creek system the Blackfeet use."

Bridger met his eyes. "Lots of scouts in Montana Territory."

"Not many who ride alone into Blackfeet country in winter."

"I go where the trails are."

"And what did you find on those trails?"

A beat. Just long enough.

"Snow," Bridger said. "And more snow."

Thornton held his gaze for a long moment. Something moved behind his eyes. Not belief, not quite disbelief. The calculation of a man deciding whether to press further or save it for later.

He stepped back. The tension broke like a thread pulled too tight.

"Dismissed," he said.

Bridger stood, nodded to Hargreaves, and walked out.

He didn't look at Thornton again.

Outside, the fort was settling into night. Lanterns glowed in the barracks. A few soldiers laughed near the cookhouse, their voices carrying thinly on the cold air.

Bridger walked past them, past the stables, past the last ring of firelight, until he stood alone at the edge of the parade ground. The sky above him was wide and dark, stars sharp as flint.

He let out a long breath.

Behind him, the fort gates creaked as they closed for the night.

Bridger didn't turn around.

22

Fate

The meeting had been going since dusk.

Elias was not there. Nitááhkii had asked him to stay near the horses, said it quietly, without explanation. Elias had agreed.

Now he sat at the edge of camp, mending a bridle strap by firelight, the Winchester leaning against a tree, close at hand. He could see Makóyi's lodge from where he sat. The glow of firelight through the hides, the shadows of men moving inside.

He knew what they were deciding.

The pup lay across his boots, chin on his paws, watching the lodge with the same uneasy attention Elias felt.

"You and me both," Elias murmured.

The pup's ears flicked. Ksisstaki walked across the camp, basket of herbs in her hands. The pup stood, watching her, and took off across the field to jump on her legs.

Inside the lodge, voices rose and fell, muffled, indistinct. Elias couldn't make out words. Only tone. And the tone had been tense.

He went back to his work.

The leather was stiff in his hands.

* * *

"…the people grow fond of him," an elder was saying. "The children follow him. Even the dogs."

A few men nodded.

Makóyi stirred the fire with a stick. "Fondness does not change the danger."

Across the circle, the oldest elder, the one they still called Old Bear Chief, though he had not led a war party in twenty winters, sat slumped against his blanket. His white hair spilled over his shoulders. His eyes were half-closed. He looked as though he might be asleep.

A younger warrior leaned forward, jaw tight. "The soldiers are coming because of him. If he stays, they find us. If he goes…" He let the silence finish the thought.

Another warrior, older, shook his head. "The soldiers were always coming. Harlan is just the excuse."

"Then we give them no excuse," the younger man said. "We send him south. Alone. They find him, they stop looking for us."

Makóyi's expression didn't change. "And if they don't stop?"

The warrior didn't answer.

A third man spoke, his voice careful. "There is another way."

The lodge went quiet.

"We could…" He hesitated. "We could leave him where they will find him. Dead. A sign that we are not with him."

The fire popped.

No one moved.

Nitááhkii stared into the flames, his face unreadable. His hands were fists on his knees.

Makóyi's voice came low and steady. "You speak of killing a man who fought beside us. A man who saved one of our own."

The warrior who had spoken looked away.

Another elder, gray-haired and thoughtful, said quietly, "He could have let Nitááhkii die. He did not. That cannot be ignored."

Makóyi nodded. "No. It cannot."

The young warrior spoke again, frustrated. "Then what do we do? Wait for the soldiers to come? Let them find us because we are too soft to make the hard choice?"

Old Bear Chief did not stir.

The debate continued, voices layering over each other, the same arguments circling, finding no purchase.

Just then, a small shape burst through the lodge flap.

The pup skidded across the packed earth, tail wagging wildly. He barked once, then bounded straight toward Nitááhkii.

A few elders chuckled despite themselves.

Makóyi shook his head. "That little one fears nothing."

"Ksisstaki!" someone called. "Your wolf pup is here."

The lodge flap lifted.

Ksisstaki stepped inside, cheeks flushed from the cold, eyes wide at the sight of the gathered men. She kept her gaze low, respectful.

"Come," Makóyi said gently. "Take him."

She crossed the lodge, scooped the pup into her arms. He wriggled, licking her chin.

She turned to leave.

But she paused.

Just long enough to hear an elder say, "The people grow fond of him. That matters."

Another added, "A man who wins the hearts of children is not a danger by choice."

Ksisstaki froze.

And then, a sound.

A soft clearing of a throat.

Old Bear Chief lifted his head, his blanket shifting.

His eyes, clouded with age, fixed on her with sudden clarity.

"Girl," he said, voice rough with disuse. "You see much. What do you see in this white man?"

The lodge went still.

Ksisstaki swallowed. She looked at the fire, not at the men.

"He is lonely," she said. "And he is kind. He carries sorrow, but he does not let it make him cruel."

She shifted the pup in her arms. "He tries. That is all."

Old Bear Chief nodded once, as if she had confirmed something he already knew.

Makóyi's voice was gentle. "Go on now."

She bowed her head and slipped out into the cold.

Old Bear Chief turned his gaze to the circle of men.

"It is not ours to decide his path," he said. His voice was quiet, but it carried. "He was put among us by Ihtsipaitapiiyo'pa. The Source of Life. The One who moves all things."

No one spoke.

He went on.

"And what is this talk of giving him to the whites? Dead, staked out like a goat?" His eyes swept the circle, sharp despite the years. "Have we decided to give the white men the ones they seek?"

The young warrior shifted uncomfortably.

Old Bear Chief's voice hardened. "Where does it stop? Do we give them this council? They surely seek us. Do we give them our sons? Our daughters? Our lodges? Our land?"

Silence.

"If we give them this white man," he said, "we have given them ourselves."

The fire cracked.

No one argued.

Makóyi bowed his head in respect. "Your words are heard, grandfather."

Old Bear Chief closed his eyes again, as if the effort had exhausted him.

Makóyi lifted his chin. "He stays, if he wants. For now. We teach him. When the time comes to move again, we decide together."

One by one, the elders nodded.

The young warrior who had spoken of killing Elias looked down at his hands. He did not nod. But he did not argue.

Nitááhkii let his shoulders relax.

Makóyi stood. "It is decided."

The fire crackled, and the decision settled over the room like snow.

The men began to rise, to file out into the cold.

* * *

Outside, the night air hit her hard.

She knelt beside the fire, holding the pup close, her heart pounding.

Inside, the voices rose again, muffled, urgent.

She couldn't hear the words.

She didn't need to.

She knew they were deciding whether Elias would live or die.

Nitááhkii emerged a few minutes later.

He saw her.

He knelt beside her.

For a moment, neither spoke.

Then he said, "You spoke truth."

She didn't look up. "I only said what I saw."

"That is why it mattered."

She held the pup tighter. "He is not safe."

"No," Nitááhkii said. "But he is safer than he would be alone."

She nodded, though her eyes were wet.

Nitááhkii watched her for a long moment, something unspoken in his gaze, something protective, something patient.

"He will stay," he said. "For now."

Ksisstaki closed her eyes, relief and fear tangled together.

She looked toward the edge of camp, where Elias sat by the horses, distant and small in the firelight.

"Does he know?" she asked.

"Not yet," Nitááhkii said. "Makóyi will tell him."

She nodded.

The pup wriggled free and dropped to the ground, shaking himself. He looked toward Elias, ears perked, then looked back at Ksisstaki as if asking permission.

She let him go.

He tore across the camp, a small streak of fur and energy, barking once as he ran.

Ksisstaki watched him go.

Nitááhkii watched her.

"You care for him," he said quietly.

She looked at her hands. "He is kind to the pup. And to me. "

Nitááhkii nodded. He understood what she meant. And what she didn't say.

"He sees you as a child," Nitááhkii said. Not unkindly. Just truth.

Ksisstaki's cheeks flushed. "I know."

"That is good," Nitááhkii said. "He is a good man. But you are young. And he is… broken."

She looked at him then. "We are all broken."

Nitááhkii's mouth twitched, not quite a smile. "Yes. But some breaks do not mend the same way."She was quiet for a moment. Then she said, "You care for him too."

Nitááhkii didn't answer.

He stood, brushed snow from his leggings, and walked back toward the camp.

Ksisstaki sat alone for a while longer, watching the pup run to Elias, watching Elias catch him, watching the small shape settle against the man's leg.

She thought about what Old Bear Chief had said.

He was put among us by Ihtsipaitapiiyo'pa.

She didn't know if that was true.

But she was glad he was staying.

Even if it meant the danger stayed too.

* * *

The pup hit him like a small avalanche, all paws and tongue and wriggling joy.

Elias caught him, laughing despite himself. "Where've you been?"

The pup squirmed in his arms, licking his face, his hands, anything he could reach.

Elias set him down. The pup immediately climbed onto his boots and sat, tail thumping against the ground.

"You're a menace," Elias said.

The pup grinned up at him, tongue lolling.

Elias looked toward Makóyi's lodge. The elders were leaving now, walking slowly through the camp, their voices low. Makóyi stood outside, speaking with two of the older men. He glanced toward Elias once, then turned back to his conversation.

Elias felt his chest tighten.

He didn't know what had been decided.

He didn't know if he'd be told to leave in the morning.

He didn't know if they'd decided on something worse.

The pup leaned against his leg, heavy and warm.

Elias put his hand on the pup's head and felt him breathe.

The fire crackled. The stars burned cold overhead. The camp settled into the rhythm of evening, voices fading, children quieting, the world pulling in close against the dark.

Makóyi walked toward him.

Elias stood.

The pup stood too, tail wagging.

Makóyi stopped a few paces away. His face was unreadable in the firelight.

For a long moment, he said nothing.

Then he spoke.

"You stay."

Elias let out a breath he hadn't known he was holding.

Makóyi continued. "The council has decided. You stay with us. You work. You learn."

He paused.

"For now."

Elias nodded. "Thank you."

Makóyi's expression softened, just slightly. "Do not thank me. Thank the girl who spoke for you. And the old chief who reminded us what we are."

He turned to go, then stopped.

"The soldiers are still coming," he said. "This does not change that."

"I know," Elias said.

Makóyi looked at him a long moment. "Then you know what it means to stay."

"I do."

Makóyi nodded once. "Good."

He walked back toward his lodge.

Elias sat down slowly, the weight of it settling over him.

The pup climbed into his lap, curled into a ball, and closed his eyes.

Elias looked up at the stars.

He was still here.

Somewhere to the south, Thornton was riding.

He sat with the pup in his lap, the Winchester near, the fire burning low.

23

The Grulla

Morning came cold and pale, the kind of light that made everything look washed clean. Elias woke to the sound of horses snorting in the corral and the pup whining softly at the lodge flap, eager to be outside.

He stepped into the crisp air, breath fogging, the pup bounding ahead of him. The camp was already moving, women tending fires, children chasing each other between lodges, men checking tack and gear. The smell of woodsmoke and frost hung in the air.

Nitááhkii was waiting for him near the horses.

"You come," he said, jerking his chin toward the far end of the corral. Elias followed.

Nitááhkii led Elias past the main herd, toward the small training corral at the far end of camp. Elias had worked with the horses for days now. He knew every mare, every gelding, every buffalo runner by sight. But he hadn't seen the grulla before.

He soon learned why.

Three young warriors were gathered at the fence, laughing and giving Káto no mercy. Káto stood scowling, his forearm wrapped in a strip of hide.

"You traded a rifle for that?" one of them said. "A good rifle?"

"A *fine* rifle," another added, grinning.

Káto muttered something under his breath.

The warriors roared.

"And now you have no rifle," the first man said, "and no horse."

"He bit me," Káto snapped, lifting his arm. "Twice."

"You got close enough for twice?" someone said. "That's your mistake."

More laughter.

Nitááhkii stopped beside them. "When did he come?"

"Last night," Káto said. "Traded for him near the river. Took me half the night to get him here. He fought the rope the whole way."

Elias looked down.

A rope lay in the dirt inside the corral, trampled, muddy, half-buried in the churned ground.

"He shook it off," Káto said. "Wouldn't let me near him to take it. I'm lucky I still have fingers."

The warriors laughed again.

Inside the corral, the grulla stallion paced the far fence, head high, ears pinned, muscles tight beneath his winter coat. He was young, three, maybe four, but already powerful, already proud. His coat was the color of storm clouds over the prairie. His mane and tail were black as coal. His eyes were sharp, watchful, untrusting.

He stopped pacing long enough to glare at the men, then bared his teeth.

"See?" Káto said. "Meat. That's all he's good for."

Elias didn't answer.

He stepped closer to the fence.

The stallion froze, nostrils flaring, breath steaming in the cold air. He didn't bolt. He didn't strike. He just watched Elias with a hard, assessing stare.

Nitááhkii noticed.

The warriors noticed.

Even Káto fell quiet.

Elias lifted the latch on the gate.

"What are you doing?" Káto hissed.

Elias didn't answer.

He stepped inside the corral, then turned his back to the horse and closed the gate behind him.

The warriors went silent.

The stallion snorted, pawing at the ground, ears flicking forward and back. He didn't charge. He didn't retreat. He simply watched Elias with a predator's focus.

Elias stood still for a long moment, letting the horse see him, smell him, understand him. Then he began to walk, not toward the stallion, but around the edge of the corral, slow and steady, eyes on the ground, shoulders loose.

The stallion followed him with his eyes, head turning, muscles coiled.

Elias stopped near the trampled rope.

He didn't look at the horse.

He didn't reach for it.

He simply crouched, picked it up, and coiled it in his hands.

The stallion snorted sharply, stamping once, but didn't move.

Elias walked back to the gate, opened it, and stepped out.

He closed the gate behind him.

The warriors stared at him, unsure what they'd just seen.

Nitááhkii's expression didn't change, but something in his eyes softened, respect, maybe, or recognition.

Káto looked at Elias, then at the stallion, then back at Elias.

"You're crazy," he said.

Elias shrugged. "Maybe."

The stallion stood in the center of the corral now, watching Elias through the rails, ears forward, breath rising in slow, steady plumes.

Not trusting.

Not accepting.

But no longer dismissing him.

The first step had been taken.

* * *

Elias coiled the rope in his hands, testing its weight, the feel of it. Then he walked to Káto and held it out.

"You'll want this back," Elias said.

Káto blinked, surprised. He took the rope as if it might bite him too.

Elias nodded toward the stallion. "Let him stay there tonight. Let him get used to the corral. If he doesn't jump the fence and run off, we'll see if he'll talk to us tomorrow."

Káto stared at him. "Talk to us? You are a crazy man. Horses don't talk."

Elias gave a small, tired smile. "You don't listen."

The warriors laughed, not at Elias, but at Káto, who scowled and muttered something about "white men and their strange ideas."

Nitááhkii didn't laugh.

He watched Elias with a new kind of attention, something measuring, something respectful.

Inside the corral, the grulla stallion stood still for the first time since they'd arrived, ears forward, eyes fixed on Elias as if trying to decide what kind of creature he was.

The pup trotted to Elias's side and sat, tail thumping, as if he too were waiting for the horse's answer.

Elias rested his hands on the top rail, not looking at the stallion directly, just standing there, breathing the same cold air.

"We'll try again tomorrow," he said softly.

The stallion snorted once, not a challenge, not a warning.

Something closer to acknowledgment.

And the men around Elias fell quiet, each of them feeling, in their own way, that something had just begun.

* * *

The sun rose slow and soft, a pale wash of gold over the prairie. Frost clung to the grass, glittering like ground glass. The camp was still quiet. Fires just beginning to stir, smoke drifting low in the cold air.

Ksisstaki stepped out of her family's lodge with a small clay bowl cupped in her hands, steam curling from it. She had seen him from across the camp before anyone else was awake.

Elias.

Asleep on the ground beside the training corral.

The pup was curled against his chest, nose tucked under Elias's arm, both of them breathing in the same slow rhythm. Elias's coat was pulled tight around him, but the night had been cold, and she could see the stiffness in his shoulders even from a distance.

She walked toward him, careful not to spill the broth.

As she drew closer, she saw something else.

The grulla stallion stood near the fence, closer than he had come to anyone since arriving. Not pacing. Not striking. Just standing there, head lowered slightly, ears forward, watching the sleeping man and the small dog pressed against him.

Ksisstaki slowed her steps.

The horse's breath rose in soft plumes. His dark mane stirred in the morning breeze. He looked… curious. Almost gentle. As if the wildness in him had eased for a moment in the quiet of dawn.

She stopped a few paces away.

"Elias," she said softly.

He stirred, blinking awake, the pup stretching and yawning beside him.

Elias pushed himself upright, rubbing the sleep from his eyes. "Morning."

"You slept here," she said.

He shrugged, embarrassed. "Didn't mean to. Just wanted to keep an eye on him."

Ksisstaki held out the bowl. "Hot broth. For the cold."

He hesitated, then took it with a grateful nod. "Thank you."

The pup sniffed at the bowl hopefully. Elias nudged him away with a knee.

Ksisstaki's eyes drifted to the stallion. "He watched you all night."

Elias followed her gaze.

The grulla stood only a few feet from the fence now, closer than he'd allowed anyone. His eyes were fixed on Elias, not with fear, not with aggression, just a steady, measuring interest.

"He's thinking," Elias murmured.

"Horses think?" Ksisstaki asked.

Elias smiled faintly. "More than most men."

She looked at him, then at the horse, then back again. "He is different this morning."

"So am I," Elias said quietly.

The stallion snorted, pawing once at the ground, but he didn't move away.

Elias set the empty bowl aside and rose slowly to his feet. The pup trotted to the fence, tail wagging, as if greeting an old friend.

Elias stepped toward the corral.

The stallion didn't retreat.

Ksisstaki held her breath.

Elias stopped at the fence, resting his hands lightly on the top rail.

He didn't reach for the horse. He didn't speak. He just stood there, letting the morning settle around them.

The stallion stretched his neck, nostrils flaring, breath warm in the cold air.

For a moment, the world held still.

Then the stallion took one step closer.

Ksisstaki felt something tighten in her chest. Fear, hope, she couldn't tell.

Elias didn't move.

The stallion lowered his head, ears flicking, eyes softening just a fraction.

A beginning.

A possibility.

A fragile thread of trust, barely formed, but real.

Ksisstaki whispered, "He knows you."

Elias shook his head. "Not yet."

But the way he said it, quiet, certain, made her think he wasn't talking about the horse alone.

* * *

The sun climbed higher, burning off the frost, turning the prairie gold. The camp stirred fully awake now, children running between lodges, women tending fires, men preparing for the day's work.

Elias stood at the corral again, the pup at his heels, Ksisstaki watching from a distance with the empty broth bowl in her hands.

Nitááhkii joined him, arms folded. "You want to work him today."

Elias nodded. "If he'll let me."

Nitááhkii didn't argue. He simply stepped back, giving Elias space.

A few warriors drifted over, curious. Káto among them, still nursing his pride and his bitten arm.

"Watch this," Káto muttered. "He'll get himself killed."

But he didn't sound convinced.

Elias opened the gate and stepped inside.

The stallion's head shot up.

Ears pinned.

Muscles tight.

A warning snort.

Elias didn't move.

He stood in the center of the corral, hands loose at his sides, eyes on the ground. He didn't look at the horse. Didn't speak. Didn't reach.

He simply existed in the same space.

Minutes passed.

Then more.

The warriors shifted, restless.

"What is he doing?" one whispered.

"Nothing," another said.

"Exactly," Káto muttered.

But Nitááhkii watched with a different kind of attention.

The stallion circled the edge of the corral, snorting, pawing, tossing his head. Every time a warrior stepped too close to the fence, the horse bolted to the far side, kicking out, wild and furious.

But when it was only Elias in the corral, the stallion slowed.

Watched.

Measured.

An hour passed.

Then another.

Elias didn't move.

The sun climbed higher.

The camp went about its business.

But the warriors stayed, drawn in despite themselves.

Ksisstaki stayed too, silent, her eyes never leaving the corral.

Finally, finally, the stallion stopped pacing.

He stood still.

Head high.

Breath steady.

Then he took one step toward Elias.

Just one.

The warriors fell silent.

Elias didn't react.

Didn't reward.

Didn't reach.

He simply breathed.

Another long stretch of time passed, the kind of time only a horseman understands, the kind that feels like prayer.

The stallion took another step.

Then another.

He was close now, close enough that Elias could feel the heat of him, hear the soft rush of his breath.

Still Elias didn't move.

The stallion stretched his neck, nostrils flaring, breath warm against Elias's shoulder.

Then, with a slow, tentative motion, he pressed his nose against Elias's chest.

A touch.

A question.

A beginning.

Elias lifted his hand, slowly, gently, and laid it on the stallion's neck.

The horse didn't flinch.

Didn't bolt.

Didn't bite.

He stood there, trembling slightly, but not from fear.

From a choice made.

From trust.

Ksisstaki let out a breath she hadn't realized she was holding.

Nitááhkii nodded once, a small, private gesture of respect.

Káto stared, speechless.

Elias stroked the stallion's neck, feeling the warmth, the strength, the wildness still coiled beneath the skin.

"Easy," he whispered.

The stallion closed his eyes.

It had taken all morning, hours of silence, patience, and stillness, but Elias had touched him.

And the horse had allowed it.

* * *

Elias stepped out of the corral, closing the gate behind him. His shoulders were stiff from standing so long, his legs half-numb, but there was a lightness in him he hadn't felt in months.

The warriors were waiting.

Káto crossed his arms. "That's it? You touch him once and call it a day?"

Another snorted. "You spent all morning standing like a dead tree. You think that's training?"

A third shook his head. "You'll never ride that horse like that."

Elias handed Káto the coiled rope. "That's it for today."

They stared at him.

"That's it?" Káto repeated, incredulous.

Elias shrugged. "I'm not trying to train him."

The warriors exchanged looks.

Elias started walking toward his lodge, the pup trotting at his heels. Over his shoulder he added, "I'm trying to know him."

Káto blinked. "Know him? What does that mean?"

Elias didn't slow. "Means I listen first."

The warriors burst out laughing.

"Horses don't talk!" one shouted.

Elias lifted a hand in a lazy half-wave. "That's why you think they don't. You're not listening."

The laughter faltered.

Káto scowled, unsure if he'd been insulted or taught something.

Elias kept walking, the pup bounding ahead, tail wagging. He paused once, glancing back at the corral.

The grulla stallion was still standing where Elias had left him, head over the fence, watching him go.

Elias nodded once, almost imperceptibly.

Then he said, loud enough for the warriors to hear, "But you're welcome to go in there and ride him if you want."

The braves fell silent.

Káto looked at the scar on his arm.

"No," he muttered. "I'm good."

Nitááhkii's mouth twitched, not quite a smile, but close.

Ksisstaki, watching from the edge of camp, felt something warm bloom in her chest. Not pride. Not exactly. Something quieter. Something she didn't have a word for.

Elias walked on, the pup dancing around his boots, the morning sun warming his back.

Behind him, the grulla stallion snorted once, a soft, almost approving sound.

24

The Departure

Thornton stood over the map table, hands flat, the wood creaking under the pressure. Morning light cut across the room in a hard line. His officers waited, hats in their hands, boots dusty from the yard.

"There's a band of Blackfeet north of the Teton," Thornton said. "Off-reservation. Moving fast. They've been taking horses. Spooking settlers."

No one spoke. A few exchanged glances.

"How many?" Hargreaves asked.

"Thirty. Maybe forty. Women and children with them, but that doesn't make them harmless."

Lieutenant Hargreaves shifted his weight. "Objective?"

"Apprehend or disperse," Thornton said. "Bring them back to the reservation. Use force if needed."

He didn't blink.

He didn't need to.

Everything he said was true.

None of it was the truth.

Harrington came in without knocking. He closed the door behind him.

"I told you to stand down," he said.

Thornton didn't move his hands from the table. "This is a separate matter, sir. Raiders. Federal mandate…"

Harrington narrowed his eyes, "This is about Harlan, isn't it Captain?"

"This is about securing the territory."

"This isn't about raiders." Harrington said, the words tight.

Thornton's jaw worked once. A small tic. Then stillness.

"I'm following my orders," he said. "All of them."

Harrington studied him for a long moment. Long enough to understand the truth: Thornton was going north with or without permission.

"You have one week," Harrington said. "Seven days. Then you return."

"Understood."

"Captain," Harrington said quietly. "If this goes wrong, I can't protect you."

Thornton straightened, hands leaving the table at last. "I don't need protection, sir."

He saluted, turned, and walked out.

* * *

Bridger was behind the stables, tightening the cinch on his horse. His gear was packed. He was ready to disappear.

Bootsteps crunched in the frost behind him.

He didn't turn. "You're riding north."

Thornton stopped a few paces away. "We leave at dawn."

Bridger let out a slow breath. He kept his eyes on the saddle. "You'll want a scout."

Thornton didn't answer. He didn't need to.

Bridger nodded once, as if he'd made the decision himself. "I'll take the lead."

Thorton didn't move.

Bridger tightened the cinch one last time. "Trail's thin this time of year. Might take a while."

Thornton's jaw twitched. "You'll find it."

Bridger didn't look at him, just let out a grunt.

Thornton turned and walked away.

Bridger waited until he was gone before he let his shoulders sag. He rested a hand on the horse's neck.

He would go.

He would scout.

And he would slow them every mile he could.

"Forgive me," he murmured.

* * *

Private Cady sat on his bunk, cleaning his rifle. He'd already cleaned it twice. His hands wouldn't stop moving.

Outside, the sergeants talked in low voices.

"This ain't about raiders," one said.

"What then?"

"Captain's got a grudge. Some white man who went native."

Cady swallowed. "So why are we going?"

"Because he's the captain," the sergeant said. "And we follow orders."

Cady looked down at the rifle in his lap.

He wrote a letter home and folded it into his coat.

He didn't send it.

He didn't know what to say that wouldn't sound like goodbye.

Dawn came cold. Frost on the ground. Horses stamping, breath rising in white plumes.

The gates of Fort Shaw opened with a long groan.

Thornton rode at the head of fifty men.

Bridger scouted ahead, shoulders hunched against the wind.

Wagons creaked behind them.

People watched from doorways.

Some waved.

Some didn't.

A woman held a child on her hip. The child waved at the soldiers. A few waved back.

They thought it was a patrol.

A week out.

A week back.

Only two men knew better.

*   *   *

That night, the first camp.

Thornton sat by his fire, cleaning his pistol. Slow, methodical strokes. The same motion again and again. The ritual steadied him.

He thought of Elias.

Of the Little Bighorn.

Of the years between then and now.

Of the shame that had never left him.

He didn't think of the Blackfeet as people.

He thought of them as a line he had to cross.

"Where are you, Harlan?" he whispered to the fire.

The flames snapped in the cold air.

"I'm coming."

*   *   *

Bridger sat apart from the soldiers, turning a small stone over in his hand. He didn't remember picking it up.

He looked north.

Ksisstaki with the children.

Makóyi's steady voice.

Nitááhkii's quiet strength.

Elias with the Winchester.

The pup snarling at danger.

He was leading fifty armed men toward them.

He couldn't stop it.

He could only slow it.

He didn't sleep.

Dawn broke again.

The column moved north.

Dust rising behind them.

Thornton at the head.

Bridger ahead of him.

Fifty men following.

Miles away, Elias stood beside a grulla stallion, the pup at his feet, unaware of the storm riding toward him.

The distance between them narrowed with every mile.

* * *

Colonel Harrington sat at his desk long after the column had vanished. The parade ground was empty. The fort felt hollow.

He pulled a blank sheet toward him.

To: Department of Dakota, Helena

Re: Northern patrol under Captain Thornton

He hesitated, pen hovering.

What could he write that wouldn't damn him? What could he say that would matter?

He began carefully:

Captain Thornton departed Fort Shaw this morning with fifty cavalry and supply train. Stated objective: apprehend off-reservation Blackfeet band north of Teton River. Estimated 30–40 individuals, including women and children.

Request clarification of rules of engagement regarding non-combatants.

He read it back.

Dry.

Factual.

Safe.

He didn't write what he knew, that Thornton wasn't hunting raiders, that this was personal, that people would die.

He couldn't put that on paper.

He signed the report, folded it, sealed it.

"Courier," he called.

A young corporal appeared. "Sir?"

"Telegraph to Helena. Priority."

"Yes, sir."

The corporal took the envelope and left.

Harrington sat alone, staring at the empty desk.

He'd done what he could.

He'd covered himself.

It wasn't the same thing.

Outside, the telegraph key began tapping, a thin, metallic sound carrying a warning southward. Helena. Then headquarters. Maybe Washington. If anyone bothered to read it.

Words on paper.

Reports and replies.

The machinery grinding while men rode toward something irreversible.

Harrington stood and looked north through the window.

Somewhere out there, Thornton was already a day closer to what he wanted.

And Harrington's message would take a week to reach anyone who might care.

By then it would be over.

He closed the window.

Closed the door.

The message traveled.

Too slow to matter.

Too late to stop anything.

25

The Last Sunrise

Dawn came pale and cold.

Smoke drifted low over the lodges. Women moved quietly between fires, stirring pots, shaking out hides. Children chased each other through the frost, their breath white in the air. The pup darted among them, yipping, tail high.

Elias carried a bucket from the creek, shoulders stiff from the night. He set it down near the lodge rubbing his hands together, watching the camp wake.

Nitááhkii was already at the corral, checking the ponies.

Makóyi knelt beside a boy with a cut hand, wrapping it with clean cloth.

Ksisstaki shook out a hide, her hair catching the early light.

Life.

Ordinary.

Fragile.

Elias felt it settling into him, the rhythm of the place, the quiet trust, the sense that he belonged here more each day.

The pup tore past Elias with a stick barely longer than his own body, growling as if dragging a fallen tree. Two children chased him, laughing, slipping in the frost. The pup darted behind Elias and planted himself between his boots, stick clamped sideways in his teeth.

Káto reached for it.

The pup's growl deepened, a tiny, ridiculous warning.

The children stopped, wide-eyed.

Elias bent, took the stick, and the pup released it instantly, sitting back on his haunches like he'd planned it that way.

Káto stared. "He hates me."

Elias tossed the stick. The pup bolted after it, skidding in the dirt, triumphant again. The children followed, shouting, the three of them disappearing toward the creek.

Ksisstaki laughed softly from where she worked near the lodge. Nitááhkii shook his head, trying not to smile.

For a moment, just a moment, the camp felt untouched by anything beyond its own borders.

The grulla watched him from the far corner of the corral, ears flicking, breath rising in thin white streams. Elias walked toward him with a halter over his shoulder. The stallion didn't move away. Not anymore.

He slipped the rope over the horse's neck. The grulla stood still, muscles tight but not braced to flee. Elias stroked the warm hide along his jaw, feeling the strength there, the patience, the waiting.

Nitááhkii leaned on the fence. "He is ready," he said.

Elias wasn't sure if he meant the horse or the man.

He led the grulla into the center of the corral. The pup trotted behind them, tail thumping. Ksisstaki paused with her basket of roots, watching. She'd been watching every morning. He knew that now.

Elias set a hand on the horse's withers. The grulla shifted, not in fear, just settling. Elias swung a leg over and eased himself onto the stallion's back.

The horse stood still beneath him, tense but steady, ears forward. It had taken days to get here, weeks, maybe. Elias had lost count.

Nitááhkii crossed his arms, face unreadable. But he'd come to watch. That meant something.

Elias touched the horse's neck. "Easy."

A soft snort.

He pressed his heels in gently.

The horse took one step.

Then another.

Around the corral, slow and steady, with a man on his back for the first time in his life.

Káto stared. "I don't believe it."

Another warrior laughed. "You owe me a knife."

Elias smiled despite himself. The morning was cold and bright. The camp was quiet. Spring was coming.

He only knew the grulla was walking beneath him, trusting him.

Two days' ride south, Thornton was breaking camp, the same sunrise melting the frost on his saddle. He looked north.

26

The Gathering

The scout came in fast, his pony blowing hard, foam on its chest. Men straightened. Women paused at the fires. Even the dogs went quiet.

Nitááhkii stepped forward. "What do you see?"

The scout slid off his horse, breath ragged. "Soldiers," he said in Blackfoot. "Two days south. Riding north."

A stillness moved through the camp. Not fear. Not yet. But something colder.

Elias felt the truth settle in him, heavy and unwelcome.

Thornton.

He turned and walked quickly toward the lodge. The pup followed, whining, sensing the shift.

Ksisstaki stepped out as he reached the doorway. "What is it?"

He didn't answer. He was already gathering his coat, his rifle, and the small bundle of things he owned. He dropped the strap once, then forced himself to slow, to breathe, to keep moving.

Ksisstaki caught his arm. "Elias."

He looked at her, and the fear in her eyes nearly stopped him.

"If Thornton is looking for me, then I'll give him what he wants. Once he has me, he'll turn. I won't bring blood here."

The pup barked once, sharp and confused. Elias knelt and put a hand on the warm head. The pup licked his face, tail wagging slowly.

"Stay," he whispered.

The pup whined, pushing his nose into Elias's palm.

"Stay,"

The pup jumped up against him, then backed toward Ksisstaki, tail low.

Elias stood and walked to the corral. The grulla lifted his head, ears pricked. Elias turned to see Nitááhkii walking towards him.

Elias tightened the cinch, as Nitááhkii said, "I'll get my pony," already turning.

"No."

Elias caught his arm.

Nitááhkii jerked free. "You think I let you ride alone?"

"If you come with me, you die," Elias said. "And it won't stop him."

Nitááhkii stepped closer, eyes hard. "Then I die with you."

Elias shook his head. "No. Not you."

That stopped him.

Not the danger.

Not the soldiers.

Not Thornton.

But *that*.

Nitááhkii's breath hitched, anger and hurt twisting together. "You think I would stay behind, like a child?"

"I won't lead you to a death that means nothing," Elias said. "Not after everything you've done for me. Not after Scout. Not after…"

He swallowed.

"Not you."

Nitááhkii's jaw worked. His hands curled into fists. For a moment, Elias thought he might swing at him.

Then, slowly, painfully, Nitááhkii stepped back.

"Come back," he said, voice rough. He glanced away. "The horses need you."

He turned and walked off.

Elias nodded once, mounted the grulla, and rode out of camp.

***

Elias rode south through the long afternoon, the grulla moving steadily beneath him. The land opened wide: rolling grass, scattered cottonwoods, the far blue line of the mountains. The sun climbed, burned, then began its slow fall. He didn't look back.

He rode until the light thinned and the shadows stretched long across the flats. The air cooled. A hawk drifted overhead, circling once before sliding away toward the river breaks.

By dusk, he saw a faint glow ahead. A small fire tucked in a shallow draw, half-hidden by willows. A single horse stood nearby, reins dropped. A man sat beside the flames, hat low.

Bridger didn't look surprised.

He lifted a hand. "Figured you'd come this way."

Elias stopped the grulla ten yards off. "I'm going to him."

Bridger poked the fire with a stick. "I know."

"If he wants me, he can have me."

Bridger snorted softly. "He doesn't want you. He wants a reason."

Elias dismounted, legs stiff from the long ride. He walked closer to the fire and held his hands toward the heat.

"If I ride into his camp—"

"He'll shoot you," Bridger said. "And then he'll keep riding north anyway."

The fire cracked. A coyote called somewhere out on the flats. The night felt too wide.

Elias stared into the flames.

"What then," he said. "I can't turn my back on them."

Bridger tossed the stick aside. "You're not. You're going back with me to warn them."

Elias didn't answer. He sat down across from him, the fire between them. The grulla grazed quietly in the dark.

For a long time, they didn't speak. The stars came out one by one. The wind moved through the grass in slow waves.

Bridger finally said, "You think he's after you."

"I know he is."

Bridger nodded. "Maybe. But he's riding blind. He doesn't know what's north of him. He doesn't know who's gathering."

Elias looked up. "Gathering?"

Bridger shrugged. "Saw smoke trails today. More than one. Could be Blackfeet bands coming down from the north. Could be Cree slipping south from Canada. Maybe some Assiniboine. Gros Ventre if they're hungry enough. Folks trying to stay ahead of the forts and the hunger both."

Elias looked out into the dark. "How do they know where to go? No one sent word."

Bridger shrugged. "They don't need to. Same valley, same time of year, going back longer than anyone remembers. The place is the message."

Elias felt something shift inside him.

Bridger leaned back on his elbows. "These aren't war parties. They're families. Starving folks. People who don't want trouble. But there'll be a lot of them in one place."

Elias stared into the fire. "Thornton won't expect that."

"No," Bridger said. "He won't."

***

They slept in turns, the fire burning low, the horses shifting in the dark. Elias dreamed of nothing he could hold onto.

They rode north at first light.

The land felt different now. Not empty, not quiet. Smoke trails rose in the distance. A faint drumbeat carried on the wind. The smell of woodsmoke thickened as they climbed a low rise.

When they reached the top, Elias stopped.

The valley below was filling with life.

Lodges dotted the flats. Dozens more than when he'd left. New fires burned. Horses grazed in widening circles. People moved between camps, carrying bundles, leading children, greeting kin. He saw Blackfeet lodges, but also others. Different cuts of hide, different painted patterns, different ways of tying the poles.

Bridger reined in beside him. "Told you."

Elias felt his breath catch. "Who are they?"

"Off-reservation bands," Bridger said. "Like I said, Blackfeet from the north. Cree from Canada. Assiniboine. Gros Ventre. Folks who've been scattered all winter and don't want to starve alone."

Elias watched the movement below. The slow, steady convergence of people who had been wandering the cold months, now drawn together by the promise of spring.

A gathering, not a war.

A people trying to survive.

"He's not ready for what's up there," Bridger said.

Elias nudged the grulla forward, down toward the swelling camp, toward the people who had taken him in, toward whatever waited next.

***

They rode into camp mid-morning, the sun already warming the valley. Smoke drifted low over the lodges. Children ran between them, weaving through horses and dogs. The air smelled of woodsmoke and boiling meat, thin, but more than yesterday.

People looked up as Elias passed. Some nodded. Some stared. Some didn't recognize him at all.

Ksisstaki saw him first.

183

She froze where she stood, a bundle of firewood in her arms. The pup popped its head out from behind her legs and bounded toward the grulla, yipping. Elias swung down and caught the pup before it could leap at the horse's legs.

Ksisstaki didn't move.

Didn't speak.

Just watched him with something tight in her face. Relief. Anger. Fear. All braided together.

Elias opened his mouth, but she turned away before he could say anything, carrying the wood toward her mother's lodge. The pup stayed pressed against his boots.

Nitááhkii appeared a moment later, breathless, as if he'd run from the far side of camp. He stopped a few feet away, eyes fixed on Elias.

"You came back," he said.

Elias nodded.

Nitááhkii's gaze swept over him, the dust, the tired slump of his shoulders, the fact that he was unhurt. His jaw tightened.

"What happened?" he demanded. "Did you find him? Did he turn? Did you kill him?"

Elias shook his head once.

Makóyi approached then, slow and steady, as if he'd been watching from the moment they crested the rise. His face was unreadable.

"You left," Makóyi said.

"Yes."

"And you returned."

"Yes."

Makóyi studied him for a long moment. "Good," he said finally. "A man who runs toward death too quickly is no use to the living."

Elias's shoulders eased.

Makóyi looked past him, toward the far edge of camp where new lodges were being raised. "More will come," he said. "Winter pushed them hard."

Bridger nodded. "We saw smoke trails all morning."

Makóyi's eyes narrowed slightly. "And soldiers?"

"Close," Bridger said. "Too close."

Makóyi didn't flinch. "Then we prepare."

He turned and walked away, calling for the men who served as his runners.

Elias stood there a moment longer, the pup pressed against his leg, the camp shifting and swelling around him. A living thing, growing by the hour.

27

The Weight of Regret

Morning came slow, gray and cold, the kind of light that didn't so much rise as seep into the valley. Elias woke before the camp stirred. The fire outside Makóyi's lodge had burned down to a bed of coals, faint red beneath a skin of ash. Smoke drifted low, clinging to the frost-hardened ground.

He stepped out into the cold and let the air bite at him. It felt deserved.

The camp was larger than it had been the day before. He could feel it before he saw it. More voices, more movement, more horses shifting in the half-light. The valley had taken on a different sound, a different weight. It wasn't the quiet of a small band anymore. It was the restless murmur of too many people in one place, all of them waiting for something they didn't want.

He walked without thinking, letting his boots find their own path through the maze of lodges. Smoke curled from dozens of small fires. Women knelt beside kettles, coaxing thin broth to boil. Children huddled close to their mothers, wrapped in blankets that weren't warm enough. A few dogs trotted between the lodges, ribs showing beneath their coats.

He hadn't noticed how thin the dogs were before.

A woman he didn't recognize looked up as he passed. Her eyes were hollow, the kind of hollow that came from weeks of hunger, not a single hard winter. She didn't speak. She didn't need to. Her gaze slid past him, toward the far end of camp where more families were arriving. Two men leading a sway-backed mare, a woman carrying a child whose head lolled against her shoulder.

Elias stopped walking.

He had brought danger north. He had brought soldiers. He had brought Thornton.

But hunger had brought these people.

He watched the new arrivals move through the camp, their steps slow, their faces drawn. They weren't warriors. They weren't raiders. They were families who had run out of places to go.

A boy no older than eight led a pony with a torn ear and a coat dull from lack of feed. The boy's feet were wrapped in strips of hide. Frost clung to the edges.

Elias felt something twist in his chest. He looked away.

He kept walking.

The grulla stallion stood apart from the other horses, tied to a long picket line that had been extended overnight to make room for the new arrivals. The stallion's ears flicked forward when Elias approached, nostrils flaring. He was restless, shifting his weight, tail lashing once at the cold morning air.

Elias laid a hand on the horse's neck. The stallion's skin twitched beneath his palm.

"You feel it too," Elias murmured.

The horse blew out a breath, warm against the cold.

He checked the cinch, though he wasn't planning to ride. It gave his hands something to do. The stallion tossed his head, impatient. Elias stepped back and let him settle.

A small shape pressed against his leg. The pup. He hadn't seen it approach. It looked up at him with dark eyes, tail wagging once before it sat down, leaning into him as if it belonged there.

He crouched and scratched behind its ears. The pup closed its eyes, content.

"You don't know any better," Elias said softly. "Lucky for you."

He straightened and looked out over the camp. Smoke rose from a hundred fires. Horses stamped and snorted. Children cried. Women moved with the slow, tired rhythm of people who had been cold too long.

He had brought soldiers north. He had brought Thornton. He had brought danger.

But winter had brought all of this.

The camp wasn't just growing. It was swelling, like a river rising against its banks.

* * *

The sun had climbed only a hand's width above the ridge when Bridger found him. He came across the camp with his hat pulled low, his rangy bay already saddled and trailing behind him.

He didn't say anything at first. He just jerked his chin toward the horse line.

"Come on," he said. "Ride with me."

They rode out of camp at a slow walk, letting the horses pick their way through the frost-stiff grass. Behind them, the camp murmured and shifted, a living thing growing larger by the hour.

They were nearly clear of the lodges when Elias heard it, a low growl, more indignant than threatening, and then a burst of laughter.

He turned in the saddle.

A young woman crouched near the edge of a lodge, a strip of dried meat in both hands, leaning back against the pull of something at the other end. The pup had it in his teeth and was working it with the solemn dedication of an animal who had decided this was his life's purpose. His back legs were braced, his whole body corded with effort, tail going hard despite the seriousness of the enterprise.

The woman laughed again and said something Elias didn't understand, and tugged, and the pup tugged back, and neither of them gave an inch.

Elias watched.

The sharp word had already formed in his throat. The old reflex. The same one that used to rise whenever Scout got into the chickens, or dragged something dead up onto the porch, or decided the best place to be was exactly where he wasn't supposed to be.

He never got to use it. Clara always beat him to it, but not the way he would have. She'd laugh first. Then she'd say the dog's name like it was a question she already knew the answer to, and whatever trouble Scout had gotten into would somehow become a story worth telling rather than a thing worth stopping.

That dog, she'd say. *Look at that dog.*

Like it was the best thing she'd seen all week.

The pup lost his grip and sat down hard in the frost, blinking. The young woman held out a small piece of the meat. The pup took it with elaborate gentleness, as if he'd meant to do that all along.

Elias turned back to the trail ahead.

Bridger hadn't noticed. He was already a length ahead, studying the hoofprints in the frozen grass.

"Trail's fresher than yesterday," Bridger said. "More families coming in from the west."

Elias leaned forward in the saddle, studying the sign. The prints were shallow, the edges crisp. A few smaller tracks, colts or ponies, walked close beside the larger ones.

"They're moving slow," Elias said.

"Too slow," Bridger replied. "Means they're tired. Means they're hungry. Means they've been walking a long damn time."

Elias didn't answer.

Bridger turned north, toward a low rise that overlooked the valley. They rode in silence, the only sound the creak of leather and the soft thud of hooves on frozen ground.

When they reached the rise, Bridger pulled up and looked out over the land.

Smoke trails rose in thin lines from the west, three, maybe four of them, barely visible against the pale sky.

"More bands," Bridger said. "Maybe a day out. Maybe less."

Elias felt the weight of it settle on him. "They're all coming here."

"Where else would they go?" Bridger asked. "No rations at the agency. No buffalo. No shelter. Winter's been hard. Harder than most."

They rode down off the rise and along the edge of the valley, keeping to the higher ground. From here, Elias could see the full sweep of the camp, hundreds of lodges, horses tied in long lines, people moving like slow currents through the cold morning.

Bridger pointed toward a cluster of lodges near the far end. "That's a band from the Two Medicine. Lost half their horses last month. Wolves took some. Hunger took the rest."

Elias's stomach tightened.

Bridger pointed again. "Those are Piegan families. Been walking for weeks. Some of the children can't keep up anymore."

Elias looked away.

"You're carrying something heavy," Bridger said.

Elias kept his eyes on the horizon. "I brought Thornton north. I brought soldiers. I brought danger."

Bridger let out a slow breath. "You think this is your doing."

"It is."

Bridger snorted. "You give yourself too much credit."

Elias turned then, anger rising. "I led him here."

"You led him to a camp," Bridger said. "Not to a war." He paused. "You think he wouldn't have come anyway? You think winter wouldn't have pushed these people together? You think Washington wouldn't have sent someone sooner or later?"

Elias looked away.

Bridger's voice softened, but only a little. "This was coming long before you."

"That doesn't change what I did."

"No," Bridger said. "But it changes what you think you can fix."

Elias didn't speak.

Bridger nodded toward the camp. "They're not here because of you. They're here because they're starving. Because the buffalo are gone. Because the government cut their rations. Because they've got nowhere else to go."

Elias swallowed.

"Thornton's coming because he's scared," Bridger continued. "Because he wants a clean victory. Because he thinks he's chasing a handful of raiders. Not this." He gestured at the valley below. "He doesn't have the steel for this."

Elias frowned. "You think he'll back down?"

"I think he'll freeze," Bridger said. "I think he'll see the size of this camp and realize he's in over his head. I think he'll wait for orders. Or he'll stall. Or he'll try to talk."

"And if he doesn't?"

Bridger's jaw tightened. "Then it only takes one scared man to start a war."

Elias looked back at the camp. Near the northern edge, a group of young men were practicing with their bows, arrows thudding into a target made from bundled hides. Nitááhkii was among them, his movements sharp, precise.

"They're ready to fight," Elias said quietly.

"They think they are," Bridger replied. "But they don't know what a fight like this looks like."

Elias felt the truth of that settle in him.

Bridger nudged him with an elbow. "You can't stop this alone. But you can help keep those boys from doing something foolish."

Elias didn't answer.

Bridger let the silence stretch. Then he said, "Come on. Makóyi's looking for you."

They rode back toward the camp. The sun had climbed a little higher, though it didn't bring much warmth. Smoke drifted through the air, carrying the thin smell of boiling meat.

Makóyi stood near the center of camp, speaking quietly with a young woman Elias didn't recognize. Her face was tired, patient. She listened without moving. As Elias watched, Ksisstaki appeared and put her arms around the woman, the easy familiarity of someone known from before. Elias drifted closer without thinking.

Makóyi's voice was low. "He stood straight at the end. He was not afraid."

The young woman smiled. Nodded once.

Ksisstaki drew her away, whispering, her arm still around her shoulders.

Makóyi watched them go for a moment. Then he turned to Elias.

"You walked the camp," Makóyi said.

Elias nodded.

"You saw what is here."

"I did."

Makóyi studied him. "You understand now."

Makóyi looked toward the young men at the target. "They are

restless. They want to ride out. They want to show strength."

"They'll get themselves killed," Elias said.

Makóyi nodded once. "Yes."

He turned back to Elias. "You know the soldiers. You know this Thornton. You know how they think."

Elias hesitated. "I know some of it."

"It is more than we know," Makóyi said. "Speak to the young men. Tell them what you told me. Tell them what Bridger told you. Keep them from riding out."

Elias felt the weight of that settle on him. "They won't listen to me."

"They will," Makóyi said. "Because you came back."

Elias looked away.

Makóyi placed a hand on his shoulder. "You cannot stop what is coming. But you can keep our young men alive long enough to see it."

Elias nodded slowly.

Makóyi stepped back. "Come. It is time."

Elias followed him toward the group of young warriors. Nitááhkii looked up as they approached, his expression guarded. The others paused in their practice, watching.

Elias felt their eyes on him. Felt the weight of what he had to say. Felt the truth of it settle in his bones.

He drew a breath, steady and controlled, and stepped forward.

28

Makóyi's Council

The council gathered as the sun climbed higher, though the light stayed thin and cold. Makóyi chose a place near the center of camp, where the ground was flat and the wind broke against the lodges. A circle had been cleared, trampled snow, a few scattered bones from last night's meal, the ash of a fire long gone cold.

Elias stood at the edge of the circle, unsure whether he belonged inside it. Bridger stood beside him, arms folded, hat pulled low against the wind. The pup sat between Elias's boots, tail curled around its body.

Makóyi arrived first, walking with the steady, unhurried gait of a man who had carried responsibility for too many winters. His hair was tied back, streaked with gray. His face was calm, but his eyes were sharp, taking in every movement of the camp.

Behind him came elders from the arriving bands. Men with lined faces and tired eyes, wrapped in worn blankets and buffalo robes. Some walked with canes. Some leaned on younger men. All of them carried the weight of their people on their shoulders.

Nitááhkii stood a short distance away with the other young warriors, arms crossed, jaw tight. He watched Elias without looking directly at him.

Makóyi raised a hand, and the murmurs around the circle quieted.

"We speak now," he said. "Because we must."

The elders settled into place. Elias remained standing at the edge, unsure whether to step forward. Bridger nudged him with an elbow.

"Get in there," he muttered. "He asked for you."

Elias hesitated, then stepped into the circle. The pup followed, then sat down again, as if this were all perfectly normal.

Makóyi nodded once in acknowledgment.

He began without ceremony.

"More families are coming," he said. "You have seen them. You have seen their horses. You have seen their children."

A murmur of agreement rippled through the elders.

Makóyi continued, "They come because winter has been hard. Because the buffalo are gone. Because the agency gives nothing. Because they have nowhere else to go."

One of the elders, a man with a scar across his cheek, spoke. "We cannot feed them all."

Another said, "We cannot turn them away."

A third added, "If we move, they will follow. If we stay, they will stay."

Makóyi listened without interrupting.

When the elders fell silent, he said, "The soldiers are coming."

A low rumble of voices rose, tense and uneasy.

Makóyi lifted a hand. "We do not know when. But they come."

An elder from the Two Medicine band leaned forward. "Do they come to fight?"

Makóyi looked at Elias.

Elias felt every eye turn toward him. He swallowed, then stepped forward.

"I don't know," he said. "Thornton… he's unpredictable. He wants a victory. He wants to prove something. But he doesn't know what's here. He thinks he's chasing a small band."

The elders exchanged glances.

Elias continued, "When he sees this camp, when he sees how many people are here, he may stop. He may wait. He may try to talk."

"And if he does not?" an elder asked.

Elias hesitated. "Then it only takes one scared man to start something no one can stop."

Silence settled over the circle.

Makóyi nodded. "This is why we speak."

An elder with white braids said, "We should move the camp. Go into the hills. Hide."

Another shook his head. "We cannot move so many people. Not in this cold. Not with so few horses."

A younger elder said, "We should send a delegation. Speak to the soldiers. Show them we are not raiders."

A man beside him scoffed. "And be shot on sight?"

"They will not shoot a delegation," the younger elder insisted.

"They have before," someone muttered.

The circle broke into low arguments, voices rising, hands gesturing, frustration simmering beneath the surface.

Makóyi let it go on for a moment, then raised his hand again. The voices quieted.

"We cannot fight," he said. "Not with so many children. Not with so many hungry. Not with so many who cannot run."

The elders nodded reluctantly.

Makóyi went on, "But we cannot flee. Not with winter still here. Not with so few horses."

Another nod of agreement.

"So we stay," Makóyi said. "But we prepare."

"How?" an elder asked.

Makóyi looked toward the young warriors. "We keep the young men close. We keep them from riding out. We keep them from giving the soldiers a reason to attack."

Nitááhkii stiffened.

Makóyi continued, "We move the horses to the far side of camp. We keep them hidden. We keep them quiet. We do not let the soldiers think we are preparing for war."

An elder added, "We should send scouts. Watch the soldiers. Know where they are."

Makóyi nodded. "Yes. Scouts will go."

Another elder said, "We should send a delegation. Not to speak for peace. To show we are not raiders. To show we are families."

Makóyi considered this. "Perhaps."

He looked at Elias again. "You know this Thornton. You know the soldiers. You know how they think."

Elias shook his head. "I know some of it."

"It is more than we know," Makóyi said. "Speak."

Elias took a breath. "If you send a delegation, send elders. Not young men. Not warriors. Thornton will see warriors as a threat."

The elders murmured.

Elias continued, "And don't send too many. A small group. Slow. Open. No weapons."

Nitááhkii muttered something under his breath.

Makóyi heard it. "Speak, nephew."

Nitááhkii stepped forward, eyes flashing. "We should not crawl to them. We should not show weakness."

Makóyi's voice stayed calm. "We show survival. Not weakness."

Nitááhkii shook his head. "They will think we are afraid."

Makóyi looked at him steadily. "We are afraid."

Nitááhkii's jaw tightened.

Makóyi went on, "Fear keeps us alive. Pride kills."

The words hung in the air.

Nitááhkii looked away, anger and shame warring in his expression.

Makóyi turned back to the elders. "We will send scouts. We will move the horses. We will keep the young men close. And we will consider a delegation."

The elders nodded.

Makóyi looked at Elias. "You will speak to the young men."

Elias felt the weight of it settle on him. "They won't listen."

"They will," Makóyi said. "Because you came back."

Elias didn't answer.

Makóyi stepped closer. "You cannot stop what is coming. But you can keep our young men alive long enough to see it."

Elias nodded slowly.

Makóyi turned to the elders. "We are done."

The council broke apart. Elders rising slowly, leaning on canes, wrapping blankets tighter around their shoulders. The young warriors drifted away, some glancing at Elias, others avoiding his gaze.

Nitááhkii lingered a moment, eyes fixed on Elias. There was anger there, yes, but also something else. Confusion. Hurt. Fear he didn't want anyone to see.

He turned and walked away.

Bridger stepped up beside Elias. "Well," he said. "That went about how I figured."

Elias didn't respond.

Bridger nudged him with an elbow. "Come on. You've got boys to talk to."

Elias looked out over the camp, over the lodges, the smoke, the tired faces, the restless horses.

He drew a breath, steady and controlled, and walked toward the young warriors.

29

The Retreat

Dawn came cold and gray.

Thornton's column had been riding north for two days. Fifty cavalry. Six supply wagons. Bridger scouting ahead.

They were close now. The scouts had reported Makóyi's band two days' ride north, small group, maybe forty people, moving slow. Easy to corner. Easy to disperse.

Thornton sat his horse at the head of the column, back straight despite the cold. His hip ached where an old bullet was buried. He ignored it.

Two days from ending this.

Two days from Elias Harlan.

The first day, they'd covered twenty miles through open country. The second day, less, the land turned rough, forcing them into coulees and draws. By evening, they'd made camp in a stand of cottonwoods, no fires, cold rations, sentries posted at every approach.

Thornton sat apart from the men, cleaning his pistol by starlight. The ritual steadied his hands. Kept his mind focused.

He thought about what he'd say to Harlan when they found him. Thought about the arrest. The charges. The trial that would never happen because Harlan would resist, and Thornton would have no choice but to.

"Captain."

Bridger stood at the edge of the firelight. Thornton hadn't heard him approach.

"Report," Thornton said.

"Tracks heading northeast. Fresh. Maybe a day old." Bridger paused. "More than what we expected."

"How many more?"

"Hard to say. Fifty horses, maybe. Could be they picked up another band."

Thornton reassembled the pistol, loaded it, and holstered it. "We continue north at first light."

Bridger nodded and walked away.

Thornton sat in the dark, listening to the men settle into uneasy sleep. The wind rattled through bare branches. Somewhere distant, a coyote called.

He didn't sleep.

Dawn broke gray and cold.

The column moved at first light, riding single file through narrow draws. The land changed as they went. Less open prairie, more broken country. Hills and coulees. Frozen creeks cutting through rock. Better cover but harder going.

The men were quiet. They'd been riding hard, sleeping cold, eating jerky and hardtack. No complaints. Thornton had trained them for this.

By midday, they reached rougher terrain, low ridges, sparse timber, wind-scraped rock. The horses labored up steep grades, hooves slipping on ice.

Bridger rode back from his forward position and pulled up beside Thornton.

"Smoke," he said. "Next ridge over."

Thornton felt his chest tighten. "How far?"

"Mile. Maybe less."

"Guards posted?"

"Saw two. High ground on the north side."

Thornton nodded. If the camp had posted scouts, it would have known soldiers were coming. But they hadn't fled. That meant they were too weak to run or too confident to worry.

Either way, he had them.

"We dismount here," Thornton said, "Officers only. The rest stay with the horses."

Six men followed him up the slope, Lieutenant Hayes, Captain Morris, and four others. They moved slowly, staying low, using what cover the terrain offered. The wind was in their favor, blowing south, carrying sound away from the camp.

At the base of the ridge, Thornton signaled a halt. He pulled his field glass from inside his coat, checked the lens, and gestured the men forward.

They crawled the last twenty yards on their bellies.

Thornton reached the crest first. He rose just enough to see over, raised the glass, and looked down into the valley.

He stopped breathing.

The valley spread wide below, maybe two miles across, timber on the far side, a frozen creek cutting through the middle.

And filled with lodges.

Not forty people.

Hundreds.

Lodges arranged in wide circles, some painted, some plain. Smoke rising from countless fires, thin columns that bent in the wind and merged into a gray haze above the camp. People moving everywhere, women carrying water from the creek, children running between lodges, men working with horses.

The horse herds stretched along the frozen creek. Hundreds of animals. Maybe a thousand.

Lieutenant Hayes crawled up beside him and looked down. His breath caught.

"Jesus," he whispered.

Captain Morris came up on the other side. Stared. Said nothing.

The other officers spread along the ridge, each one going still as they saw what waited below.

Thornton swept the glass across the camp, trying to count lodges. Lost track after sixty. Started over. Lost count again.

Too many.

Way too many.

He could see different styles, some Blackfeet, some Cree, maybe Assiniboine. Different bands. Different tribes. A gathering.

"Sir," Hayes said quietly, voice tight. "That's not what the scouts reported."

"I can see that, Lieutenant."

Thornton moved the glass slowly across the camp. He saw women scraping hides. Saw children playing near the lodges, throwing sticks for dogs. Saw elders sitting in a circle near a large painted lodge. A war council, probably, discussing what to do about the soldiers they knew were coming.

He swept toward the horse corrals on the far side of camp.

A man stood there. Tall. White. Long hair tied back. Wearing a wool coat and holding a hat in his hand. Watching the horses like he had all day to do it.

Elias Harlan.

Thornton's hand tightened on the glass. His breath came shallow, fast.

Harlan stood easy, relaxed, one hand resting on a fence rail. A dog sat at his feet, some kind of pup, tail wagging. While Thornton watched, a woman approached Harlan with something in her hands. Food, maybe. Harlan took it and said something. The woman smiled and walked away.

Like he belonged there.

Like this was his home.

Like he'd known Thornton would come and prepared for it.

Thornton lowered the glass. His hands were shaking.

"How many you figure, sir?" Hayes asked.

Thornton didn't answer immediately. He raised the glass again, swept it across the camp one more time. Counted the fires. Estimated people per lodge.

"Three hundred," he said finally. "Maybe more."

Silence along the ridge.

The wind picked up, rattling dead branches. A crow called somewhere in the timber.

Hayes said carefully: "We have fifty men, sir."

"I'm aware, Lieutenant."

Captain Morris spoke, voice low: "Even if we had twice that, sir… There are women down there. Children."

"I can see them, Captain."

More silence.

Thornton stared at the camp. Saw a group of children playing near the creek, throwing snowballs. Saw women tending fires, cooking, working. Saw the elders, old men wrapped in blankets, sitting and talking.

He thought of Custer at the Little Bighorn.

Of riding down into overwhelming force.

Of choosing to fight and dying for it.

Of becoming a hero or a fool, depending on who wrote the history.

His throat felt tight. His chest ached.

Fifty men couldn't take this camp. Not without massive casualties on both sides. Not without killing women and children. Not without it becoming a massacre that newspapers would scream about for months.

And even if they tried, even if he gave the order to charge, they might lose.

All of them.

Hayes shifted beside him. "Sir? What are your orders?"

Thornton didn't answer. He stared through the glass at Elias Harlan standing by the horses, calm as Sunday morning.

The man had warned them. Had given them time. Had brought them together into something Thornton couldn't touch.

Had beaten him without firing a shot.

"Sir?" Hayes said again.

Thornton's jaw tightened. He lowered the glass.

"We withdraw," he said.

The officers stared at him.

Captain Morris said: "Sir—"

"I gave an order, Captain."

"Yes, sir."

They crawled backward from the ridge. Slow. Careful. Like they were afraid the camp would hear them and come boiling up the slope with rifles and arrows.

Thornton stayed at the crest a moment longer.

He raised the glass one final time. Found Harlan in the lens.

The man still hadn't moved. Still watching the horses. Still calm.

A warrior approached him. Young, painted, armed. Spoke to him. Harlan nodded, said something back. The warrior walked away.

Like they were friends.

Like Harlan was one of them now.

Thornton's vision blurred. He wiped his eyes, from the cold, he told himself. Just the cold.

He lowered the glass, tucked it inside his coat, and stood.

Walked back down the slope to where the men waited with the horses.

Every step felt wrong. Like walking away from a fight he was supposed to win. Like choosing survival over honor.

Like failing.

Again.

The enlisted men watched him approach. Saw his face. Looked away quickly.

"Mount up," Thornton said.

They climbed into saddles without a word. Fifty men, silent, faces carefully blank.

No one asked what he'd seen. No one had to.

"Column south," Thornton said. "Walking pace. No talking."

They moved out.

The only sounds were hooves on frozen ground and wind through dead grass. No bugles. No commands. Just the slow march of retreat.

Thornton rode at the front, back straight, jaw locked tight.

His hands shook on the reins. He clenched them until his knuckles went white, until the leather bit into his palms.

Behind him, the massive camp continued its daily life. Smoke rising. People moving. Children playing. Completely unaware, or completely uncaring, that fifty armed soldiers had just retreated from their doorstep.

The column descended into a draw. The valley disappeared behind them.

Snow began to fall. Light at first, just a few flakes drifting on the wind. Then heavier. Thick white curtains that erased the landscape.

It covered their tracks. Hid the ridge. Made the camp vanish like it had never been there.

Thornton didn't look back.

He rode south with his teeth clenched and his pride in ruins, while the snow fell harder and the world turned white around him.

He'd come north to crush a small band of raiders.

He'd found an army.

The snow swallowed the column.

The wind erased their passage.

By nightfall, it would be like they'd never been there at all.

30

The Humiliation

The column reached Fort Shaw three days after the retreat.

They rode in silence. Fifty men who'd left with purpose, returning with shame. No one talked. No one looked at each other. They just rode, eyes forward, backs straight out of habit, not pride.

Scouts had ridden ahead the day before. By the time the column arrived, everyone at the fort knew what had happened.

Thornton led them through the gates.

The soldiers on watch didn't cheer. Didn't wave. Just stared as the column filed past, men covered in trail dust, horses exhausted, supply wagons half-empty.

A patrol that had ridden north to crush raiders.

Returning with nothing.

Thornton dismounted in the yard. His hip screamed where the old bullet was buried. He ignored it. Walked toward the headquarters building without looking back.

Behind him, he heard the sergeants dismissing the men. Quiet orders. Boots shuffling. The creak of saddles as soldiers dismounted and led horses toward the stables.

No one asked how it went.

* * *

Colonel Harrington was waiting in his office.

He stood by the window, hands clasped behind his back, watching the column disperse. He didn't turn when Thornton entered.

"Sir," Thornton said.

Harrington's voice came flat. "Close the door."

Thornton closed it.

Silence stretched between them. Long enough that Thornton felt sweat gathering under his collar despite the cold.

Finally, Harrington turned. His face was stone.

"Report," he said.

Thornton's voice came tight. "We tracked them north. Found the camp two days from here."

"And?"

"It wasn't—" Thornton stopped. Started again. "The intelligence was wrong, sir. Completely wrong. Multiple bands had converged. Three hundred people. Maybe more." The words came faster now. "Women, children, elders everywhere. Armed warriors. Horse herds, thousands of them. It wasn't a raiding party. It was an army."

Harrington stared at him. "You had fifty cavalry."

"Yes, sir. Against three hundred."

"So you engaged."

Thornton's throat went dry. "No, sir."

The silence was worse than shouting.

Harrington walked to his desk. Sat. Folded his hands on the surface. His knuckles were white.

"You didn't engage," he said quietly.

"Sir, the tactical situation, if we'd attacked, women and children in every direction, it would have been a slaughter. We'd have lost half our men before we even reached the lodges. The numbers alone—"

"The tactical situation," Harrington cut him off, "was that you had orders to apprehend or disperse a band of raiders. You had fifty trained cavalry. You had superior weapons, discipline, and the authority of the United States Army behind you."

"Which I would have used!" Thornton's voice rose. He caught himself. Brought it down. "I would have, sir. But what we found wasn't what we expected. The intelligence said forty people. We found three hundred. They had time to gather. Someone warned them. They had time to—"

"Time to what?" Harrington's eyes narrowed. "Time to call for help? Time to prepare? Time to become too big a target for Captain Charles Thornton?"

Thornton's hands clenched at his sides. "That's not, I'm not, " He stopped. Forced the words out steady. "I made a tactical decision to preserve my command."

"You retreated without firing a shot."

"I saved lives, sir." His voice cracked slightly. "I kept my men alive. If I'd ridden down there—" He gestured north, hand shaking. "It would have been another Little Bighorn. You want that? Another massacre on your record?"

Harrington stood. Walked around the desk. Stopped three feet from Thornton, close enough that Thornton could see the veins in his temples.

"Do you know what the difference is between you and Custer?" Harrington asked.

Thornton's jaw worked. He said nothing.

"Custer fought," Harrington said. "Custer stood his ground. Custer died with his men rather than turn and run."

"Custer died," Thornton shot back. The words came out too harsh. "He rode into a fight he couldn't win and got his entire command killed. That's what you wanted me to do?"

"I wanted you to do your duty."

"My duty was to keep my men alive!"

"Your duty," Harrington's voice rose to match his, "was to show those hostiles that the Army doesn't back down. That we don't turn tail when the odds aren't perfect. That we don't let them think they can raid and steal and gather and we'll just ride away!"

He stepped closer.

"You. Ran." Each word came sharp. "You saw overwhelming force, and you turned your column around, and you rode away. You came back here with your tail between your legs and fifty men who now know their commanding officer is a coward."

Thornton's face flushed. "I am not a coward."

"Then what are you?"

"I'm a realist! I'm a soldier who understands that throwing men into a battle they can't win is murder, not leadership!"

"Is that what you tell yourself?" Harrington's voice went cold. "That you're the rational one? The smart one? The one who made the hard choice?"

He shook his head.

"Custer made a choice, too. He chose to fight. He chose honor over survival. And yes, he died. But he died a hero." Harrington's eyes bored into him. "You'll be remembered as the man who ran."

Thornton's breath came short. His hands were shaking now. He couldn't stop them.

"Sir, I did what was right. For my men. For—"

"For yourself," Harrington said. "You did what was safe. What was easy. What let you come back here and justify it with talk about tactics and casualties and intelligence failures."

He walked back to his desk. Pulled out a sheet of paper. Started writing.

"But here's what I know, Captain. I know that you had your moment.

Your chance to prove yourself. To show that missing the Little Bighorn thirteen years ago didn't define you. To demonstrate that you're the officer you claim to be."

The pen scratched across paper.

"And you failed."

Thornton felt something crack inside him. "It was Harlan." The words burst out before he could stop them. "Elias Harlan warned them. He's the reason they gathered. He gave them time. If not for him, if he hadn't, " His jaw worked. "This is on him, sir. Not me."

Harrington looked up. His expression was ice.

"Harlan is a civilian fugitive. He has no authority. No command. No responsibility for what you do or don't do." He set the pen down. "You're a commissioned officer who failed his duty. Don't confuse the two."

He slid the paper across the desk.

"Effective immediately, you are relieved of command. You will remain at Fort Shaw under quarters arrest pending court-martial or dismissal. You are not to leave the fort. You are not to communicate with your former command. You are not to wear your rank insignia."

Thornton stared at the paper. The words swam.

Relieved of command.

Court-martial.

Dismissal.

"Sign it," Harrington said.

Thornton's hand moved. Picked up the pen. The shaft felt slick in his grip.

He signed his name. The letters looked wrong. Shaky.

Harrington took the paper. Didn't look at it.

"Dismissed," he said.

Thornton didn't move.

"I said dismissed. Get out of my office."

Thornton turned. His legs felt disconnected from his body. He walked to the door. Each step took effort.

At the threshold, he stopped.

"He did this," he said quietly. "Harlan. He cost me everything."

Harrington didn't look up from the papers on his desk.

"You did that yourself, Mister Thornton. Now get out."

Thornton stepped through the door and closed it behind him.

* * *

His quarters were small. A bunk. A chair. A desk. A trunk for his belongings.

He sat on the edge of the bunk and stared at the wall.

The room was cold. The stove hadn't been lit. He didn't move to light it.

Outside, he heard soldiers moving through the fort. Voices. Laughter. The normal sounds of garrison life.

He sat in silence.

His hands were shaking. He pressed them flat against his thighs. They kept shaking.

Custer fought. You ran.

The words echoed in his skull. Over and over. A litany of failure.

Custer died a hero. You'll be remembered as the man who ran.

He'd spent thirteen years trying to prove he wasn't a coward. Thirteen years trying to show that missing the Little Bighorn didn't define him. Thirteen years building a career, earning rank, waiting for the chance to prove himself.

And when the chance came, he'd retreated.

He'd turned his column around and ridden away.

Just like Harrington said.

He thought of the ridge. Of looking down at that massive camp. Of counting the lodges, the people, the horses. Of doing the mathematics in his head, fifty men versus three hundred.

He'd made the rational choice.

The safe choice.

The choice that kept his men alive.

And Harrington called it cowardice.

His breath came faster. His chest felt tight.

Everything he'd worked for. Everything he'd sacrificed. Gone.

Not in battle. Not in some heroic last stand.

In shame. In disgrace. In a quiet office with a colonel telling him he wasn't fit to wear the uniform.

He stood. Paced to the window. Looked out at the parade ground.

Soldiers were drilling. Young men in blue, marching in formation, rifles on their shoulders. Learning to be warriors. Learning to follow orders. Learning that courage meant facing death without flinching.

He'd taught them the opposite.

He'd taught them to run.

His hands clenched into fists.

It wasn't my fault.

The thought came unbidden. Urgent.

It was Harlan.

Harlan had warned the camp. Had given them time. Had let them gather into something too big to attack.

If not for Harlan, it would have been forty people. Maybe fifty. Easy to disperse. Easy to contain.

If not for Harlan, Thornton would be a hero right now. Successful raid. Hostiles apprehended. Horses recovered. Order restored.

If not for Harlan.

The rage built slowly. Started in his chest. Spread through his arms, his legs, his jaw.

Harlan had done this.

Harlan, a traitor, a deserter, a man who'd chosen savages over his own kind, had destroyed Thornton's career. Had humiliated him. Had made him look like a coward in front of his men and his superior.

Thornton turned from the window.

Sat at the desk.

Pulled out a sheet of paper.

Started to write. A defense. An explanation. A detailed account of why the retreat was justified, why the situation was impossible, and why he'd made the only rational choice.

He got three lines in and stopped.

His hand was shaking so badly the words were illegible.

He crumpled the paper. Threw it across the room.

It wasn't about justification.

It wasn't about reports or court martials or explanations.

It was about Harlan.

The man who'd caused all of this.

The man who was out there somewhere, free, while Thornton sat in this room under arrest.

The man who'd beaten him.

Again.

Thornton stood. Walked to his trunk. Opened it.

Inside: civilian clothes. A wool coat. Spare boots. Personal effects.

And at the bottom, wrapped in oilcloth: his pistol. His rifle. Ammunition.

He stared at them.

Outside, a bugle called. Dinner formation. The fort settling into its evening routine.

Thornton closed the trunk.

Walked back to the window.

The sun was setting. The sky had gone orange and purple, shadows lengthening across the parade ground.

He thought about Harrington's words. About Custer. About dying a hero versus living a coward.

About what happened to men who ran.

His jaw tightened.

He wasn't going to sit here and wait for a court-martial. Wasn't going to let Harrington and the Army decide his fate.

The thought arrived quietly. Not as rage. As something colder.

He'd spent his whole career inside the system. Following orders. Writing reports. Waiting for permission. And the system had just finished with him. Signed its name to his destruction and told him to get out.

He was outside it now.

He opened the trunk. Picked up the pistol. Turned it in his hand. Twenty years he'd carried one, always issued, always Army property, always subject to report and accountability. He set it back down.

Just his now.

A man outside the system could do what the system wouldn't.

He wasn't going to find Harlan and arrest him. Wasn't going to bring him back for trial. There was no trial anymore. No system. No authority except his own.

He was going to find Harlan.

And whatever happened after that, whatever he had to do, he would do it.

He closed the trunk and waited for guilt or hesitation.

Neither came.

That told him something, too.

* * *

Night fell.

Thornton sat in darkness, not lighting the lamp.

Outside, the fort grew quiet. Soldiers settling into barracks. Officers retiring to their quarters. Guards taking their posts.

Routine. Order. The machinery of military life was grinding on without him.

He waited until the sounds faded. Until the fort was as quiet as it would get.

Then he stood.

Opened the trunk.

Pulled out civilian clothes. Changed out of his uniform. Each piece he removed felt like shedding a skin, the blue coat, the brass buttons, the insignia of rank.

He dressed in wool and leather. Common clothes. Nothing that would mark him as military.

He packed a small bag: food, ammunition, a bedroll. The pistol went in his belt. The rifle in his hand.

He moved to the door. Listened.

Silence.

He stood in the shadow of the stable wall and looked back at the fort. The barracks dark. The headquarters building dark. The lanterns on the main gate, far across the parade ground, too distant to matter.

He had signed his name tonight. Shaky, illegible letters on a paper that ended everything.

He turned toward the service gate.

He opened it slowly. Stepped into the hallway.

Empty.

He walked quietly, boots soft on the wooden floor. Reached the back door of the building. The one that opened onto the supply yard, not the parade ground.

The guard would be at the front gate. At the main entrance. Not watching the back.

He slipped outside.

The cold hit him immediately. He pulled his coat tighter and moved along the wall, staying in shadow.

The stables were fifty yards away. He crossed the yard quickly and quietly, expecting a shout, a challenge, someone to see him.

Nothing.

Inside the stables, horses shifted in their stalls. He found his mount, the bay he'd ridden for two years. Saddled it by feel in the darkness.

Led it out the back entrance.

Still no alarm.

He swung into the saddle. Turned the horse toward the rear gate, the service entrance, used for supply wagons, barely guarded.

One soldier stood there, Private Henderson, rifle slung, half-asleep against the gate post.

Thornton rode toward him.

The Henderson turned. Squinted into darkness.

"Who's there?"

Thornton stepped forward, leading his horse. "It's Captain Thornton. I need to—"

The soldier's posture changed. Went rigid. "Sir, you're under arrest. You're not supposed to leave your quarters."

"I know, but I need—"

"Sir, I have to call the—"

The soldier's hand went to his mouth, about to shout.

Thornton's hand shot out before the thought formed, clamped over the soldier's mouth, cut the shout off.

The soldier was young and strong, and he didn't freeze. He grabbed Thornton's wrist with both hands and wrenched sideways, twisting hard. His elbow caught Thornton in the ribs.

They went into the gate post together. The rifle clattered into the snow.

Thornton's free hand found the knife at his belt. He pulled it without deciding to. Without thinking *knife* or *threat* or anything at all. His body was past thinking. Just the need to silence, to stop, to prevent the shout that would end everything.

The soldier felt it. Felt the blade. Went rigid.

For one second, they both froze.

Then the soldier drove his knee upward, and they lurched together, off-balance, and Thornton felt the resistance, then the give, and something left the soldier's body, some fundamental resistance, and they were both still.

Thornton stepped back.

The soldier looked down. Then up. His mouth opened.

He fell forward into the snow.

Thornton stood frozen, blood warm and sticky on his hand.

He knelt. Pressed fingers to the soldier's neck.

Nothing.

He stayed crouched there longer than he should have. The cold coming up through the snow. The soldier's face turned sideways, one cheek in the white cold. Young. Younger than he'd looked on duty.

I didn't mean—

The thought started, and he stopped it. Looked at it. Set it aside.

He had meant it. Not this boy, not this specific moment, but he had stood at the trunk an hour ago and decided he would do whatever he had to do, and this was what he'd had to do, and pretending otherwise was the kind of lie that made men useless.

He had killed a soldier.

He had crossed something that could not be uncrossed.

The only question now was whether that fact would stop him.

He looked at his hands. At the body. At the gate.

It didn't stop him.

Voices somewhere on the far side of the fort.

He grabbed the soldier under the arms and dragged him into the shadow of the gatehouse.

Only thinking: *Run. Get away. Find Harlan.*

This is his fault. All of this.

The lie was easier than the truth.

The horse moved beneath him. The night swallowed him.

Behind him, in the snow by the gate, a soldier lay face down. Twenty years old. His watch had just started.

31

The Breaking

Dawn broke cold over Fort Shaw.

The relief guard walked toward the service gate, boots crunching through fresh snow. His breath steamed in the gray light. Another night watch done. Another cold morning is coming.

He saw the gate first.

Open.

Standing wide, the bar was lying in the snow.

He stopped. Stared.

No one opened that gate without authorization. Especially not at night.

He walked closer, rifle coming up.

Saw the dark shape in the shadow of the gatehouse.

Thought it was a bundle of rags. Or supplies left out.

Then he saw the boots. The legs. The uniform.

At first, it looked like a man slumped over, sleeping. Then he saw the wet hair glued to the cheek. The blood frozen on the boards.

He wanted to scream, but the sound stuck in his throat.

He fumbled the bugle from his belt and blew two shrill notes.

The fort woke hard.

Within minutes, the yard was filled with soldiers.

Officers appeared from headquarters, half-dressed, pulling on coats. Sergeants barking orders. Men forming a perimeter around the body.

Colonel Harrington arrived last. He walked through the crowd without speaking and knelt beside Henderson.

Studied the wound. The position. The open gate.

Throat slit clean through. Knife work. No powder burn, no sign of a gun. Just the cut.

He stood and turned to his adjutant. "Check Captain Thornton's quarters."

The lieutenant ran.

Harrington looked at the gate. At the tracks in the snow, boot prints, hoof prints, leading north.

The lieutenant returned, breathing hard. "Sir. Quarters are empty. Personal effects gone. Horse missing from the stables."

Harrington's jaw tightened. He looked down at Henderson's body one more time. Twenty years old. Wet hair frozen to his cheek. Eyes open.

"Cover him," he said quietly. "Get him out of the snow."

Two soldiers moved forward with a blanket.

Harrington turned to face his officers. "Captain Thornton has deserted. He murdered Private Henderson and fled the fort sometime during the night."

Murmurs rippled through the gathered men.

"I want a patrol assembled within the hour. Twenty men. Best trackers. Follow those prints north. Find him."

"Sir," one of the officers said carefully. "If he's already got a night's head start—"

"I don't care if he's got a week's head start," Harrington snapped. "He murdered a soldier. He's not just a deserter now. He's a murderer. And we will find him."

He looked around at the faces watching him.

"Spread the word to every fort, every trading post, every settlement between here and Canada. Captain Charles Thornton is wanted for murder and desertion. Anyone who sees him is to report immediately to the nearest Army authority."

He paused.

"Dead or alive."

The officers nodded and began moving, shouting orders.

The yard erupted into activity, men running to saddle horses, check weapons, gather supplies.

Harrington stood alone by the gate, staring north.

Bridger heard the news in the stables.

He was checking his horse's shoes when one of the sergeants came in, face grim.

"You hear?"

Bridger looked up. "Hear what?"

"Thornton killed Henderson. Deserted last night."

Bridger's hands went still on the hoof pick. "Henderson?"

"Gate guard. Knifed him. Rode out before dawn."

Bridger set the horse's hoof down slowly and straightened. "Where'd he go."

"North. Harrington's sending a patrol. Wants you to scout."

Bridger looked at the stall wall. He thought about Thornton's face in that tent. The rage was barely contained. The obsession with Harlan.

"I'm not going," he said quietly.

The sergeant blinked. "What?"

"Tell the Colonel I'm done. I quit."

"You can't just—"

"I can. And I am." Bridger looked at him. "I'm not tracking that man. Not for Harrington. Not for the Army. Not for anybody."

The sergeant stared at him. "You know what they'll do to you."

"Don't care." Bridger picked up his saddle. "I'm leaving. Today. Now."

"Where?"

"North. Canada. Somewhere the Army doesn't reach."

He saddled his horse with quick, practiced movements. Tied his bedroll. His gear.

The sergeant watched. "They'll call you a deserter too."

"Let them." Bridger swung into the saddle. "I've seen enough. Done enough. I'm not doing this anymore."

He rode toward the main gate.

No one stopped him.

The fort was too busy organizing the manhunt to notice one scout leaving.

Bridger rode through the gates and turned north.

Behind him, Fort Shaw grew smaller.

Ahead, the land opened up, empty, white, waiting.

He thought about Thornton out there somewhere. Hunting Harlan. Hunted himself now.

Two men chasing each other across a winter landscape.

And nothing good is waiting at the end of either trail.

Bridger touched his heels to his horse.

He'd warned them once. He'd helped Harlan escape. He'd done what he could.

Now he was done.

The fort disappeared behind him.

He didn't look back.

* * *

Three days' ride north, the Blackfeet camp woke to scouts returning.

Makóyi stood outside his lodge as the two riders came in fast, horses blowing steam. The morning was cold, the sky heavy with clouds. Wind rattled the lodge poles, battering the smoke flaps until they sounded like bones in a sack.

Snow still clung to the shaded places, but the ground was soft where the sun reached. The river had started to break, black water snarling under the ice, gnawing its way through.

One of them, a young warrior named Apiistoomska, dismounted and walked straight to Makóyi.

"The soldiers turned back," he said.

Relief rippled through the people who'd gathered.

"But they will return," Apiistoomska continued. "We saw their fort. Saw more soldiers gathering. They will come with many more next time."

Makóyi nodded slowly. He'd known this. Had hoped otherwise, but knew.

"How long do we have?"

"A week. Maybe two if the weather turns bad."

Makóyi looked across the camp. The gathering that had saved them was now their greatest danger. Too many people. Too many fires. Too easy to find.

"Call the council," he said.

They met in the largest lodge. Elders from each band. Warriors. Women who'd earned voice through wisdom or loss.

Makóyi spoke first.

"The soldiers will return. With many more. Maybe a hundred. Maybe two hundred. We cannot fight them. And we cannot stay together."

An elder from the Two Medicine band leaned forward. "If we scatter now, we abandon the strength we found."

"The strength was temporary," Makóyi said. "The gathering saved us once. It will kill us if we stay."

"Where do we go?" someone asked.

"Where we came from. Each band to their own winter grounds. Spread out. Small groups. Harder to find. Harder to surround."

A woman spoke, voice quiet but firm. "The children just stopped being afraid. Now we tell them to run again?"

Makóyi met her eyes. "Yes. Because running keeps them alive."

Silence settled heavy in the lodge.

Old Bear Chief, who had spoken so powerfully before, shifted his weight. "When do we leave?"

"Tomorrow," Makóyi said. "Dawn. The longer we wait, the more danger."

The council sat with it. The weight of it.

Finally, one by one, they nodded.

The camp moved like a living thing coming apart.

Lodges came down. Fires were scattered. Horses gathered and divided. Families sorting what to take, what to leave, what to carry.

Elias stood near Makóyi's lodge, watching. The wind had picked up, carrying the smell of wet earth and melting snow.

Pup sat at his feet, tail low, sensing the change.

Makóyi approached. "You cannot stay with us."

Elias nodded. He'd known it was coming.

"Your presence brings soldiers," Makóyi continued. "Not your fault. But the truth."

"I know."

"Where will you go?"

Elias looked south. "Away. Far enough that they can't follow me back to you."

Makóyi studied him. "The scout, Bridger, he told you about the man who hunts you."

"Thornton. Yes."

"He is dangerous now. More than before."

"I know."

Makóyi pulled something from his coat. A Winchester. The one Elias had given him months ago when he'd warned the camp.

"Take this back."

Elias shook his head. "That's yours. The debt—"

"The debt is paid." Makóyi held it out. "And you will need it."

Elias hesitated, then took the rifle. His rifle. Felt its familiar weight.

"Thank you," he said quietly.

Makóyi nodded once, then turned to go.

"Makóyi," Elias said.

The chief stopped.

"I'm sorry. For all of this. For bringing this to you."

Makóyi looked at him. "You brought a warning. You brought help when we needed it. You stood with us when you could have run." He paused. "The rest, the soldiers, the pursuit, that is not yours to carry."

He walked away.

Elias stood holding the Winchester, throat tight.

Later, Káto approached, leading the grulla.

The horse was saddled. Ready.

Káto stopped a few feet away, jaw tight.

"Makóyi says you take him," Káto said.

Elias looked at the grulla. At Káto.

"You traded a rifle for him," Elias said.

"A good rifle." Káto's voice was bitter. "For Sspommitaa'poka."

Elias frowned. "What does that mean?"

Káto lifted his hand, showing the scar on his palm. Then the one on his forearm. "Bites People." He glared at the horse. "He has earned his name."

The grulla stood calm, ears forward.

"He doesn't bite anymore," Elias said.

"He bites me." Káto held out the reins. "Take him before I butcher him."

Elias went to his gear and pulled out the second Winchester. The one Nitááhkii had given him after the Cree raid. He held it out to Káto.

"Trade," Elias said.

Káto's eyes widened. He took the rifle, checked the action, and sighted down the barrel. Good weapon. Well-maintained. Better than the one he'd lost.

"This is a good rifle," he said carefully.

"Better than what you traded."

Káto looked at the Winchester in his hands. At the grulla. At Elias.

His expression shifted. This wasn't charity. This was business. A fair trade between men.

"This is fair," Káto said.

He handed over the reins and walked away, the Winchester on his shoulder. His back a little straighter now.

Elias stood with the grulla's reins in one hand. The horse waited, patient.

"Biter," Elias said quietly.

The horse's ears flicked toward him.

Good enough.

Nitááhkii found him an hour later.

They stood at the edge of camp, not looking at each other. Just standing.

"You leave tomorrow," Nitááhkii said finally.

"Yes."

Silence.

"The grulla," Nitááhkii said. "Káto finally let him go."

"Traded for him."

Nitááhkii's mouth twitched. Almost a smile. "He will tell everyone it was a good trade."

"It was."

They stood there.

Nitááhkii looked at Elias directly now.

"You saved my life," he said. "Twice. Once from the Cree. Once from myself." He paused. "I wish I had not killed your dog."

"I know."

"But I would do it again. If the camp needed horses. If my people were starving."

"I know that too."

They stood there.

Brothers who could never fully be brothers. Enemies who'd stopped being enemies. Something in between that had no name.

Nitááhkii held out his hand.

Elias took it.

They gripped hard. Brief. Then let go.

Nitááhkii turned and walked back toward the lodges.

Elias watched him disappear into the camp.

* * *

Ksisstaki came at dusk.

She found him near the horse corral. The grulla stood nearby, already saddled, the Winchester in its scabbard.

Pup sat at her feet, watching Elias.

She didn't say anything at first. Just stood there.

Finally: "You're taking him." She looked at the grulla.

"He won't let anyone else ride him," Elias said.

"I meant Pup."

Elias looked down. The dog's ears were up, tail wagging slightly.

"He's yours," Elias said. "You found him. You raised him."

"He follows you," Ksisstaki said quietly. "He always has."

"Because I feed him."

"Because he chose you." She knelt beside Pup and ran her hand over his head. "I wanted to keep him. I tried." She looked up at Elias. "But he is not mine to keep."

She stood.

"You're going south," she said.

"Yes."

"To the Black Hills."

He looked at her, surprised. "How did you know?"

"I listen." She looked down. "Will you come back?"

"I don't know."

"You won't," she said quietly. "Once you leave, you won't come back."

He wanted to argue. Couldn't.

She stepped closer. "I know you saw me as a child. I know I am young." She met his eyes. "But I see you. I saw you when you came broken. I saw you heal. I saw you become part of us."

Elias's throat tightened.

"I wanted—" She stopped. Started again. "I hoped you would stay."

"I can't. My being here—"

"I know." Her voice was steady now. "The soldiers. The danger. I know."

She pressed her fist to his chest. Hard enough to sting.

"Don't die," she said.

He looked at her. She looked away.

Then she knelt beside Pup. Wrapped her arms around him. His head came up to her shoulder now, almost too big to hold. The dog licked her face, tail wagging.

She whispered something in Blackfoot. Too quiet for Elias to hear.

She stood, not looking at Elias, and walked a few steps away. Then she stopped.

Reached into the pouch at her belt and pulled out something small. Held it out without turning.

A carved piece of bone. A wolf. Simple. Beautiful.

"So you remember," she said.

He took it. The bone was smooth, warm from her hand.

"Thank you," he managed.

She nodded once, then walked back toward the lodges.

Pup watched her go. Whined once. Started to follow.

Elias turned away. Started checking the grulla's saddle straps.

Pup stopped. Looked at Ksisstaki's retreating back. Looked at Elias.

Ksisstaki heard the whine. She stopped walking. Didn't turn around.

Her shoulders rose. She was going to call him back.

Then they fell.

She turned. Looked at Pup. At Elias.

Smiled. Small. Sad.

Raised one hand. Not a wave. Just acknowledgment.

Then she walked on.

* * *

Pup watched until she disappeared into the camp. Then he sat beside the grulla. Waiting.

"Come on then," Elias said quietly.

Pup's tail thumped once.

Dawn came gray and cold, the sky heavy with clouds.

The camp was already separating. Bands moving in different directions, north, east, west. Spreading out across the land like water finding cracks in stone.

Elias mounted the grulla. The horse shifted beneath him, muscles tense but steady. Ready.

The ground was soft from the spring thaw, patches of snow still clinging to the shadows. A cold wind blew from the north, carrying the smell of rain.

He had two Winchesters now, one in the saddle scabbard, one rolled in his bedroll. The carved wolf in his pocket. Pup at the horse's feet.

He turned south.

Didn't look back.

Behind him, the gathering dissolved. The lodges that had filled the valley scattered. The people who'd come together for survival were going their separate ways because survival demanded it.

Makóyi's band headed northeast.

The Two Medicine band went west.

Others went north, toward Canada.

Each one is smaller. Harder to find. Harder to surround.

Safer.

Alone.

Elias rode through the morning. The grulla moving steady beneath him. Pup trotting alongside.

Everything he'd found, belonging, purpose, something like home, left behind because his presence made it dangerous.

The land stretched empty around him. Cold. Gray. The spring thaw turning the ground to mud in places, ice still thick on the shaded creeks.

He thought about Clara. About Scout. About the ranch that wasn't his anymore. About the graves under the cottonwood.

About Ksisstaki's fist pressed to his chest.

About Nitááhkii's hand gripping his.

About Makóyi saying the debt was paid.

And somewhere behind him, Thornton was coming.

Two days north, Thornton rode through country he didn't recognize.

Rain had turned to sleet, then back to rain. The ground was soft, muddy. His horse's hooves sank with every step. The animal was exhausted, ribs showing, coat dull.

He'd been following rumors. A white man traveling alone. Heading south. Maybe toward the Black Hills.

He hadn't eaten in two days. Hadn't slept except in brief, fitful stretches in the saddle.

His hands shook constantly now. His eyes burned.

He talked to himself.

"Find him. Just find him. He's out there. He has to be."

At night, he saw Harlan everywhere. Over every rise. Behind every copse. Just out of reach. Sometimes on a horse. Sometimes walking. Once, he saw his face in the surface of a melted pond, staring back at him.

He threw a rock at it and moved on.

The second night, the horse was gone. He woke to find it had broken loose and wandered off. Wolves, maybe. Or just the smell of blood.

He cursed, shouldered his pack, and walked.

Each step south was harder than the last. The mud grabbed at his boots. His feet were raw. The sun was a flat coin, no warmth in it.

He kept the knife in his hand. Just in case.

By the third day, he reached a cutbank above the river. He saw tracks in the mud. A horse, big, unshod. The grulla.

Thornton's hands shook, but he grinned.

"You're coming, rancher," he said to the empty air.

That night, he slept in a gully, jacket over his head. His boots were wet through. His toes had gone numb.

He dreamed.

In the dream, he stood on the ramparts at Fort Shaw. The river below was black glass. Harlan was at the base, rifle pointed up, silent. Thornton wanted to shout, but his throat was cut, blood pouring down his chest, hot and thick.

He woke choking.

Sat up in the dark, hands full of dirt and dead grass.

He rubbed his eyes. "No more running," he told himself. "No more mistakes."

He stood. Shouldered the pack. Set his teeth.

Each mile hurt, but it was the kind of pain that sharpened the mind.

He headed south, into the wind.

Elias was coming. He was certain now.

He would end it.

The rain fell steady. The ground turned to mud beneath his boots. The sky hung low and gray.

Two men riding toward each other across the spring prairie.

One running. One hunting.

Both convinced the other was to blame for everything they'd lost.

And the distance between them narrowing.

Mile by mile.

Day by day.

32

On the Road South

Elias woke to Pup's wet nose against his face.

Cold. Dark. Stars still out but fading at the edges.

He sat up. The fire had died to coals. Biter stood hipshot twenty feet away, ears forward, watching the horizon.

Elias pulled his coat tighter and blew on his hands. His breath steamed. Spring in the mountains came slow and the nights still bit.

Pup sat beside him, tail thumping once against the ground.

"Yeah," Elias said. "I'm up."

He built the fire back from coals, fed it dry sage and dead pine. The flames caught quick. He filled his tin cup from the canteen and set it near the heat. No coffee left. Just water.

He chewed jerky while the water warmed. Pup watched him, eyes tracking every movement.

"You already ate," Elias said.

Pup's tail thumped again.

Elias tossed him a scrap anyway. The dog caught it mid-air and swallowed without chewing.

The sun came up slow over the plains to the east. Behind him, the mountains stood dark against the lightening sky. St. Mary Lake somewhere back there. The camp scattered now, gone in every direction like seeds on the wind.

He drank the warm water and packed his gear. Rolled the bedroll tight. Checked the Winchester. One in the chamber, more in the scabbard. His father's rifle. The one Makóyi had given back.

He saddled Biter. The horse stood patient, used to the routine now. No biting. No fighting. Just stood and let Elias work.

"Good horse," Elias said quietly.

Biter's ear flicked back toward his voice.

Elias mounted. Pup stood, shook himself, and fell in beside the horse without being told.

They rode southeast.

The land opened up ahead of them. Mountains falling away behind. High plains stretching out brown and gray and endless under a sky that looked like hammered tin.

He didn't look back.

* * *

The mountains became a blue smudge, then nothing.

The land flattened into rolling prairie. Grass coming in green where the snow had melted. Mud everywhere else. Biter's hooves made sucking sounds with every step.

Pup ranged ahead, nose to the ground, then circled back. Keeping watch. He'd grown. Big enough now that when he stood on his hind legs he could put his paws on Elias's chest. Still gangly but filling out. More wolf than dog in the way he moved.

They stopped at a creek to water the horse. The water ran fast and brown, swollen with snowmelt. Elias knelt and drank from his cupped hands. Cold enough to make his teeth ache.

Pup waded in up to his chest, snapping at the current.

Elias sat on a rock and watched the dog play. Watched the prairie stretch out in every direction.

Empty.

He touched the carved wolf in his pocket. Smooth bone. Warm from his body heat.

Don't die, she'd said.

He stood and whistled. Pup came running, water streaming from his coat.

They rode on.

He saw the ranch in the afternoon light.

Hadn't meant to. Had tried to angle east, avoid it. But the land pulled him that direction anyway, following the Sun River drainage, the easiest route through the rolling country.

There. The cottonwood. The corral posts. The cabin.

He reined Biter to a stop on a low rise half a mile out.

Pup sat, looked up at him, waiting.

From this distance, it looked almost whole. Like he could ride down there, unsaddle Biter, walk inside, and find Clara at the stove.

Then the wind shifted, and he smelled it.

Char. Old smoke. Burned wood.

The cabin was gone. Just the stone chimney standing. Blackened timbers collapsed around it. The barn was leaning, and half the roof had caved in. The corral, empty.

The cottonwood stood alone at the edge of the property. Two mounds of earth beneath it. One older, settled. One newer, the dirt still dark.

Clara. Scout.

He sat there.

Pup whined once, soft.

Elias's throat was tight. He wanted to ride down there. Stand by the graves. Say something. What? He didn't know.

But his hands didn't move on the reins.

What was there to say that the land didn't already know?

He'd loved her. She'd died. He'd buried her and the dog and left, and everything that happened after, the raid, the chase, Thornton, the camp, Makóyi, Nitááhkii, Ksisstaki, all of it, had happened because he'd ridden north that day looking for stolen horses.

And now the ranch was ash and bone, and he was riding away again.

He touched his heels to Biter's flanks.

The horse started forward, then stopped. Turned his head back toward the ranch. Ears forward.

"I know," Elias said quietly.

Biter stood a moment longer, then turned and walked on.

Elias didn't look back.

* * *

Behind him, the cottonwood stood over two graves no one would tend. The wind moved through the bare branches. The prairie stretched out silent and empty and the only sound was the creak of saddle leather and Biter's hooves in the mud.

He kept riding southeast.

Pup caught the rabbit at dusk.

Elias heard the yelp, then the thrashing in the sage. He reined Biter around and saw Pup shaking something brown and furious.

The rabbit went limp.

Pup trotted back, proud, the rabbit hanging from his jaws.

"Good dog," Elias said.

He dismounted and took the rabbit. Still warm. He gutted it quick with his knife, tossed the entrails to Pup. The dog gulped them down and sat waiting for more.

They camped in a draw out of the wind. Elias built a small fire and roasted the rabbit on a green stick. The fat dripped and hissed in the flames. The smell made his stomach clench.

He gave Pup half. Kept half for himself.

They ate in silence, the fire crackling between them.

When the meat was gone, Elias wiped his hands on his pants and stared into the flames.

Pup lay down beside him, head on his paws, eyes reflecting the firelight.

Elias reached out and scratched behind the dog's ears. Pup's tail thumped twice against the ground.

"Just us now," Elias said quietly.

Pup's eyes closed.

Elias sat there after the fire burned down. The stars came out cold and bright and infinite. The wind died. Somewhere far off, a coyote called and another answered.

He thought about the camp. About Makóyi's voice in council. About Nitááhkii's hand gripping his. About Ksisstaki's fist pressed to his chest.

Don't die.

He pulled his coat tighter and lay down, using his saddle as a pillow. Pup shifted closer, warm against his side.

The stars turned overhead.

He slept.

The river came up fast.

Not the Sun. Some tributary, he didn't know the name of. Swollen from snowmelt, brown and angry, littered with broken branches and debris.

Elias sat on Biter at the bank and studied it. Maybe thirty yards across. Current fast. No way to tell how deep.

Pup paced the edge, whining.

"Yeah," Elias said. "I don't like it either."

But there was no going around. The river bent east and west as far as he could see and he needed to keep heading southeast.

He checked the saddle straps. Made sure the Winchester was secure. Touched the carved wolf in his pocket.

Then he put his heels to Biter.

The horse balked.

"Come on," Elias said.

Biter tossed his head, backed up two steps.

Elias leaned forward and spoke low. "I know. But we're going."

He urged the horse forward again. This time, Biter took a step. Then another. Then his front hooves hit the water, and he stopped, trembling.

"Easy," Elias said. "Easy."

He touched his heels again, gently.

Biter stepped in.

The water came up to his knees. Then his chest. The current grabbed at them, pulling sideways. Biter's nostrils flared wide, eyes rolling.

"Steady," Elias said. "Steady."

The horse pushed forward. The water rose to Elias's boots, then his thighs. Cold, shockingly cold, soaking through his pants.

Behind them, Pup barked once, sharp.

Then he jumped in.

Elias saw him swimming, head up, legs churning. The current pulled him downstream fast.

"Pup!" Elias shouted.

The dog's head went under, came up again. He was fighting it, swimming hard, but the current was stronger.

Biter lunged forward, maybe sensing Elias's panic. The horse plunged deeper, water up to his shoulders now. His hooves found purchase on the bottom, and he drove forward, powerful, surging through the current.

Elias grabbed the saddle horn with both hands as Biter fought across. The far bank came closer. Closer.

Biter's front hooves hit gravel, and he scrambled up, water streaming from his coat, blowing hard.

Elias slid off, boots squelching, and ran downstream along the bank.

There. Pup's head, twenty yards down, still fighting.

"Come on!" Elias shouted. "Here!"

Pup saw him. Changed angle. Swam toward the bank with everything he had.

The current pushed him into the shallows, and he got his feet under him, stumbled, nearly went down, then lunged forward onto the bank.

He collapsed in the mud, his sides heaving.

Elias dropped to his knees beside him. Pup's eyes were wide, tongue lolling.

"You damn fool dog," Elias said.

Pup's tail thumped once, weakly.

Elias sat back in the mud and laughed. Couldn't help it. Pup was half-drowned and still wagging his tail. Biter was standing twenty yards upstream, dripping and watching them both like they were idiots.

Maybe they were.

But they were across.

Elias stood and whistled. Biter walked over, still blowing hard. Elias checked his legs, his hooves. No injuries. Just tired and wet.

"Good horse," Elias said.

He pulled off his boots and dumped the water out. Wrung out his socks as best he could. Put them back on wet.

Pup shook himself, spraying water everywhere.

They stood there on the far bank, all three of them soaked and cold and alive.

Elias swung back into the saddle. Pup fell in beside Biter without being told.

They rode on, wet and shivering, toward a horizon that never seemed to get closer.

* * *

He smelled the settlement before he saw it.

Woodsmoke and something else. Garbage. Cooking. People.

He topped a low rise, and there it was. Maybe twenty rough buildings clustered along a bend in the river. Tents scattered around the edges. Wagons. Horses tied to hitching posts. Men moving between buildings.

A trading post. Supply stop for miners and trappers heading west or south.

Elias reined Biter to a stop.

He could go around. Swing wide, avoid it entirely.

But his supplies were low. He needed ammunition. Coffee. Maybe grain for Biter.

And he needed to know if anyone had seen Thornton.

He touched his heels to the horse and rode down the slope.

The trading post was a squat log building with a crooked chimney. Furs hung from the eaves. A sign nailed over the door said HUTCHINS in faded paint.

Elias tied Biter to the rail. Pup sat beside the horse, eyes tracking every person who walked past.

"Stay," Elias said.

Pup's ears went back, but he stayed.

* * *

Inside, the trading post smelled like tobacco and damp fur and unwashed men. Shelves lined the walls, stocked with tins and sacks and coils of rope. A man behind the counter looked up when Elias walked in.

"Help you?"

"Ammunition," Elias said. "Forty-four-forty. Coffee, if you've got it."

The man nodded and turned to the shelves.

An older man sat near the stove, weathered and quiet, drinking from a tin cup. He looked at Elias, then at the window where Biter stood tied outside.

"Gray horse," the man said.

Elias looked at him.

"Saw another fellow asking about a gray horse. Week or so back, up near Heart Butte." The man sipped his coffee. "Military man. On foot, but hadn't lost himself yet. Asking about someone named Elias. Real specific questions, what'd he look like, which way, how long back." He paused. "Had a book. Wrote things down. Professional about it."

He looked at Elias.

"But the way he said the name. 'Elias.' Made me glad I wasn't who he was looking for."

"Which way'd he go?" Elias asked.

The man shrugged. "Don't know. I was heading southeast when I saw him. But he was asking about a man with a gray horse heading this direction. Figured he'd follow once he got what he needed."

The storekeeper came back with ammunition and coffee. "Two dollars."

Elias paid. Took the supplies.

"That you?" the old man asked. "Elias?"

"No," Elias said.

He walked out.

Outside, Pup stood when he saw him. Elias untied Biter and swung into the saddle.

Elias touched his heels to Biter and rode out of the settlement heading southeast.

Behind him, the old man looked out the window of the trading post, watching him go.

That night, Elias didn't build a fire.

He sat in the dark with his back against a rock, the Winchester across his knees. Pup lay beside him, ears up, alert.

The stars came out. The wind died. The prairie stretched empty and black in every direction.

Somewhere behind him, Thornton was riding.

Somewhere ahead, the Black Hills waited.

And Elias was caught between them, moving south because there was nowhere else to go.

He thought about the miner's words. *Eyes kind of wild. Like he hadn't slept in a month.*

Thornton was coming apart. Had been since the retreat. Maybe before.

And he wouldn't stop. Not until one of them was dead.

Elias touched the carved wolf in his pocket.

Don't die.

He pulled his coat tighter and closed his eyes.

Pup shifted closer, warm against his leg.

The stars turned overhead.

And in the morning, Elias rose, saddled Biter, and rode south.

33

The Hunt

He'd been walking for six days when he saw the buildings.

Heart Butte sat in a fold of land where the creek ran east. A dozen structures. Trading post. Corrals. Blacksmith. Enough.

Thornton stopped on the rise and studied it. His boots were worn through at the heels. His feet were raw. But he'd kept moving, Army pace, thirty miles a day when the ground allowed it.

He'd lost the horse but not the discipline.

He walked down into the settlement.

The trading post had a room for rent above the store. Two dollars a night. Thornton paid for two nights.

"You need anything else?" the storekeeper asked.

Thornton looked down at his boots. The right one had a hole worn through the sole. The left wasn't much better.

"Boots," he said. "Size ten."

The storekeeper nodded and went to the shelves. Came back with a pair of heavy work boots. Leather, well-made. Not Army issue, but solid.

"Three dollars."

Thornton paid and took them upstairs with him.

The room was small. A cot. A chair. A basin for washing. A window that looked out over the corrals.

Thornton dropped his pack on the floor and sat on the edge of the cot. His feet screamed when he pulled off his ruined boots. Blisters had opened and bled and opened again. The socks were stiff with dried blood.

He poured water from the pitcher into the basin and washed his feet carefully. The water turned pink. He dried them and wrapped them in strips torn from a spare shirt.

The new boots sat on the floor beside the cot. He'd break them in tomorrow.

He lay back and stared at the ceiling.

His body wanted sleep. Demanded it. But his mind wouldn't settle.

Harlan was out there somewhere. Moving. Every hour Thornton rested was another hour of distance.

But he couldn't catch anyone on foot with ruined boots and bleeding feet.

He needed a horse. Needed rest. Needed to be smart about this.

Two days. He'd give himself two days to recover and get what he needed.

Then he'd be back on the trail.

He closed his eyes.

Sleep came fast and hard.

He woke to gray light coming through the window. Morning. He'd slept through the afternoon and night without moving.

His feet were stiff. He unwrapped them and checked the blisters. Some had scabbed over. Others were still raw.

He washed again. Re-wrapped them. Pulled on the new boots slowly, grimacing. Stiff leather. They'd need breaking in, but they were whole. That was what mattered.

Downstairs, the trading post served breakfast. Biscuits and gravy.

Coffee. Thornton ate methodically, forcing himself to go slow. His stomach had shrunk during the days of walking and eating light.

The storekeeper, a heavyset man with a gray beard, refilled his coffee.

"You look like you came a ways," the man said.

"Fort Shaw," Thornton said.

"On foot?"

"Horse ran off."

The man grunted sympathetically. "Happens. You looking to buy another?"

"I am."

"Fellow down at the corrals has a few for sale. Fair prices, mostly."

Thornton nodded. "I'll see him today."

He finished his coffee and went back upstairs. Sat by the window and watched the settlement wake up. A woman hanging laundry. A blacksmith firing his forge. Two children chasing a dog through the mud.

Normal life. People going about their business.

None of them knowing what he was doing. What he'd done.

He thought about Henderson again. Couldn't help it.

The young soldier's face. The surprise. The blood spreading across his uniform.

I didn't mean to, part of him whispered.

He tried to stop me, another part answered. *He reached for his weapon. I had no choice.*

Thornton stood and pulled the small notebook from his coat pocket. Opened it. Looked at the notes he'd been keeping.

Dates. Locations. Distances. Details about anyone who might have seen Harlan or heard of him.

Most of it was old. Rumors from Fort Shaw. Reports that the gathering had been somewhere north of the Marias. Nothing solid.

Nothing recent.

But Harlan was out there somewhere. And if Thornton kept asking, kept searching, eventually someone would have seen something. A traveler. A trapper. Someone who'd crossed paths with him.

He just had to be patient. Methodical.

He'd find him.

* * *

He put the notebook away and walked through the settlement. Testing the new boots. They rubbed at the heels but held. His feet ached but didn't bleed.

Good enough.

The man at the corrals was shoeing a roan mare when Thornton arrived. He looked up. Took in Thornton's appearance, dusty, lean, worn gear, but still squared shoulders. Military bearing.

"Help you?"

"I need a horse," Thornton said.

The man straightened and wiped his hands on his apron. "Got three for sale. That roan there once I finish with her, the bay in the far pen, and the sorrel by the water trough."

Thornton walked to the fence and looked them over. The roan was sound but too much spirit for long travel. The bay was old, maybe fifteen, but steady. Deep chest. Strong legs. The kind of horse that could cover ground all day without complaint. The sorrel was young, green, not ready for what Thornton needed.

"The bay," Thornton said. "How much?"

"Forty dollars. Saddle and tack another ten."

Thornton pulled the leather pouch from inside his coat. His savings. Army pay accumulated over months. He'd never spent much. Had nothing to spend it on.

247

Now it was buying him the means to finish this.

He counted out bills. "Fifty."

The man took the money and nodded. "You know horses."

"I know what I need."

"Army?"

"Was," Thornton said.

The man studied him a moment, then seemed to decide not to ask more questions. "I'll get the tack."

Thornton spent the afternoon with the bay. Led him around the corral. Saddled and unsaddled him twice. Checked his hooves, his teeth, his legs.

The horse was sound. Patient. Used to work.

Good enough.

He paid the storekeeper to stable the horse for the night and walked back to the trading post. The new boots had raised blisters on top of the old ones, but his feet weren't bleeding. Progress.

* * *

He ate dinner, stew and bread, and went back upstairs. Lay on the cot and stared at the ceiling as the light faded.

Tomorrow he'd leave. Two days of rest. That was enough.

Harlan had maybe a week's lead now. Maybe more. But Thornton would find the trail. Would ask questions. Would track him the way the Army had taught him to track.

Patient. Methodical.

He'd find him.

He had to.

Everything depended on it.

The second morning, Thornton woke before dawn. Washed. Dressed. Wrapped his feet one more time and pulled on the new boots. They were breaking in. Still stiff, but better.

Downstairs, he ate quickly. Biscuits. Coffee. He didn't linger.

At the corrals, he saddled the bay himself. The horse stood patiently while Thornton worked. He checked the cinch twice. Adjusted the stirrups. Tied his bedroll behind the saddle. The Winchester went in the scabbard on the right side, where he could reach it quickly.

His pack, what little he had, went behind the saddle, secured with a rope.

He was tying down the last knot when he heard them.

Two men near the water trough, filling canteens. Cowboys by their look, wide hats, worn chaps, the lean build of men who lived in the saddle. They had that early-season look. Probably heading south looking for ranch work. Spring roundup starting soon.

The younger one was talking.

"...never seen a grulla like that. Beautiful animal. Wild-looking, you know? But calm. Just stood there while the fellow watered him."

The older cowboy grunted. "Rare color. Don't see many."

"I asked if he was selling. He just shook his head and kept moving. Didn't say ten words the whole time."

Thornton stopped. His hands went still on the rope.

Grulla. Gray horse. Rare.

He walked over.

The two men looked up.

"The horse you're talking about," Thornton said. "Grulla. When did you see it?"

The men exchanged glances. The older one straightened slightly, wary.

"Three, four days back. Why?"

"Where."

The younger cowboy frowned. "Why you asking?"

Thornton kept his voice level. Polite. Professional. "I'm looking for someone. White man. Traveling alone. Gray horse."

The older cowboy studied him a moment, then nodded slowly. "That'd be him. Had a dog with him, too. Big one. Looked half wolf."

Thornton's jaw tightened slightly. "Which direction was he heading?"

"Southeast. We were coming up from the Missouri breaks, passed him on the trail. Asked if he needed anything, water, food, directions, but he just nodded and kept riding." The cowboy paused. "Wasn't unfriendly. Just focused. Like he had somewhere to be."

"Southeast," Thornton repeated.

"That's right. Toward the Missouri, looked like. Maybe heading for the Black Hills. A lot of folks are going that way these days."

"You know him?" the younger cowboy asked.

"I'm looking for him," Thornton said.

He turned and walked back to his horse.

Behind him, he heard the younger one say something quiet. The older cowboy's response was too low to make out.

Thornton didn't care what they thought.

He had a direction now.

Southeast. Three or four days ahead.

He could close that gap.

* * *

Thornton led the bay to the water trough and let him drink. The horse took his time, unhurried. Thornton stood beside him, one hand on the saddle, thinking.

Harlan had warned them.

That was the fact that mattered. Everything else followed from that.

Thornton had been doing his duty. Following orders. The raiders had stolen from settlers, Harlan himself had reported it. The Army had mobilized to recover the property and apprehend the thieves. Standard procedure. Nothing unusual.

Then Harlan disappeared from Fort Shaw. Bridger brought his horses back in the night. And when the column reached the Marias, the camp was gone. Empty. Like they'd known the Army was coming.

Because Harlan had told them.

He'd chosen them over his own kind. Warned them. Given them time to scatter or gather, Thornton still wasn't sure which. But the result was the same.

When Thornton found them, there were too many. Three hundred people. Maybe more. Warriors, women, and children, all mixed together in one massive camp. Attacking would have been suicide. A massacre. He'd made the only tactical decision possible and withdrawn.

And Harrington had called him a coward.

Relieved him of command. Compared him to Custer. Said Custer had fought while Thornton ran.

But Harrington didn't understand. Couldn't understand. He hadn't been there. Hadn't seen the size of that gathering. Hadn't done the mathematics, fifty men against three hundred.

Custer had fought, and Custer had died, and his entire command with him. That was courage, maybe. Or stupidity. Thornton wasn't sure anymore which was which.

But it didn't matter. What mattered was that Harlan had created the situation. Harlan had made the camp too big to engage. Harlan had forced Thornton into an impossible choice and then let him take the blame for it.

And when Thornton tried to leave Fort Shaw, to fix this, to find Harlan and make it right, Henderson had tried to stop him.

Thornton closed his eyes briefly. Saw Henderson's face in the darkness. The young soldier's expression. Surprise. Then pain. Then nothing.

The knife going in. The warmth of blood. The weight of the body as it slid down.

I didn't want to, part of him whispered.

He reached for his weapon, the other part answered. *He was going to raise the alarm. I had no choice.*

Both things were true. Both things had to be true.

Because if Henderson's death wasn't necessary, then Thornton was a murderer. And if he was a murderer, then everything else, leaving the fort, tracking Harlan, all of it, was wrong.

But it wasn't wrong.

It was justice.

Harlan had destroyed his career. His reputation. Everything he'd worked for. And Harlan was out there now, free, riding south like none of it mattered.

That couldn't stand.

The bay finished drinking and lifted his head. Water dripped from his muzzle.

Thornton opened his eyes. The sun had broken through the clouds. The day was cold but clear.

He checked the girth one more time. Adjusted the rifle in its scabbard. Touched the notebook in his pocket to make sure it was secure.

Then he swung into the saddle.

The leather creaked. The horse shifted beneath him, solid and steady and ready.

Thornton touched his heels to the bay's flanks and rode out of Heart Butte heading southeast.

* * *

The land stretched out ahead of him. Rolling prairie cut by creeks swollen with snowmelt. The sky vast and gray above. No trees. No cover. Just open country that went on forever.

Somewhere out there, three or four days ahead, Harlan was riding. Gray horse. Big dog. Heading southeast toward the Missouri.

Thornton knew where to go now.

He settled into the saddle and let the bay find his pace. Not fast. Steady. The kind of pace that ate up miles without burning out the horse.

Three days. Maybe four. Maybe a week if Harlan kept moving hard.

But eventually, Thornton would catch him.

And then it would be over.

The horse moved steady beneath him. Southeast. Toward the Missouri. Toward the man who'd destroyed everything.

Thornton didn't look back.

Behind him, Heart Butte faded into the distance, smoke from morning fires rising straight up in the still air.

Ahead, the land opened up empty and cold and endless.

And somewhere out there, getting closer with every mile, Elias Harlan was riding south.

34

The Witness

The land changed as Elias rode southeast.

The prairie gave way to broken country, rolling hills cut by ravines, scattered pine on the ridges, grass going from brown to green in patches where the snow had melted. The air smelled different. Drier. The wind carried dust instead of the clean bite of mountain cold.

He'd been riding for four days since the trading post.

The old man's words stayed with him. *Military man. Asking about someone named Elias. Had a book, took notes. Professional about it.*

Probably Thornton.

Maybe still following. Maybe not.

Elias couldn't know. But he rode carefully anyway. Watched his back trail. Took the high ground when he could. Chose campsites where he could see anyone approaching.

Pup ranged ahead, nose to the ground, circling back. Alert but not agitated. Just doing what he always did.

Biter moved steadily beneath him. The horse had settled into the rhythm of long travel, head down, ears forward, covering ground without complaint.

The country showed more traffic now. Wagon ruts cut deep in

the soft earth. Abandoned campsites. Trash scattered in the sage, broken bottles, tin cans, rotted canvas. The detritus of people heading somewhere in a hurry.

The Black Hills.

Elias had heard about them at the trading post. Gold. Thousands of men flooding in. Deadwood. Lead. Camps springing up overnight. Fortunes made and lost. Lawlessness.

And all of it on land that wasn't supposed to be touched.

Treaty land. Lakota land.

He'd heard that too.

Late morning on the fifth day, he topped a rise and saw them.

The camp sat in a fold of land below, tucked against a creek where cottonwoods grew thick. Maybe six lodges. Eight at most. Horses grazing nearby. Smoke rising thin and straight in the still air.

Lakota.

Elias reined Biter to a stop.

People moved around the camp. Women at cook fires. Children were playing near the creek. Men working with horses in the corral they'd built from deadfall.

Normal life.

Except it wasn't normal. Not anymore.

A child saw him first. Pointed. The playing stopped. One of the women looked up. Then another. Men near the horses turned.

Everyone watching now.

Elias sat his horse on the ridge. Pup at Biter's feet, ears up.

No one moved toward him. No one raised a weapon. Just watched.

He was maybe three hundred yards away. Close enough to see faces. Far enough that neither side felt immediately threatened.

Elias understood what they were seeing: a white man, alone, a gray horse, a big dog, heading southeast. Toward the Black Hills. Toward the gold. One more invader in a flood of invaders.

He understood what he was seeing, too: people living their lives. Temporarily. A small camp, probably a fragment of something larger that had scattered. Watching the land get taken. Watching men like him ride past on their way to take more.

The woman at the nearest fire said something to the child. The child went inside a lodge.

An older man walked out from the horses. Stood at the edge of the camp. Looked up at Elias.

They held each other's gaze across the distance.

The man's expression was unreadable. Not hostile. Not welcoming. Just… watching.

Elias touched his hat brim. A gesture. Acknowledgment.

The man didn't respond.

Elias turned Biter east, giving the camp a wide berth. Rode along the ridge rather than down through the valley.

When he looked back, they were still watching him.

He rode on.

* * *

That evening, he camped in a draw sheltered by a stand of pine.

No fire. The sky was clear, and he didn't want smoke giving away his position. Just jerky and water. The air turned cold as the sun went down.

He unsaddled Biter and hobbled him where the grass was good. The horse grazed, tearing at the new green shoots with a steady rhythm.

Pup circled the camp perimeter, nose down, checking. Then came back and lay down near Elias's bedroll.

Elias sat with his back against his saddle and looked at the stars coming out. Thought about the camp he'd seen. The people watching him pass.

Thought about Makóyi's camp. The gathering. The council. The scattering.

Different people. Different place. Same pattern.

Treaties made. Treaties broken.

Land promised. Land taken.

People pushed. People scattered.

White men flooding in for gold, for land, for something they wanted and would take regardless of who had it first.

He'd witnessed it with the Blackfeet. Warned them. Lived with them. Watched them break apart because staying together made them a target.

And now he was riding toward the Black Hills, Lakota sacred land, treaty land, where the same thing was happening. Where thousands of white men were tearing up the earth looking for gold on land they'd been told was off-limits, and didn't care.

And he was one of them now.

Not looking for gold. Just looking for a place to disappear. But still. Riding toward land that wasn't his, that had been promised to people who'd had everything taken already.

He was a witness.

But he was also part of it.

The carved wolf was in his pocket. He pulled it out, ran his thumb over the smooth bone.

Don't die, Ksisstaki had said.

He hadn't. But he'd lost everything anyway. The ranch. Clara. Scout. The camp. Makóyi. Nitááhkii. Ksisstaki.

Pup was here. That was something.

And Biter. The horse Káto had called Bites People and traded away in frustration. Now Elias's only constant other than the dog.

He put the wolf back in his pocket.

Lay down and pulled his coat over him. Pup shifted closer, warmth against his side.

The stars turned overhead.

Tomorrow he'd reach the Black Hills. The chaos. The gold camps. The violation of everything the Lakota had been promised.

And somewhere behind him, maybe a day, maybe a week, maybe not at all, Thornton might be following.

Or might not.

Elias couldn't know.

He closed his eyes and slept.

* * *

Elias woke to Pup's growl.

Low. Continuous. The sound the dog made when something was wrong.

He opened his eyes.

The sun was just breaking over the hills to the east, light spilling gold across the prairie. His breath steamed in the cold air. Frost had settled on his coat during the night.

Twenty feet away, a man sat on horseback. Lakota. Leading a second horse. Watching him.

Elias went still.

The man was maybe forty. Long hair with a single feather tied in it. He wore buckskin leggings and a cotton shirt, a beaded belt. A rifle rested across his lap. Not pointed at Elias. Just there.

How long had he been sitting there?

Long enough.

Pup took a step forward, hackles up, growl deepening.

The man's horse shifted, ears pinning back. Started to sidestep.

"Stay," Elias said. Quiet but firm.

Pup stopped. Grumbled low in his throat but stayed.

The man's horse settled. The man himself hadn't moved. Hadn't reached for the rifle. Hadn't shown concern. Just sat there, calm, eyes on Elias.

Elias sat up slowly. His Winchester was five feet away, leaning against his saddle. Might as well have been a mile.

The man could have killed him. Could have shot him in his sleep. Could have counted coup. Could have taken his horse, his gear, everything.

But he was just sitting there.

Watching.

The man said something. A few words in Lakota. The tone was flat. Matter-of-fact. Not hostile. Not friendly. Just… speaking.

Elias didn't understand the words.

He nodded anyway. Acknowledgment. *I hear you. I don't know what you're saying, but I hear you.*

The man's expression didn't change. He looked at Elias a moment longer. Then he spoke again. Two words this time. Slow. Deliberate.

"Paha Sapa."

The way he said it, weight behind it. Sacred and stolen both.

Elias understood that much.

The Black Hills. Where Elias was heading. Where white men were tearing apart something holy.

The man held his gaze.

Then he turned his horse. The led horse followed. He rode north along the tree line, moving easy, unhurried.

Didn't look back.

Elias watched him go until he disappeared into the pines.

Pup stood tense, watching too. When the man was gone, the dog shook himself and came back to Elias, tail low.

Elias reached out and scratched behind the dog's ears. "Good boy," he said quietly.

He sat there as the sun climbed higher and the frost burned off his coat.

The man could have killed him. Easily.

Had chosen not to.

Why? Pity? Contempt? Just not worth the effort?

Or maybe a different message: *You're already dead. You just don't know it yet.*

Elias stood. Saddled Biter. Checked the Winchester. The carved wolf was still in his pocket.

He mounted and rode southeast.

Toward the Black Hills.

Toward Paha Sapa.

Toward the thing the man had named, and Elias was riding into it anyway.

* * *

By midday, the traffic increased.

Wagons heading south, loaded with supplies. Men on horseback. Men on foot. All heading in the same direction.

Toward the gold.

No one paid Elias much attention. Just another man heading to the Hills. Another hopeful. Another fool.

He passed a wagon train. Six wagons, families inside, heading to set up shop wherever the miners gathered. A woman looked out at him as he rode past. Tired eyes. A baby on her hip. She didn't smile.

He passed men on foot, carrying everything they owned on their backs. Young men mostly. Hungry-looking. Desperate-looking.

He passed a group of Chinese workers heading south with tools and packs. They kept to themselves, eyes down.

Everyone heading toward something. Running toward or running from. Hard to tell the difference sometimes.

Elias kept Biter to a steady pace. Pup stayed close now, wary of the crowds.

Late afternoon, he topped a rise and saw it spread out below.

Not Deadwood. Not yet. But a camp. Maybe five hundred people. Maybe more. Tents and shanties sprawled along a creek. Smoke from cook fires. The sound of hammering. Shouting. A piano playing somewhere, out of tune.

Chaos.

And beyond it, in the hills to the west, riders on a distant ridge.

Lakota.

Maybe a dozen of them. Too far to make out the details. But Elias knew what they were seeing.

Their sacred land. Paha Sapa. Being torn apart.

And they couldn't stop it.

Just like Makóyi couldn't stop the Army. Just like the gathering couldn't stay together. Just like the treaties meant nothing when white men wanted something.

The pattern.

Elias sat on Biter and looked at the camp below. Looked at the Lakota on the ridge.

Witness to both.

Part of both.

He thought about the man this morning. Sitting on his horse. Watching Elias sleep. Saying the sacred name.

Paha Sapa.

Elias touched his heels to Biter and rode down toward the camp.

Behind him, the Lakota watched from the ridge.

And somewhere behind him, maybe close, maybe not, Thornton might be riding too.

He rode into the chaos and let it swallow him.

35

The Encounter

Elias had been in the Black Hills four days when the drunk grabbed him.

He was outside Hendrick's Supply, loading sacks of flour onto a freight wagon. The work was simple. Heavy. It paid enough to keep him and the animals fed while he figured out what came next.

Pup lay in the shade of the wagon, watching the street. He'd grown massive in the months since leaving the camp. When he stood, his shoulder came to Elias's hip. Lean and muscled, gray coat thick, pale eyes that tracked every person who passed. People crossed the street to avoid him.

The drunk came from the saloon across the way. Stumbling. Loud. He'd been watching Elias work for the past hour, muttering to himself, working up to something.

He crossed the street fast, boots unsteady in the mud.

"You," he said. "You took my job."

Elias straightened, wiping his hands on his pants. "Don't know you."

"Hendrick gave you my job. I worked that freight line all winter."

"I don't know anything about that," Elias said. Kept his voice even. "You'll have to talk to Hendrick."

The man's hand shot out. Grabbed Elias's shoulder. Hard.

"I'm talking to—"

Pup moved.

No bark. No warning. Just speed.

The dog's jaws closed on the man's forearm. Not tearing. Not ripping. Just holding. Teeth through wool, pressure on flesh. The man froze mid-word.

Pup's eyes locked on him. A sound came from deep in the dog's chest. Not his throat. Deeper. A rumble that seemed to come from somewhere ancient. Low. Continuous. A sound that makes the hair stand up on a man's arms.

Pure killing sound.

The man felt the power in those jaws. Felt how easy it would be for Pup to bite down. To snap bone.

"Jesus Christ," the man whispered.

Elias didn't move. Didn't grab the dog. Didn't panic.

"Pup," he said. Calm. Quiet. "Let go."

The dog didn't release. Just held. The growl didn't stop.

"Now."

Pup's jaws opened. He stepped back. But he didn't look away from the man. Another growl rose. Sharper. *Try that again, and I'll finish it.*

The man stumbled backward, clutching his arm. The sleeve was wet with spit, dented where the teeth had pressed. No blood. Not yet. But the warning was clear.

"That thing should be shot," the man said. His voice shook.

"You shouldn't have grabbed me," Elias said.

The man backed away. Turned. Walked fast toward the saloon, looking over his shoulder twice.

People had stopped to watch. A woman with a basket. Two miners. The freight driver on the wagon seat. They looked at Pup. Looked at Elias.

No one said anything.

Elias turned back to the flour sacks.

Pup stood beside him now. Still tense. Still watching the saloon door where the man had disappeared.

Elias put his hand on the dog's head. Felt the muscles tight beneath the fur. The readiness.

"Good boy," he said quietly. "Easy now."

Pup leaned into his leg. The tension didn't leave completely, but the growl stopped.

Elias loaded the last two sacks. The freight driver climbed down, inspected the load, and paid him four bits without a word. Climbed back up and drove off.

* * *

Pup followed Elias into the shade. Lay down. Put his head on his paws. But his eyes stayed on the street. Watching.

Elias sat beside him. Pulled a canteen from his pack and drank. Poured water into his hand for the dog. Pup lapped it up, eyes never leaving the street.

"You're getting mean," Elias said.

Pup's tail thumped once against the dirt.

"Gonna get us both killed."

The tail thumped again.

Elias looked at him. Really looked. The pup Ksisstaki had given him was gone. This was something else now. Something wild and loyal and deadly in equal measure.

Partner.

He scratched behind the dog's ears. Pup closed his eyes briefly, then opened them again. Still watching. Always watching.

"I know," Elias said. "I know."

The work dried up by afternoon. Hendrick had no more freight to move. Told Elias to come back in two days.

Elias needed ammunition. Coffee. The last of his supply was gone.

He walked to where Biter stood tied in the shade behind the supply building. The horse lifted his head, ears forward. Elias untied him, checked the cinch, and swung into the saddle.

Pup fell in beside them as they moved through camp.

The place was chaos. Tents packed so tight you could barely walk between them. Mud everywhere. The smell of unwashed bodies, wood smoke, and rotting garbage. Men shouting. Hammering. A piano playing badly somewhere, the same three chords over and over.

Gold fever. Desperation. Greed. All of it packed into one churning, filthy sprawl.

They passed a claim where two men were arguing over boundaries. Walked past a woman calling out prices from a tent flap. Passed a group of Chinese workers hauling water, silent, eyes down.

Pup stayed close to Biter's legs. Ears back. He didn't like the crowds. Too many people. Too much noise. Too much threat.

They passed the edge of the diggings. Raw earth torn open. Sluice boxes. Men bent over pans. The hillside was scarred and broken.

Beyond, on a distant ridge, Elias saw them.

Lakota.

Maybe a dozen riders. Too far to see clearly. Just silhouettes against the sky. Watching.

Watching their sacred land get torn apart.

Elias thought about Mountain Chief. About the promises. About the pattern.

Different people. Different land. Same thing happening.

He kept riding.

* * *

The trading post sat at the center of camp. A rough plank building with canvas stretched over the roof. Barrels and crates stacked outside. A hand-painted sign above the door said LANG'S SUPPLY.

Elias had come here on his first day in camp. The man who ran it was fair. Didn't gouge on prices like some of the others.

He tied Biter to the rail outside. The horse stood patient, one hip cocked, resting.

"Stay," Elias said to Pup.

The dog's ears went back, but he sat.

Elias pushed through the door.

Inside, the trading post smelled like tobacco, damp fur, and un-washed men. Shelves lined the walls, stocked with tins and sacks and coils of rope. Three men stood at the counter. Two more near the stove.

Elias moved to the shelves. Found the ammunition. Forty-four-forty. Took two boxes.

Then he saw him.

Thornton stood near the back of the store, looking at a display of knives. He held one up to the light, testing the edge with his thumb.

Elias went still.

For a moment, neither man moved.

Then Thornton looked up.

Their eyes met across the room.

Recognition.

Instant. Complete.

Thornton's hand stopped moving. The knife stayed half-raised.

Elias felt his heart kick once, hard.

The men at the counter kept talking. The stove crackled. Someone coughed.

But between Elias and Thornton, the air went dead quiet.

Thornton set the knife down slowly. His hand moved toward his coat. Stopped. His eyes never left Elias.

Elias's hand moved toward his hip. Empty. He'd left the pistol at camp. Work day. Hadn't thought he'd need it.

The Winchester was with his saddle outside. Might as well be a mile away.

Pup was outside too.

He was alone.

Three men between them. The counter. Shelves. Innocent people who didn't know what was happening.

Thornton took a step forward.

The storekeeper's voice cut between them. "Not here, boys."

Both men stopped.

The storekeeper had a shotgun under the counter. Everyone knew it. His hand was out of sight now.

"You got business, take it outside. You got business with me, state it. Otherwise, one of you leaves. Now."

Silence stretched.

The men at the counter shifted away. Watching. Wary.

Thornton looked at the storekeeper. Back at Elias.

His jaw worked.

Then he spoke. Quiet. Just loud enough for Elias to hear.

"Harlan."

Elias said nothing.

"Knew I'd find you."

"You found me."

Silence.

Thornton's eyes stayed locked on Elias. Not wild. Not broken. Just focused. Absolute.

"Soon," he said.

Then he turned. Walked to the door. Stopped with his hand on the frame. Looked back once.

Then he was gone.

Elias stood there, ammunition still in his hand.

The men at the counter stared at him.

The storekeeper cleared his throat. "You want those?"

Elias looked down. Forty-four-forty. Two boxes.

"Yeah," he said.

The storekeeper wrapped them. Took Elias's money. Put the boxes in a sack.

Then he looked at Elias.

"Seems you might be needing them," he said quietly.

Elias didn't answer.

He took the sack and walked out.

* * *

Outside, Pup stood immediately. Looked at the door like he could smell what had just happened.

Thornton was gone. Horse and rider disappeared into the chaos of the camp.

But he was here. In the Black Hills. Close.

Elias untied Biter. Mounted. Pup fell in beside the horse.

They rode back to the edge of camp where Elias had been staying. A small clearing near a stand of pine. Far enough from the noise for some quiet.

He unsaddled Biter. Hobbled him where the grass was good.

Sat down with his back against a tree.

Pup lay beside him, head on Elias's thigh.

Elias looked at the ammunition in his hand. Looked at the Winchester leaning against his saddle.

He thought about Thornton's face. The steadiness in his eyes. The calculation.

Soon.

Elias put his hand on Pup's head. The dog's breathing was steady. Warm.

"He's here," Elias said quietly.

Pup's eyes opened. Looked up at him.

Elias sat there as the sun went down. As the noise from the camp drifted through the trees. As the stars came out cold and bright.

Somewhere out there, Thornton was preparing too.

36

The Vigil

The morning after Lang's Supply, Elias woke to Pup's nose against his face.

The dog hadn't slept. Elias could tell. The tension in his body. The way his eyes tracked every movement through camp. The low rumble in his chest whenever someone passed too close.

Elias sat up. Checked the Winchester. The pistol. Both where he'd left them. Both loaded.

Biter stood hobbled nearby, grazing. Calm. The horse didn't sense what the dog did.

But Pup knew.

Thornton was here. In the Black Hills. Close.

Elias stood. Stretched. His shoulder ached where the drunk had grabbed him days ago. Felt like weeks.

He saddled Biter. Slid the Winchester into the scabbard. The pistol went on his belt. He wouldn't be without them again.

Pup followed him through camp. Pressed against his leg. Eyes moving. Watching.

They passed miners heading to their claims. Passed women hauling water. Passed the chaos and noise and stink of too many people packed into too small a space.

Elias found work at a stable. Mucking stalls. Moving hay. The owner paid two bits for the morning. Didn't ask questions about the rifle or the dog or why Elias kept looking toward the tree line.

By noon the work was done.

Elias took his pay and walked to the edge of camp where it met the forest. Found a spot in the shade. Sat with his back against a pine.

Pup lay beside him. Facing camp. Watching.

Elias pulled jerky from his pack. Broke it in half. Gave Pup his share.

They ate in silence.

Across the camp, beyond the tents and shanties, Elias saw movement on the far ridge.

Lakota.

Still there. Still watching. Witnesses to everything.

He thought about Mountain Chief. About the promises. About the pattern repeating.

Then he saw him.

Thornton.

Just for a moment. Across the main thoroughfare. Maybe a hundred yards away. Standing near a freight wagon. Looking.

Their eyes met.

Neither moved.

Then a wagon rolled between them and when it passed, Thornton was gone.

Pup's growl deepened.

"I know," Elias said quietly.

He couldn't live like this. Looking over his shoulder. Waiting for a bullet. Jumping at every sound.

It had to end.

On his terms. Not Thornton's.

* * *

Thornton watched from the shadow of a canvas awning.

Harlan sat against a tree at the camp's edge. The wolf-dog beside him. Both of them alert. Ready.

Smart.

Thornton had been watching since dawn. Learned Harlan's pattern. Where he worked. Where he camped. How he moved.

Always armed now. Always careful. The dog was never more than a few feet away.

That dog was a problem.

Big. Fast. Protective. It had taken down the drunk outside Hendrick's Supply with barely a sound. Thornton had watched that too. Seen the speed. The control. The warning.

The dog would sense him coming. Would alert Harlan. Would attack.

Thornton would have to account for that.

But not today. Not yet.

He needed to know more. Needed to understand Harlan's routine completely. Needed to find the right moment. The right approach.

Patience.

He'd tracked men before. In the war. After. Knew how to wait. How to watch. How to learn everything about a target before making a move.

Harlan wasn't going anywhere. The Black Hills had swallowed him just like it had swallowed thousands of others. Gold fever. Desperation. Men running from something or running toward something, and not sure which.

Thornton could wait.

He pulled back into the camp's flow. Disappeared among the miners, freight wagons, and noise.

But he'd be watching.

Always watching.

* * *

The next morning, Elias rode out before dawn.

He'd thought about it all night. About where it would happen. Where it had to happen.

Not in camp. Too many people. Innocents. Children.

Not in the diggings. Same problem.

Somewhere away. Somewhere open. Somewhere he could see Thornton coming.

He found it a quarter mile northeast of camp.

A clearing where the forest opened up. Maybe sixty yards across. Good grass. A few scattered pines. Rocky ground rising on the west side. Forest on the other three sides.

Open enough to see. Small enough to defend.

Elias rode Biter around the perimeter. Studied the approaches. The sight lines. Where someone could come from.

The western rocks rose at the clearing's edge. Steep. He looked at them briefly. Turned back to watch the forest approaches.

Those were the ways someone would come. Through the trees. From cover.

Pup ranged through the clearing. Nose down. Checking. Then sat in the center and looked at Elias.

"Yeah," Elias said. "Here."

He dismounted. Tied Biter at the clearing's edge. Took a position in the center. Facing east, where the sun would rise.

The Winchester across his knees.

And waited.

An hour passed.

Birds moved through the trees. A squirrel chattered. The wind shifted pine branches overhead.

No Thornton.

The sun climbed higher. The day warmed.

Still nothing.

By midmorning, Elias stood. Stretched. Mounted Biter.

Not today.

But soon.

He rode back to camp.

* * *

Thornton saw Harlan leave camp at dawn.

Heading northeast. The dog and horse were with him.

Thornton waited ten minutes. Then followed.

He stayed in the trees. Moving quietly. Watching where Harlan went.

The clearing appeared through the pines. Harlan in the center. Waiting.

Thornton stopped. Studied it from the tree line.

Smart choice. Open ground. Good sight lines. Away from people.

Harlan was setting the terms. Choosing the ground.

Thornton circled wide. Stayed hidden. Studied the clearing from all sides.

The western rocks caught his attention. Steep. Someone could climb the back side. Come over the top. Get behind Harlan while he watched the forest.

Perfect.

Thornton marked it in his mind.

Then he pulled back into the forest.

Harlan waited in the clearing for two hours. Then left.

Thornton stayed another hour after he was gone. Studying. Planning.

This is where it would happen.

Now he just needed to choose when.

*　*　*

The second day, Elias went to the clearing at dawn again.

Same routine. Biter tied at the edge. Elias in the center. Winchester ready. Pup watching.

Waiting.

The sun rose. The frost melted. The day began.

No Thornton.

Elias sat there until mid-morning. Then rode back to camp. Found work. Earned enough to buy coffee and ammunition.

Pup stayed closer than ever. At night, pressed against Elias's ribs. During the day, never more than a few feet away.

The dog knew what was coming.

That evening, Elias sat at his camp and cleaned the Winchester. Checked every part. The action. The barrel. The sights.

Loaded it. Worked the lever. Smooth. Ready.

The pistol next. Same process. Clean. Check. Load.

Tomorrow maybe.

Or the day after.

But soon.

*　*　*

Thornton spent the second day watching the clearing from the trees.

Harlan came at dawn. Same as before. Waited. Left.

Patient. Disciplined.

Like a soldier.

Thornton understood that. Respected it even. Harlan was making a stand. Choosing his ground. Waiting for the fight to come to him instead of running.

Most men would run. Keep running. Try to disappear.

Not Harlan.

That told Thornton something. This wasn't a man who would beg. Wasn't a man who would plead or try to talk his way out.

When it happened, it would be clean. Direct. The way it should be.

After Harlan left the clearing, Thornton moved in. Walked the ground Harlan had chosen. Looked at it from Harlan's position.

Then he walked to the western rocks.

Found the route up the back side. Loose stone. Difficult. But climbable.

He climbed it. Slow. Testing each hold.

Reached the top. Stood where the rocks met the clearing's level.

From here, he could see Harlan's position perfectly. Harlan would be facing east. Watching for someone to come from that direction. From the forest. From the obvious approaches.

Not from behind. Not from the rocks he'd have his back to.

Thornton marked the route in his mind. Every handhold. Every loose stone. How long it would take to climb.

Then he climbed down.

Tomorrow at dawn.

That's when it would be.

* * *

The third night, Elias couldn't sleep.

He lay on his back staring at the stars. Pup against his side. The dog's breathing steady but the tension never leaving his body.

Elias thought about Clara. About Scout. About the ranch and the graves under the cottonwood.

Thought about Makóyi. Nitááhkii. Ksisstaki. The camp scattered to the wind.

Thought about Mountain Chief's words.

The right thing doesn't stop soldiers. Doesn't bring back the dead. But it matters anyway.

He didn't know if leaving Thornton that choice would matter.

Didn't know if it was right or wrong or something in between.

The carved wolf was in his pocket. He pulled it out. Ran his thumb over the smooth bone in the darkness.

Don't die.

He'd try not to.

He put the wolf away. Closed his eyes. Didn't sleep but rested.

The stars turned overhead. Cold and distant and uncaring.

Somewhere in the camp, Thornton sat at his own fire.

Both men waiting for dawn.

Thornton checked his rifle for the last time.

Lever action. Smooth. Ammunition loaded. Sights true.

He'd fired it yesterday. Put three rounds into a tree trunk at sixty yards. All clustered tight.

The rifle was ready.

He was ready.

* * *

He thought about Henderson. About the gate at Fort Shaw. About the knife going in and the boy's surprised expression. The weight of him sliding down.

Harlan's fault. All of it. Had to be.

Tomorrow at dawn, he would climb the western rocks. Come over the top. Get behind Harlan. End it clean with one shot.

Then ride south. Find someplace else. Start over.

The fire burned low. Thornton sat watching it until the coals went dark.

Then he lay down. Closed his eyes.

Didn't sleep.

The night passed slow.

When the stars began to fade, both men rose.

Dawn was coming.

37

The Face-off

Elias woke an hour before dawn.

He'd barely slept. Pup hadn't slept at all. The dog was tense against his ribs, staring toward the tree line.

Elias sat up. Checked the Winchester. The pistol. Both loaded. Both ready.

He built no fire. Ate jerky cold. Gave Pup half.

The camp was dark around them. Quiet. Just snoring and wind through canvas.

The sky lightened gradually. Gray, then pale gold along the eastern ridges.

He saddled Biter in the darkness. Led him to the clearing. Away from the tents and miners.

If it happened, it would happen away from innocents.

He tied Biter to a pine at the clearing's edge. The horse stood calm, one ear back, listening.

Elias took a position in the center of the clearing. Facing east where the sun would rise. Where Thornton would expect him to watch.

The Winchester across his knees.

Pup sat beside him. Alert. Watching.

They waited.

The sun broke over the ridge.

Light spilled across the clearing, turning the frost to gold.

Elias squinted into it. Watching the tree line. The approaches. Any movement.

Nothing.

Minutes passed.

The sun climbed higher.

Still nothing.

Elias's shoulders were tight. His jaw ached from clenching.

Then Pup's ears swiveled. Not toward the east. Toward the west.

The dog's lip curled. That low sound started in his chest. Not his throat. Deeper. A rumble that seemed to come from somewhere ancient.

Elias turned. Scanned the western tree line where the clearing met the rocks.

A rabbit burst from the brush at the base of the cliff. Bounded across the open ground and disappeared into the sage.

Elias watched it go.

Just a rabbit.

He turned back to face east. The sun. Where Thornton would come from.

Behind him, Pup's growl didn't stop.

Elias frowned. Glanced back over his shoulder.

The dog stood rigid. Hackles up. Eyes fixed on the rocks. Not on where the rabbit had gone. On the rocks themselves.

That didn't make sense. Pup didn't growl at rabbits. He chased them. Caught them. Killed them.

Elias felt it then. Something wrong.

He started to turn.

Pup launched.

The shot cracked across the clearing.

The bullet whipped past Elias's ear. So close he felt the heat. Heard it snap.

It hit a tree behind him and tore bark into splinters.

Elias spun. Brought the Winchester up.

Thornton stood at the edge of the western rocks. Not above the clearing. Level with it. He'd climbed the back side of the cliff. Come over the top. Had Elias's back perfectly.

Rifle in his hands. Working the lever to chamber another round.

Pup was already there.

The dog hit him low and fast. All muscle and speed and teeth.

Pup's jaws closed on Thornton's forearm. The rifle flew from his hands. Clattered on stone.

Thornton stumbled backward. Tried to stay upright. Tried to shake the dog off.

But the cliff edge was right behind him. The drop he'd just climbed.

Pup let go.

Thornton went over.

Backward. Arms windmilling. A shout cut short.

Thirty feet of granite and broken trees and nothing to grab.

He hit hard.

The sound carried across the clearing. Impact. Breaking. Something snapping. Then silence.

Pup stood at the cliff edge. Looking down. The growl still rumbling in his chest.

Elias ran.

∗ ∗ ∗

When Elias reached the edge, Pup was still there. Watching. Ready.

Elias looked over.

Thornton lay on the rocks below. On his back. A broken pine branch beside him. The fall had driven him onto it. The sharpened end had gone through his side, just below the ribs.

His left leg was bent at the wrong angle. Bad break. But the bone wasn't showing through the skin.

Thornton's eyes were open. Staring up at the sky. His chest moving. Shallow breaths.

Still alive.

Elias looked for the easiest way down. Found where Thornton must have climbed up. Loose rock. Treacherous. He started down slow, testing each step.

Pup stayed at the top. Watching. Guarding.

Elias reached the bottom. Stood over Thornton.

Thornton's eyes found him. Focused.

They looked at each other.

No words yet.

Just breathing, distance, and cold morning light on the stones.

Elias knelt. Looked at the wound.

The branch had gone through below the ribs. Four, maybe five inches deep. Through muscle and fat. Bleeding steady, but not the dark flow that meant gut or liver. Not arterial.

He looked at the leg. Bad break. The angle told him that. But the bone wasn't showing. No tear through the skin.

Thornton could survive this. If the branch came out clean. If the wound got packed. If the leg got set. If someone found him soon.

A lot of ifs.

"How bad," Thornton said. Barely a whisper.

Elias met his eyes.

"Bad," he said. "But maybe not impossible."

Thornton's breath hitched. Something like hope flickered across his face. Then pain pushed it away.

"Could you—" he started.

"No," Elias said.

He stood.

Thornton closed his eyes. Opened them.

"Please."

Elias shook his head.

"I won't."

Silence.

Thornton's breathing was fast now. Shallow. Pain, shock, and cold are all fighting each other.

Elias climbed back up. Walked to where Biter was tied. Came back down with his canteen. His blanket. His knife.

He set the canteen beside Thornton. Within reach.

Cut a long strip from the blanket with his knife. Handed it to Thornton.

"Press that on the wound," Elias said. "Hard as you can. It'll slow the bleeding."

Thornton took it with shaking hands. Pressed it against his side. His face went white. A sound escaped him.

Elias laid what was left of the blanket over him. Thornton was shaking now. The cold getting in.

Then Elias pulled the pistol from his belt.

Thornton watched him.

Elias checked the cylinder. Six rounds. He emptied five into his hand. Dropped them in his pocket.

One bullet left.

He set the pistol on the blanket beside Thornton's hand.

Thornton looked at it. Looked at Elias.

"Your choice," Elias said. "You can wait for help. Or you can use that. Up to you."

The silence stretched.

Thornton's hand moved toward the pistol. Stopped. His fingers were trembling.

"You could end it," Thornton said. Voice barely there. "Quick. Clean."

"I could," Elias said.

He didn't move.

"But I won't."

"Why?"

"Because I'm not what you think I am."

Thornton stared at him. Something breaking behind his eyes. The story he'd told himself. The justification he'd carried all these miles. The reason he'd killed a boy at a gate and hunted a man across Montana.

All of it, crumbling.

His hand touched the pistol. Rested there.

"Henderson," he said. Voice cracking. "At the gate. I didn't—it wasn't—"

"I don't want to know," Elias said.

He turned toward the rocks. Started climbing.

"Harlan."

Elias stopped. Didn't turn around.

Silence. Just wind and the creak of pine branches and Thornton's ragged breathing.

Then Thornton's voice. Broken. Small.

"I was wrong. About you."

Elias stood there a moment.

Then he climbed.

* * *

At the top, Pup pressed against his leg. The dog looked back at the cliff edge once. Ears up. Listening.

No sound came from below.

Elias walked to where Biter stood. Untied him. Mounted.

Pup fell in beside the horse.

They rode southeast. Away from the clearing. Away from the rocks. Away from the man lying broken with a canteen, a strip of blanket, and a pistol with one round.

Elias didn't look back.

The sun climbed higher. The frost burned off the grass. The day warmed.

Behind him, silence.

Just wind through the pines and the slow drip of blood on stone.

He rode for an hour before he stopped.

A creek ran through a stand of aspen. The leaves were turning. Gold against white bark against blue sky.

Elias dismounted. Let Biter drink. Pup waded into the shallows, lapping at the cold water.

Elias sat on a rock and stared at nothing.

His hands were shaking.

He looked at them. Turned them over. Looked at the palms. The fingers.

They'd almost reached for the Winchester. Almost fired back. Almost become what Thornton had called him.

But hadn't.

He'd left Thornton alive. Dying maybe. Or maybe not. Given him water. A way to slow the bleeding. A choice.

Was that mercy? Cruelty? Justice?

He didn't know.

Didn't know if Thornton would use the bullet. Didn't know if anyone would find him. Didn't know if he'd bleed out or freeze or somehow pull through.

Would never know.

And maybe that was right.

Mountain Chief's words came back.

The right thing doesn't stop soldiers. Doesn't feed hungry children. Doesn't bring back the dead.

But it matters anyway.

Elias didn't know if what he'd done mattered.

Didn't know if it was right.

Just knew he couldn't pull that trigger. Couldn't finish what Thornton had started. Couldn't become the thing Thornton needed him to be to make his story work.

He pulled the carved wolf from his pocket. Ran his thumb over the smooth bone.

Don't die, Ksisstaki had said.

He hadn't.

But he'd left a man to die. Or to live. He didn't know which.

He put the wolf back in his pocket.

*　*　*

Pup came out of the creek and shook, spraying water everywhere. Came and sat beside Elias. Leaned into his leg. Warm and solid and real.

Elias put his hand on the dog's head.

"Good boy," he said quietly.

Pup's tail thumped once.

They sat there for a while. The creek running. The aspen leaves bright against the sky. The mountains rising blue in the distance.

Then Elias stood. Mounted Biter. Pup fell in beside them.

They rode southeast.

Toward the Black Hills. Toward whatever came next.

Behind them, on the rocks at the bottom of a cliff, Captain Charles Thornton lay with a canteen, a strip of blanket pressed to his wound, and a pistol with one round in the cylinder.

What he did with them, Elias would never know.

The land kept no record of men who died alone.

Or of men who survived.

38

What Remains

Elias rode back to camp through the morning light.

Pup trotted beside Biter. Quiet. Alert. The dog's eyes tracked movement through the trees, but the tension was gone. The threat was gone.

Or maybe not.

Elias didn't know.

The camp appeared through the pines. Canvas and wood smoke and the sound of hammering. Men shouting. A piano is playing somewhere badly.

Life was going on as if nothing had happened.

Elias rode through it. Past miners heading to their claims. Past women hauling water. Past the chaos that never stopped, never cared, never noticed, one man riding back from the rocks with questions he couldn't answer.

He reached his campsite at the edge of town. Dismounted. Unsaddled Biter. Hobbled him where the grass was good.

Sat down with his back against a tree.

Pup lay beside him. Put his head on Elias's knee.

They sat like that for a long time.

The sun climbed higher. The day warmed.

Elias stared at nothing.

That evening, he couldn't sleep.

He lay on his back watching stars appear one by one. Pup pressed against his ribs. The dog's breathing steady.

Elias kept seeing it. Thornton on the rocks. The branch through his side. The leg bent wrong. The pistol on the blanket beside him.

One bullet.

What had he done with it?

Elias didn't know. Would never know.

Had Thornton died there? Bled out slow? Frozen in the night?

Or had someone found him? Pulled out the branch? Carried him to a doctor?

Or had he used the bullet?

The not-knowing was worse than knowing.

Elias turned on his side. Pup shifted with him. The dog's warmth, solid and real.

He closed his eyes.

Didn't sleep.

Morning came gray and cold.

Elias saddled Biter. Mounted. Rode north.

Not into camp. The other direction. Toward the rocks. Toward where he'd left Thornton.

He needed to know.

Pup followed, watching him. Curious.

Elias rode for ten minutes. The clearing appeared ahead through the trees. The rocks to the west, falling away behind it.

He could see the cliff edge from here.

Could ride to it. Look down. See if Thornton was still there.

See if he'd used the bullet.

What would knowing change?

Nothing.

If Thornton was dead, Elias had left him to die. If he were alive, Elias had abandoned him.

Either way, the choice was made.

Going back wouldn't unmake it.

He turned Biter around. Rode back to camp.

He didn't look back.

* * *

The second day, he went into town looking for work.

The chaos was the same. Miners everywhere. Freight wagons. Tents packed tight. The smell of too many people in too small a space.

Elias walked through it. Pup at his side. The dog following close now. Not aggressive but watchful. Men gave them space.

He found the livery stable near the center of camp. A long, low building. Corrals out back. The smell of hay and horses and manure.

An older man was shoeing a bay mare when Elias walked in. Maybe sixty. Gray beard. Thick shoulders. The kind of careful hands that came from forty years working with animals that could kill you if you weren't paying attention.

He looked up. Saw Elias. Saw Pup. Went back to work.

"Help you?" he said.

"Looking for work," Elias said.

"What kind?"

"Anything. But I know horses."

The man straightened. Wiped his hands on his apron. Walked past Elias to the stable entrance.

Biter stood tied to the rail outside. One hip cocked. Resting.

The man approached slow. Reading the horse. Extended his hand toward Biter's neck.

Biter's ears went flat. Tossed his head, pawed the ground. He showed his teeth. A warning. *Don't.*

The man stopped. Pulled his hand back. Looked at the horse. Looked at Elias.

Laughed.

"Mean son of a bitch," he said. Respect in his voice.

"Yeah," Elias said.

"You handle him?"

"Every day."

The man nodded. Walked back into the stable. "Then you can handle anything I've got. Show me."

Elias walked to a chestnut gelding in the nearest stall. The horse was nervous. Ears back. Shifting.

Elias stood beside the stall door. Didn't reach for the horse. Just stood. Quiet. Patient.

The horse's ears came forward. He stepped closer. Sniffed Elias's hand.

Elias scratched under the horse's jaw. The animal leaned into it.

The man grunted. "Two dollars a day. Start now."

"All right," Elias said.

"Name's Hendricks."

"Elias."

Hendricks went back to the bay mare. Picked up her hoof. "That dog gonna be a problem?"

"No," Elias said.

"Good. I don't need him eating my customers."

Pup's tail thumped once against the dirt.

Hendricks almost smiled.

The work was simple. Familiar.

Mucking stalls. Moving hay. Grooming horses. Checking hooves. Feeding. Watering.

Elias fell into the rhythm of it. The motions he'd done a thousand times on the ranch. Before everything.

The horses didn't ask questions. Didn't care what he'd done. Just wanted grain, water, and someone with steady hands.

Pup lay in the shade near the stable door. Watching. Dozing sometimes. Still protective but calmer here.

The horses didn't mind him. A few came to their stall doors and sniffed toward him. Pup's tail would thump once against the dirt. Then he'd settle again.

By afternoon, Elias had cleaned six stalls. Groomed three horses. Reset shoes on a mule that tried to kick him twice and missed both times.

His back ached. His hands were sore.

It felt good. Real. Grounding.

* * *

He was mucking the last stall when he heard the children.

Three of them. Two boys and a girl. Maybe six to ten years old. Dirty faces. Bare feet despite the cold.

They stood at the stable entrance. Staring at Pup.

"Is he mean?" the smallest boy asked.

Elias leaned the rake against the wall. Walked to the door.

"You'll have to find out," he said.

The girl looked at him. Looked at Pup. Stepped closer. Brave.

"Can we pet him?"

Elias shrugged. "That's up to him."

The girl approached slow. Hand out.

Pup stood. Tail wagging. Slow. Careful. Lowered his head. Let her touch his ears.

She giggled. "He's soft!"

The other two came running. Pup's tail went wild. He play-bowed. Front legs down, rear up, tail wagging so hard his whole back end moved.

The oldest boy laughed. "He wants to play!"

What happened next, Elias just watched.

The oldest boy was wearing a hat. Too big. Must've been his father's. Floppy brim hanging over his eyes.

He took it off. Put it on Pup's head.

The dog shook it off. Grabbed it in his mouth. Tail wagging.

The children shrieked with laughter.

The smallest boy grabbed Pup's tail. Gentle. Just holding it.

Pup spun. Play-hopped. Bounded after them.

The children ran. Not scared. Laughing. Running in circles around the stable yard.

Pup chased. Not fast. Play-speed. Letting them stay ahead.

He caught the smallest boy. Knocked him down gently. The boy landed in the dirt laughing. Pup licked his face.

"Stop! That tickles!"

The girl hugged Pup's neck. Buried her face in his fur. "Good dog!"

Pup's tail wagging so hard Elias thought it might fall off.

The oldest boy threw the hat. Pup chased it. Brought it back. Dropped it at the boy's feet.

They did it again. And again.

Elias stopped working. Leaned against the stable wall. Watched.

The smallest boy climbed onto Pup's back. The dog stood patiently. Tail still wagging. Let the child sit there like Pup was a pony.

The girl kissed the top of his head. "You're the best dog in the whole world!"

A miner walked past on the street. Big. Bearded. Drunk maybe.

Pup's head snapped up. The children slid off his back.

The growl came. Deep. That chest-sound that made men's skin

crawl.

The miner saw the dog. The size. The teeth showing now. He crossed to the other side of the street. Walked faster.

The children didn't notice. They were picking up the hat again.

Pup went back to being gentle immediately. Chasing the hat. Knocking the girl down. Letting the smallest boy pull his ears.

Pure. Simple. Good.

Elias felt something crack open in his chest.

The oldest child hugged Pup one more time. Squeezed tight. "You're a good dog. The best dog."

A woman's voice called from somewhere in camp. "Supper!"

"We have to go," the girl said. She kissed Pup's nose.

The children ran off. Waving. "Bye, dog! Bye, mister!"

Pup watched them go. Tail still wagging. Then he walked to Elias. Sat beside him. Leaned into his leg.

Elias put his hand on the dog's head.

"Good boy," he said.

Meant it more than he'd meant anything in a long time.

Hendricks came out of the stable. Watched the children disappear into the camp.

"That's something," he said.

"What's that?" Elias said.

"Dog that mean to men. That gentle with children."

"Yeah."

"He know the difference?"

"I guess."

Hendricks nodded. Looked at Pup. Back at Elias. "You can bring him every day. So long as he doesn't bite paying customers."

"He won't bite paying customers, I reckon."

"What if they don't pay?"

"Well, I figure they might need a little bitin' then."

Hendricks laughed. "Good." He pulled two silver dollars from his pocket. Handed them to Elias. "See you tomorrow morning."

Elias took the money. Put it in his pocket.

First honest pay he'd earned since the ranch.

It felt like something. Not much. But something.

* * *

That evening, Elias headed back to his camp. The sun was setting. Gold light on the hills. Long shadows stretching through the trees.

He walked back to his campsite. Built a small fire. Shared jerky with Pup. The dog lay with his head in Elias's lap. Warm and solid and real.

Elias thought about everything he'd lost. Clara and Scout. The ranch. The camp scattered to the wind. Makóyi and Nitááhkii and Ksisstaki. The words of Mountain Chief. *Unless someone remembers.* Thornton.

But some things remained.

Pup was here. Biter was here. Elias was still breathing. Children still laughed in the streets. Work still needed doing. The sun would rise tomorrow same as always.

He pulled the carved wolf from his pocket. Ran his thumb over the smooth bone.

Don't die, Ksisstaki had said.

He hadn't.

What came next, he didn't know.

He put the wolf away. Lay down. Pup shifted against his ribs. The dog's breathing steady and slow.

Sleep came.

Finally.

39

Winter Coming

Six weeks passed.

October came to the Black Hills. The air turned cold at night. Frost on the grass in the mornings. The aspen leaves went gold then fell.

Elias worked at Hendricks's stable six days a week. Two dollars a day. Sometimes three when freight came heavy and extra hands were needed.

He'd saved twenty-eight dollars. Kept it in a leather pouch in his pocket.

Rented a small room above the general store. Six dollars a month. One window. A cot. A stove. Enough.

Most nights he still camped outside town with Pup and Biter. The room was for bad weather. For when winter came hard.

The work was steady. Familiar at first. Mucking stalls. Moving hay. Feeding and watering.

But by the third week Hendricks had him doing more. Shoeing horses under supervision. Then alone. Gentling nervous animals. Working with the difficult ones that kicked or bit or wouldn't stand.

Elias was good at it. Patient. Steady hands. The horses sensed it.

By October Hendricks had him handling customers' horses without asking first. Just assumed Elias would do it right.

That was trust. In Hendricks's world, that meant something.

Elias felt it. Didn't say anything about it. Just kept working.

* * *

He was coming back from the barber when he heard it.

Biter's whinny, not the idle complaint the horse made when he wanted water, but the high sharp sound he made when something was happening that he didn't approve of.

Elias turned toward the corral behind the stable. Walked faster.

Two young men, boys really, maybe seventeen, eighteen, had Biter cornered against the fence. One had a loop of rope swinging in his hand. The other stood off to the side, ready to grab a halter. They were working together the way you did when you didn't know what you were doing but had agreed to do it anyway.

Biter's ears were flat. His eyes showed white. He'd already spun once, Elias could see the churned dirt, and now stood with his haunches against the fence, watching the rope.

Hendricks leaned against the corral rail, arms folded, watching.

Elias came to stand beside him. "What's this?"

"Shoeing him," Hendricks said. "Or trying to."

"He's never been shod."

"I know it." Hendricks glanced at him. "Rocky ground around here. Granite. Horse that size working it unshod, he'll split a hoof before spring. Wanted to do it before winter set in."

Elias looked at him.

Hendricks looked back, steady. "Just trying to save you a problem later."

In the corral, the boy with the rope swung the loop. Biter exploded sideways, all sixteen hands of him moving faster than something that size had any right to, and hit the fence hard enough to make the rails shake. The boy stumbled back. The other one dropped the halter and scrambled for the fence.

Biter put his nose in the air and screamed.

Hendricks pulled at his beard. "Hell of a horse."

"Yeah." Elias climbed through the rails.

"Harlan—"

He was already walking toward Biter.

Not fast. Not slow. Just walking. The way he'd walked toward that horse a hundred times in the Blackfeet camp when Biter was still wild and hadn't decided anything about him yet.

Biter's ears snapped forward. He blew hard through his nose, that sound, half warning, half question.

Elias kept walking. Eyes soft. Shoulders down. Hands loose at his sides.

He stopped a few feet away and stood there. Didn't reach. Just stood.

Biter's head came down an inch. His breathing slowed.

Elias waited.

The horse took a step toward him. Nostrils working. Then another.

He pushed his nose against Elias's chest and stood there, sides heaving, still worked up but done with it.

Elias let him breathe for a moment. Then reached up and scratched along his jaw the way he liked.

Biter's eyes half closed.

Elias reached up and took hold of the halter, easy, no fuss, and turned and walked him toward the barn.

Biter walked beside him like a dog on a lead.

Behind him, Elias heard one of the boys say something under his breath.

Hendricks said, "Don't feel bad. He'd have killed you."

Elias didn't look back.

In the barn he cross-tied Biter and ran his hands down each leg, letting the horse feel him, letting him understand what was coming. Biter shifted once, stamped once, then went still.

Hendricks appeared in the barn doorway. Watched.

"You want me to shoe him or you?" he asked.

"I'll do it," Elias said. "He doesn't know you yet."

Hendricks nodded. He brought the tools and set them down within reach and stepped back.

It took the better part of an hour. Biter pulled his right hind twice, the second time nearly catching Elias in the shoulder. Elias just waited, hand on the horse's flank, until the tension went out of him. Then he picked the hoof back up and kept working.

When it was done he led Biter back to the corral and turned him loose. The horse stood in the center, head up, surveying the world. Then he walked to the water trough and drank.

Hendricks came to stand beside Elias at the rail.

"How long did it take you?" he asked. "With that horse."

Elias thought about it. The Blackfeet camp. The cold mornings. The way Biter used to take three steps sideways every time he approached, and then two, and then one, and then none.

"Months," he said.

Hendricks nodded. Watching the horse drink.

"Worth it," he said.

"Yeah," Elias said. "He is."

* * *

Pup came to the stable every day. Lay in his spot near the door. The children still played with him when they could. The miners gave him space.

Biter stayed mean. Hendricks laughed about it every time the horse showed his teeth at a customer.

"That animal hates everyone but you," he said once.

"Yeah," Elias said.

"Good trait in a horse. Means he's honest."

Elias didn't disagree.

The days had rhythm now. Wake before dawn. Work until dark. Eat. Sleep. Repeat.

It wasn't the ranch. Wasn't the camp. But it was something.

Life. Routine. Survival.

He didn't think about Thornton much anymore. The not-knowing had settled into something he carried but didn't examine. Like the carved wolf in his pocket. Present. Heavy. But not consuming.

The Black Hills kept growing. More miners every week. More tents. More noise. More men with gold fever and guns and no sense.

And something else growing too.

Tension.

* * *

It started small.

A morning in early October. Elias was grooming a bay mare when he heard shouting outside.

Two miners arguing over a claim boundary. Both had guns. Both were drunk even though it wasn't yet noon.

Hendricks stepped to the stable door. Watched. Didn't move.

Elias came to stand beside him.

"Shouldn't we—" Elias started.

"No," Hendricks said. "Not our fight."

The miners shouted. Shoved. One drew his pistol.

The other backed down. Walked away. Kept his hand near his gun the whole time.

Hendricks went back to work.

Elias stood there a moment longer. Then followed.

Three days later a group of miners rode past the stable. Eight of them. Surveying equipment loaded on pack mules.

Elias was outside replacing a broken hitch rail.

One of the men called out. "Which way to them hills with the markers?"

Hendricks looked up from shoeing a horse. "Don't know what you're talking about."

"The stone markers. Indian territory. We're opening it up."

"That so," Hendricks said. Tone flat.

"Company hired us. Good money. You interested?"

"No."

The men laughed. Rode on.

Hendricks went back to the hoof in his hand. Didn't say anything.

Elias watched them go. Toward the western hills. Where the stone markers were. Where the boundaries were supposed to mean something.

That evening, shots echoed from that direction.

Distant. But clear.

Elias was walking Biter to water. Stopped. Listened.

The shots came again. Maybe six. Then silence.

No one else in camp seemed to notice. Or care.

A week later a miner came to the stable leading a limping horse.

Arrow in the saddle. Broken off but the shaft still there.

"Goddamn savages," the man said. He was big. Bearded. Smelled like whiskey even though it was morning. "Shot at me for no reason."

Hendricks was shoeing a mare in the center aisle. Didn't look up. "Put him in the second stall. I'll look at him when I'm done here."

"I ain't got time to wait."

"Then take him somewhere else."

The man's face went red. He tied his horse to a post. Stood there fuming. Watching Hendricks work.

Elias was in the back stall replacing a broken board. He could hear everything.

After a few minutes the man spoke again. Louder. "You people gonna help me or what?"

Hendricks set down the mare's hoof. Straightened. Walked to the miner's horse.

Lifted the front leg. Examined it. Pulled a stone from the hoof. Not arrow-related. Just a stone wedged deep.

"That's your problem," Hendricks said. "Stone bruise. Keep him off it for a few days."

"What about the arrow?" The man pointed at his saddle. "They shot at me."

Hendricks walked to the horse. Grabbed the arrow shaft. Pulled it out quick. Clean.

"There," he said.

Handed the shaft to the miner.

The man looked at it. Then threw it on the ground. "That's it?"

"You cross any boundaries?" Hendricks asked.

"What?"

"Did you cross into territory you weren't supposed to be in."

The man's face went darker. "It's all open territory now. Company says so."

"Company doesn't own the land."

"Government does. And government says I can go where I damn well please." The man stepped closer to Hendricks. Big. Aggressive. Using his size. "You got a problem with that, old man?"

Pup stood up.

The growl came. Not loud. Just that deep chest-sound that made the hair stand up on a man's arms.

The dog was ten feet away. Eyes locked on the miner. Hackles raised. Not moving forward. Just standing. Ready.

The miner looked at Pup. Looked at the teeth showing. Looked at the size of him.

Stepped back.

"That thing should be chained up," the man said. But his voice was different now. Smaller.

"He's fine where he is," Hendricks said. Calm. Like nothing had happened. "That'll be two dollars for the stone removal."

The man threw money on the ground. Took his horse. Led it out fast. Didn't look back.

After he left, Hendricks bent down. Picked up the coins. Put them in his pocket.

Then picked up the arrow shaft from where the miner had thrown it. Examined it. Turned it in his hands.

"Lakota," he said. "Good craftsmanship."

He handed it to Elias.

Elias took it. The break was clean. Deliberate. The fletching still intact. Beautiful work.

"Warning shot," Hendricks said. "Could've put it through him if they wanted. Chose not to."

Elias turned the shaft in his hands. Felt the weight. The balance.

"Won't matter," Hendricks said. "He'll go back to camp. Tell everyone the savages attacked him unprovoked. They'll believe him. Send more soldiers. Take more land. Same story every time."

He looked at Pup. The dog was still standing. Still watching the direction the miner had gone.

"Good dog," Hendricks said.

Pup's tail wagged once. Then he lay back down.

Hendricks went back to the mare. Picked up her hoof again. Kept working.

Elias put the arrow shaft in his pocket. Stood there a moment.

Pup had stood up for Hendricks. Not because the man was threatening Elias directly. Because he was threatening someone Elias cared about. Someone who mattered.

The dog was learning. Watching. Understanding what was important.

Elias went back to fixing the board.

* * *

Two days later Elias was stacking hay when the woman approached.

Mrs. Patterson. Mother of Sarah, the girl who'd played with Pup that first day.

She was carrying a basket. Looked like she'd been doing errands in town.

Pup was lying in his usual spot. Lifted his head when she approached. Tail wagged once.

"Mr. Harlan," she said.

"Ma'am," Elias said. Set down the hay bale.

"I wanted to thank you."

"For what."

"For letting the children play with your dog." She smiled. "Sarah talks about him every night. Asks when we can visit the stable again."

"He likes children," Elias said.

"I can see that." She paused. Looked at Pup. Back at Elias. "I wanted to tell you something else too."

Elias waited.

"I feel safer with him around," she said. "With you both here."

Elias didn't know what to say to that.

"This town," she continued. "It's getting rougher. More men every day. Not all of them good men." She looked toward the main street. The noise. The chaos. "But I know if my children are playing near your stable, they're safe. That dog of yours… he knows things. Knows who to watch."

Elias looked at Pup. The dog was watching Mrs. Patterson. Calm. Tail still.

"He's a good judge," Elias said.

"So are you." She touched his arm briefly. Just a moment. Gratitude. "Good to have you here, Mr. Harlan. Both of you."

She walked away.

Elias stood there. Felt something shift in his chest. Not large. Just a small adjustment.

Belonging maybe. Or responsibility. Or both.

He went back to stacking hay.

* * *

That afternoon Hendricks asked him to help move a wagon from the back lot.

They worked in silence for a while. The way they usually did.

Then Hendricks spoke.

"Town's changing."

"Yeah," Elias said.

"Not for the better."

They repositioned the wagon tongue. Elias checked the hitch.

"You planning to stay?" Hendricks asked.

Elias looked at him. The old man was watching him. Steady. Curious.

"For now," Elias said.

Hendricks nodded. They went back to work.

After a few minutes, Hendricks spoke again.

"Good. Need someone around here who isn't half-crazy with gold fever."

He tested the wagon wheel. Solid.

"Mrs. Patterson came by earlier this week," he said. "Before she talked to you. Mentioned you and that dog. Said her daughter feels safe around him."

Elias didn't respond.

"Town could use more like you," Hendricks said. "Steady. Not looking to take something that isn't theirs."

He walked to the front of the wagon. Started unhitching the team.

"Winter's coming," he said. "Going to be a hard one. Can feel it."

"Yeah," Elias said.

"You'll have work through it. If you want it."

"I do."

"Good."

They finished unhitching in silence.

Hendricks walked past him toward the stable. Stopped. Looked back.

"You're good with horses," he said. "Better than most. You ever think about doing this permanent?"

"Haven't thought that far ahead," Elias said.

Hendricks nodded. "Well. Job's here if you want it. Long as I'm running this place."

He went inside.

Elias stood there. The afternoon sun slanting through the pines. The smell of hay and horses and leather.

A job. A place. Something that might last.

He didn't know if he wanted it. Didn't know what he wanted.

Just knew it felt good to be offered.

* * *

That evening Elias walked back toward his camp at the edge of town.

The sun was setting. Long shadows across the hills. The air cold. Winter coming for real now.

He stopped at the edge of town. Looked west toward the hills.

Smoke rising from multiple places. Miners' camps spreading. More every day. The hillsides scarred from digging. Trees cut. The land changing.

He thought about the buffalo jump. The cliff where he'd found Scout. Where everything had started.

Thought about the camp. The dispersal. Ksisstaki's face when she'd given him the wolf carving.

Thought about Mountain Chief. The old man's eyes. The weight of his words.

Unless someone remembers.

Elias stood there for a long time. Just looking. Just seeing.

Then he walked to the general store.

The shopkeeper looked up when he entered. "Help you?"

"Need paper," Elias said.

"What kind? Wrapping paper? Butcher paper?"

"Writing paper."

The shopkeeper pulled out a stack. Twenty sheets. Good quality. "This do?"

"Yeah."

"Starting a business? Need a ledger book too?"

"No. Just paper."

The shopkeeper wrapped it. "Anything else?"

"Pencil."

The shopkeeper added one to the bundle. "Seventy-five cents."

Elias paid. Took the package. Left.

* * *

That night he sat by his fire outside town. Pup's head in his lap. The dog's breathing steady and warm.

Biter grazed nearby. The hobbles rattling soft when he moved.

Elias opened the paper. Smooth. Clean. Blank.

He stared at it for a while.

Then picked up the pencil.

Wrote the date: October 12, 1884.

Wrote the place: Black Hills.

Stopped.

Thought about what he'd seen. The miners crossing boundaries. The surveying equipment. The arrow in the saddle. The shots in the hills. The man bragging. Hendricks's face.

Wrote one sentence: *Miners crossed stone boundary markers today. No one stopped them.*

Stared at what he'd written.

Didn't know why he'd written it. Just knew he needed to.

He set the paper aside. Put the pencil down.

Pup shifted. Pressed closer.

Elias put his hand on the dog's head.

The fire crackled. The stars came out cold and bright.

He didn't write anything else that night.

* * *

The next few days he wrote more.

Not every day. Not long entries. Just facts. Just what he saw.

October 14: Shots fired in hills. Direction of sacred sites. Counted twelve. Maybe more.

October 16: Man came to stable with arrow in saddle. Laughed about it. Hendricks didn't laugh.

October 18: Three families left town. Woman said it wasn't safe anymore.

Husband wouldn't listen. They left anyway.

October 20: More miners arrived. Maybe thirty. All armed. All talking about opening new territory.

Simple. Direct. True.

He didn't know what he was doing. Didn't know if anyone would ever read these words.

Just knew someone should write it down.

Someone should remember what really happened here.

Not the stories the miners would tell. Not the justifications. Not the lies about savages and empty land and manifest destiny.

Just what actually happened.

He was there. He saw it.

* * *

The days got colder. The nights longer. Winter was coming for real now.

Elias kept working at the stable. Kept writing at night. Simple facts. True things. What he saw.

October became November. The paper filled slowly.

One evening he sat by his fire and looked at what he'd written. Two weeks of entries. Maybe a hundred sentences. Not much.

But it was something.

He thought about where he'd been six months ago. The ranch. Clara and Scout under the cottonwood. The life he'd thought would last forever.

Gone.

He thought about the camp. Makóyi and Nitááhkii. Ksisstaki giving him the wolf carving. Mountain Chief's words by the fire.

Scattered.

He thought about Thornton on the rocks. The pistol. The one bullet.

The choice he'd made to walk away.

Unknown.

Everything he'd been was gone. Everyone he'd known was scattered or dead or lost.

But some things remained.

Pup lay beside him. Head on his leg. Warm and solid. The dog that had saved his life.

Biter grazed nearby. The mean son of a bitch who'd carried him hundreds of miles.

The carved wolf in his pocket. Smooth bone. *Don't die.* He hadn't.

And the paper. The pencil. October 12 through November 3. Facts. True things. What he'd seen.

He picked up the pencil. Looked at the blank space at the bottom of the last page.

Wrote: *November 3: I have written it down. I don't know if anyone will ever read these words. I don't know if it matters.*

The hills are still being torn apart. The boundaries are still being crossed. The people who were here first are still hungry on land that was theirs.

And I am still here. Part of it whether I want to be or not. They are still here. Watching from the hills.

Set the pencil down.

The wind shifted. Cold. Carrying the smell of snow.

Somewhere in the darkness above the camp, the hills stood as they had always stood.

Elias put the paper away and lay down. Pup shifted closer.

He didn't close his eyes for a long time.

40

Paha Sapa

The hunting party left the reservation before dawn.

Seven of them. Three men. Two women. An elder. A boy of maybe ten winters.

They moved quiet through the darkness. No fires. No talking. Just movement.

By the time the agent did his morning count, they'd be fifteen miles away. Deep in the hills where the whites weren't supposed to go but went anyway.

The hills that had been promised. The hills that had been taken.

Paha Sapa. The heart of everything.

They would hunt. Find what game remained. Bring meat back to the families going hungry on rations that never came enough, or came spoiled, or didn't come at all.

Then return before the soldiers came looking.

It was illegal. Leaving the reservation. Hunting on land that had been theirs for generations, but now belonged to the government that had stolen it.

But children were hungry.

So they went.

* * *

The elder's name was Tȟatȟáŋka Wašté. He was seventy-two winters. Old enough to remember when the buffalo covered the plains like grass. When the people moved free. When the only whites they saw were traders and trappers who came and went and didn't try to own the earth.

He walked more slowly than the others. His grandson stayed beside him. Matched his pace.

The boy's name was Tȟašúŋke Kokípapi. He was small for ten winters. Thin. The rations didn't give children what they needed to grow strong.

But his eyes were sharp. He missed nothing.

"Grandfather," he said quietly. "Why do we hide? These are our hills."

"They were," the elder said.

"The treaty said—"

"The treaty said many things. The whites didn't mean any of them."

They walked in silence for a while. The sky lightening. The pines dark against gray.

"Will they ever give them back?" the boy asked.

The elder didn't answer right away.

"No," he said finally. "But we remember anyway. And remembering matters."

The boy thought about that. Then nodded.

They kept walking.

* * *

By midmorning, they'd reached the place where deer used to come. A valley between two ridges. Good grass. Water. Shelter.

Thatȟáŋka Wašté remembered hunting here as a young man. Remembered his father hunting here. His grandfather.

The valley was scarred now.

Trees cut. Stumps everywhere. The creek muddy from digging upstream. The grass tore up where wagons had passed.

No deer.

One of the younger men knelt. Studied the ground. Found tracks. Three days old, maybe. Heading west.

Away from the mining camps. Away from the noise and destruction.

The animals were learning. Like the people had learned. Run or die.

They followed the tracks.

They moved through a country that had changed.

Every ridge they crossed showed more scars. More camps. More smoke rising. More of the sacred places torn apart.

The boy saw it all. Said nothing. Just watched.

Thatȟáŋka Wašté saw the boy watching. Saw him trying to understand.

"When I was young," the elder said quietly, "these hills were silent. Just wind and birds and the sound of our people when we came here for ceremony."

"What ceremonies?" the boy asked.

"Vision quests. Coming of age. Healing. The hills were holy. The spirits lived here. Still do, though the whites don't see them."

"Can you still feel them? The spirits?"

The elder stopped. Looked around. At the stumps. The scars. The smoke in the distance.

"Yes," he said. "But they're angry. And sad. Like we are."

The boy nodded. He understood anger. He understood sad.

They kept walking.

* * *

By afternoon, they found the deer.

A small herd. Six of them. In a hidden valley the miners hadn't found yet.

The hunters moved careful. Quiet. The old way.

Tȟatȟáŋka Wašté stayed back with the boy. Let the younger ones do the stalking. His hunting days were mostly behind him now.

But he could still teach.

"Watch," he whispered to his grandson. "See how they move with the wind. How they stay low. Patient."

The boy watched.

One of the men had a rifle. Army surplus. Old but functional. They'd traded for it years ago. Used it sparingly. Ammunition was hard to get.

The others had bows. Traditional. Quiet.

The man with the rifle took the shot.

The deer dropped. Clean kill.

The others scattered. Gone in seconds.

One deer. Not enough for seven families. But something.

More than they'd had this morning.

They butchered the deer where it fell. Worked fast. Efficient. Nothing wasted.

Meat. Hide. Sinew. Organs. Bones for tools.

Everything had purpose. Everything was used. The old way.

The boy helped. Learning. His small hands careful as he followed his grandfather's instructions.

"We take only what we need," Tȟatȟáŋka Wašté said. "We thank the deer for its life. We waste nothing. This is how we've always done it."

"Even now?" the boy asked. "Even when the whites waste every-thing?"

"Especially now," the elder said. "We can't control what they do. But we can control what we do. We can remember who we are."

The boy nodded. Kept working.

They finished as the sun moved toward the western ridges.

One of the women looked toward the east. Toward the largest mining camp.

"We should go higher," she said. "See how many more have come."

The others agreed.

They climbed a ridge that overlooked the camp below.

What they saw made them stop.

The camp had grown.

Even since last month, when they'd hunted here, it had doubled. Maybe more.

Tents packed tight. Buildings going up. Smoke from hundreds of fires. The sound of hammering and shouting carried up the ridge even from this distance.

And the scars.

Hillsides torn apart. Trees gone. The earth itself wounded. Raw. Bleeding.

Sacred places destroyed.

Tȟatȟáŋka Wašté stood looking down at it. His face showed nothing. But his hands trembled.

The boy stood beside him. Looking. Trying to understand what it meant.

"Grandfather," he said quietly. "How many are there?"

"Too many to count."

"Will they stop?"

"No."

"Will they take everything?"

The elder didn't answer right away.

"Yes," he said finally. "They'll take everything they can. Until there's nothing left to take."

Silence.

The boy looked at his grandfather's face. Saw something there he'd never seen before.

Not anger. Not even sadness.

Just knowing.

The knowing that comes when you've lived long enough to see the pattern repeat. To see the promises break. To see the ending coming and know you can't stop it.

"What do we do?" the boy asked.

"We survive," the elder said. "We remember. We teach our children. And we wait."

"Wait for what?"

"For them to learn what we already know."

"What's that?"

"That the earth doesn't belong to anyone. That you can't own the wind or the water or the sacred places. That when you take everything, you lose everything."

The boy thought about that.

"Will they learn in time?"

The elder looked at him. Put his hand on the boy's shoulder.

"I don't know," he said. "But we'll still be here. Changed. Smaller maybe. Wounded. But still here. Still Lakota. Still remembering."

They saw him then.

* * *

The man with the wolf-dog.

Far below. Near the edge of the camp. Walking toward a stable.

The dog beside him. Large. Gray. Moving like a wolf but loyal like a dog.

They'd seen him before. Watched him over the weeks. He was different from the others.

Didn't rush. Didn't shout. Didn't seem consumed by the fever that drove the rest of them.

He worked. Cared for horses. The dog stayed close.

And sometimes at night, they'd seen him sitting by a fire. Writing something.

Writing what, they didn't know.

One of the younger men spoke. "Should we warn him? The others will come for him eventually. They turn on each other when the gold runs out."

"No," the elder said. "He's not our concern."

"He seems different."

The elder watched the stable door a moment longer. "Yes. He is different. He doesn't shout. He doesn't take more than he needs. He writes things down." He paused. "But he is here. His horses graze on our grass. His stable stands on our land. His gold, if he finds it, comes from our sacred hills." He turned away. "A gentle hand on a knife is still a knife."

"So it doesn't matter? Being different?"

The elder looked at his grandson. "It matters to him. It does not matter to the land."

They watched the man disappear into the stable.

"Come," the elder said. "We should go. We've been gone long enough."

They walked back through the hills as the sun set.

The deer meat divided among them. Heavy. Good.

It would feed families for a few days. Not long. But something.

The boy walked beside his grandfather. Quiet. Thinking about everything he'd seen.

Finally, he spoke.

"Grandfather. When you're gone… when all the elders are gone… will we remember? Will we know the old ways?"

Tȟatȟáŋka Wašté stopped walking. Looked at his grandson.

"That depends on you," he said. "On whether you listen. Whether you teach your children. Whether you remember that you are Lakota before you are anything else."

"But how can we live the old ways on the reservation? In the little houses they built? Eating their food? Going to their schools?"

"We can't," the elder said. "Not all of it. Too much has changed. Too much has been taken."

He put his hand on the boy's head.

"But we can remember the stories. Speak the language. Honor the sacred places even if we can't reach them. Teach our children who they are. Where they come from. What we believe."

He looked back toward the hills. The sacred hills. Paha Sapa.

"The land is in our blood," he said. "They can take the hills. But they can't take what we carry inside. They can't take memory. They can't take who we are."

The boy nodded.

Felt the weight of it. The responsibility.

He would remember. He would carry it.

Even when it was hard. Even when the others forgot. Even when the world tried to make him into something else.

He would remember.

* * *

They reached the edge of the reservation as darkness fell.

Fires burning in the small houses. Smoke rising. People waiting.

Families who'd sent them out, hoping they'd return with food.

Children who'd gone to sleep hungry.

The hunting party split up. Each family taking their share. The meat divided fairly.

It wasn't much. One deer among so many. But it was something.

Tomorrow there would be rations. Moldy flour. Spoiled beef. Not enough.

But tonight there would be fresh meat. Cooked the old way. Shared among family.

Tonight, they would remember what it felt like to be Lakota. To hunt. To share. To survive.

Tȟatȟáŋka Wašté sat by his fire with his grandson.

The boy's mother was cooking the meat. The smell filled the small house.

The boy leaned against his grandfather. Tired. Full of questions.

"Will we go hunting again?" he asked.

"If we can," the elder said. "If they don't catch us."

"And if they do?"

"Then we don't go again."

Silence.

The boy watched the fire. Thought about everything he'd seen today.

The scars on the land. The mining camp growing. The man with the wolf-dog writing something in the firelight.

"Grandfather," he said. "When I'm old like you. When I tell my grandchildren about these days. What should I tell them?"

The elder looked at him. Saw the child he was. Saw the man he would become. Saw the elder he might be one day if he lived that long.

"Tell them the truth," he said. "Tell them what was taken. What was lost. What we survived."

"Should I tell them we were angry?"

"Yes."

"Should I tell them we were sad?"

"Yes."

"Should I tell them we survived?"

"Yes. And tell them we remembered. Even when it would have been easier to forget. We remembered."

The boy nodded.

Leaned against his grandfather. Felt the warmth of the fire. Smelled the meat cooking.

Outside, the reservation was quiet. Small. Confining.

But inside this house, in this moment, they were still a family. Still Lakota. Still here.

The elder closed his eyes. Tired. Old. Carrying the weight of everything he'd seen. Everything he remembered.

Still here.

Still remembering.

The fire crackled. The meat cooked. The night settled in.

And in the sacred hills to the west, the spirits watched.

Angry. Sad.

But still there.

Still sacred.

Still Paha Sapa.

Historical Appendix

THE BLACKFEET NATION

Territory and People

The Blackfoot Confederacy historically consisted of four nations: the Siksika (Blackfoot), Kainai (Blood), Piikani (Peigan), and the Aamskáápipikani (South Peigan or Blackfeet). The Blackfoot people occupied vast territories across what is now Montana, Alberta, and Saskatchewan.

By the 1880s, the Blackfeet in Montana had been confined to a dramatically reduced reservation following decades of treaties, disease, and conflict.

Treaties and Broken Promises

Lame Bull's Treaty (1855): Signed at Fort Benton, this treaty established Blackfeet territory from the mountains to the Milk River and promised annual goods and protection. Like most treaties with Native peoples, its terms were systematically violated as white settlers, miners, and the U.S. government sought access to Native lands.

The pattern was consistent: treaties made, gold or resources discovered, treaties broken, land taken, Native peoples confined to smaller and smaller reservations.

The Marias Massacre (1870)

On January 23, 1870, U.S. Army troops under Colonel Eugene Baker attacked a peaceful Piegan Blackfeet camp on the Marias River. The soldiers were supposed to be targeting Mountain Chief's band, but instead attacked Heavy Runner's peaceful camp.

Heavy Runner emerged from his lodge, holding a safe-conduct paper issued by the U.S. government. He was shot dead while holding it.

The massacre resulted in approximately 173 deaths, mostly women, children, and elderly people suffering from smallpox. The village was burned. Survivors fled into the winter cold, many dying from exposure.

Colonel Baker faced no consequences. The massacre was initially celebrated in Montana newspapers as a victory.

Mountain Chief's son was among those killed, though he was in Heavy Runner's camp at the time. Mountain Chief himself was not present and survived.

The Starvation Winter (1883-84)

The winter of 1883-84 was catastrophic for the Blackfeet people. A combination of factors created conditions that led to widespread death:

- **Buffalo extermination:** By 1883, the buffalo herds that had sustained Plains peoples for millennia were gone, deliberately destroyed as U.S. policy to force Native peoples onto reservations and into dependence.
- **Ration cuts:** The U.S. government systematically reduced the rations promised in treaties, despite the Blackfeet having no other

food sources.

- **Corruption:** Indian agents often sold rations meant for Native peoples or provided spoiled, inadequate supplies.
- **Harsh winter:** The winter of 1883-84 was particularly severe.
- **Confinement:** Blackfeet people were not allowed to leave the reservation to hunt, even as they starved.

Estimates suggest that approximately 600 Blackfeet people, roughly one-quarter of the population, died that winter. Some accounts place the number higher.

The Starvation Winter was not a natural disaster. It was the direct result of U.S. policies designed to destroy Native ways of life and force assimilation.

Mountain Chief (Ninastoko)

Mountain Chief (c. 1848-1942) was a Blackfeet leader who lived through the entire period of dispossession and survival described in this novel. He witnessed the signing of treaties, the violation of those treaties, the Baker Massacre that killed his son, the buffalo's disappearance, the Starvation Winter, and decades of reservation life.

He lived to be approximately 94 years old and, in his later years, worked with anthropologists to preserve Blackfeet history and culture. He was one of the last living witnesses to the treaty period and the dramatic changes of the late 19th century.

His inclusion in this novel is meant to honor his role as a keeper of memory and truth.

THE LAKOTA AND THE BLACK HILLS

Paha Sapa: The Sacred Hills

The Black Hills (Paha Sapa in Lakota) are sacred to the Lakota, Cheyenne, and other Plains peoples. They are considered the center of the world, the birthplace of the Lakota nation, and home to spirits and sacred sites.

For thousands of years, these hills were used for ceremony, vision quests, healing, and sustenance.

The Fort Laramie Treaty (1868)

Following Red Cloud's War (1866-68), in which Lakota and Cheyenne forces successfully resisted U.S. expansion, the Fort Laramie Treaty of 1868 was signed. This treaty:

- Established the Great Sioux Reservation, including the Black Hills
- Guaranteed these lands to the Lakota "for as long as the rivers run and the grass grows."
- Specified that any changes to the treaty would require signatures from three-quarters of adult male Lakota

The treaty represented one of the few military victories by Native peoples that resulted in a favorable treaty. It would not last.

Gold and Betrayal

In 1874, Lieutenant Colonel George Armstrong Custer led an expedition into the Black Hills, ostensibly to find a location for a military fort. The expedition included miners and geologists. When gold was discovered, news spread rapidly.

Despite the treaty and despite the Black Hills being within reservation boundaries, prospectors flooded into the area. The U.S. government made token efforts to remove them but ultimately sided with the miners.

In 1876, the U.S. government demanded that the Lakota sell the Black Hills. When Lakota leaders refused, the government declared all Lakota off-reservation to be "hostile" and subject to military action. This led directly to the Great Sioux War of 1876-77, including the Battle of the Little Bighorn.

Despite their victory at the Little Bighorn in June 1876, the Lakota and Cheyenne were ultimately defeated by overwhelming U.S. military force and the systematic destruction of their food sources.

The Theft of the Black Hills (1877)

In 1877, the U.S. Congress passed an act seizing the Black Hills without the required three-quarters approval from Lakota leaders. This violated the Fort Laramie Treaty and effectively stole approximately 7.7 million acres of land.

The Black Hills Gold Rush continued through the 1880s and beyond. Towns like Deadwood sprang up. Sacred sites were destroyed. The land was scarred by mining.

By 1884 (when this novel's final chapter is set), the theft was complete. The Lakota people were confined to reservations. They could see their sacred hills being destroyed, but could not stop it.

Legal Recognition

In 1980, over a century after the theft, the U.S. Supreme Court ruled in *United States v. Sioux Nation of Indians* that the seizure of the Black Hills was illegal and violated the Fifth Amendment. The court awarded financial compensation.

The Lakota nations have refused the money (now over $1 billion with interest). They maintain that the Black Hills are not for sale. The fight for the return of the Black Hills continues today.

Lakota Leaders in the 1880s

By 1884, the era of armed resistance was largely over, though the memory was fresh:

Crazy Horse (Tȟašúŋke Witkó): Died September 5, 1877, at Fort Robinson. One of the most respected war leaders, he never signed a treaty and never chose to live on a reservation. He was bayoneted while in U.S. custody, allegedly while trying to escape.

Sitting Bull (Tȟatȟáŋka Íyotake): Returned from exile in Canada in 1881 and was living at Standing Rock Reservation during the period of this novel. He would be killed in 1890 during an attempt to arrest him.

Red Cloud (Maȟpíya Lúta): Living on Pine Ridge Reservation. Had signed treaties and taken a more accommodating stance toward the U.S. government, which made him controversial among his people but allowed him to maintain some political influence.

American Horse (Wašíčuŋ Tȟašúŋke): Oglala Lakota leader who survived the transition to reservation life and worked to help his people navigate the new reality.

Note: Chapter 40 departs from the rest of the novel by centering Lakota perspectives without Elias present. This was a deliberate choice to end Book One by honoring the Lakota people's experience and agency, rather than filtering everything through a white protagonist. However, I acknowledge the limitations and risks of writing from inside a culture and experience not my own. Lakota voices, telling their own stories in their own words, are essential and irreplaceable. This chapter is offered with respect and humility, knowing it is imperfect.

PATTERNS OF DISPOSSESSION

The Common Story

While this novel focuses on the Blackfeet and Lakota experiences, the pattern described was repeated across North America with hundreds of Native nations:

1. **Contact and initial coexistence** (often involving trade and mutual benefit)
2. **Treaties signed** (promising permanent territories and protection)
3. **Discovery of resources** (gold, timber, fertile land, water)
4. **Treaty violations** (settlers, miners, or the military entering treaty lands)
5. **Violence** (often justified as "self-defense" against Native "aggression")
6. **New treaties** (taking more land, shrinking territories)
7. **Forced removal** (to reservations, often on inferior land)
8. **Starvation and dependence** (destruction of traditional food sources)
9. **Cultural suppression** (boarding schools, language prohibition, religious persecution)
10. **Survival and resistance** (Native peoples maintaining identity and culture despite everything)

This pattern was not accidental. It was policy.

The Buffalo's Destruction

The systematic extermination of the buffalo was deliberate U.S. policy. General Philip Sheridan reportedly said, "Let them kill, skin, and sell until the buffalo is exterminated, as it is the only way to bring lasting peace and allow civilization to advance."

By destroying the buffalo, the U.S. government destroyed the economic and cultural foundation of Plains peoples, forcing them into dependence on government rations and making resistance impossible.

An estimated 30-60 million buffalo lived in North America before European contact. By 1890, fewer than 1,000 remained.

FORT SHAW

Fort Shaw was a real military fort in Montana, established in 1867 near present-day Great Falls. It served as a military post during the period of conflict with Native peoples and remained active through the 1880s.

The fort is historically significant for later becoming the Fort Shaw Indian Boarding School (1892-1910), part of the broader system of Indian boarding schools designed to "kill the Indian, save the man" through forced assimilation.

THE BLACK HILLS GOLD RUSH

The Black Hills Gold Rush began in earnest in 1876 following Custer's 1874 expedition. By 1884 (when this novel ends), the rush was in full swing:

- **Deadwood** was founded in 1876 and by 1884 was a booming mining town

- Thousands of miners flooded into the area
- Mining operations scarred the landscape
- Lakota people watched from reservations as their sacred lands were destroyed
- Violence was common as miners fought over claims
- The legal status was murky, the land had been taken in violation of the treaty, but the U.S. government supported the miners

The gold rush would continue for decades, fundamentally altering the landscape and cementing the theft of the Black Hills.

HISTORICAL ACCURACY IN FICTION

This novel takes liberties with certain details for narrative purposes:

Composite characters: While Mountain Chief was a real person, his specific dialogue and the scene in Chapter 19 are invented. The historical facts he discusses (the Lame Bull Treaty, the Marias Massacre, the Starvation Winter) are accurate, but the specific conversation is fictional.

Unnamed Lakota characters: The Lakota family in Chapter 40 is entirely fictional, though their experiences are based on documented historical realities of reservation life in the 1880s.

Timeline compression: Some events may be condensed or adjusted to improve narrative flow.

Language: Blackfeet and Lakota words are used throughout. While efforts were made to ensure accuracy, I acknowledge my limitations as an outsider to these languages and cultures.

Perspective: This novel is told primarily through the eyes of a white protagonist. This is a deliberate choice to avoid appropriating Native voices, but it means the story is inherently limited by that perspective. Native peoples' own stories, told in their own words, are essential and should be centered.

FURTHER READING

For readers interested in learning more about the historical events depicted in this novel, the following sources are recommended:

Blackfeet History:

- *The Piikani Blackfeet: A Culture Under Siege* by Hugh A. Dempsey
- *Blackfeet Heritage, 1907-1908* by George Bird Grinnell
- *The Blackfeet: Raiders on the Northwestern Plains* by John C. Ewers
- *Blackfeet* by Paula Flynn
- Contemporary Blackfeet voices and scholarship from the Blackfeet Nation

The Marias Massacre:

- *The Baker Massacre: Tragedy on the Marias, January 23, 1870* by Paul R. Wylie
- *Heavy Runner's Peace: A Massacre and Its Legacy* by Andrew R. Graybill
- Primary sources and accounts from the Montana Historical Society

Lakota History and the Black Hills:

- *Black Elk Speaks* by John G. Neihardt (Black Elk's first-person account)
- *Lakota Woman* by Mary Crow Dog
- *The Lakota Way* by Joseph M. Marshall III

- *In the Spirit of Crazy Horse* by Peter Matthiessen
- *The Black Hills: Last Hunting Ground of the Dakotah* by Watson Parker
- Contemporary Lakota voices and scholarship from Lakota nations

Broader Context:

- *Bury My Heart at Wounded Knee* by Dee Brown
- *An Indigenous Peoples' History of the United States* by Roxanne Dunbar-Ortiz
- *The Earth Is Weeping: The Epic Story of the Indian Wars for the American West* by Peter Cozzens
- *Empire of the Summer Moon* by S.C. Gwynne

Primary Sources:

- Annual Reports of the Commissioner of Indian Affairs (available through the National Archives)
- Treaty texts (Fort Laramie 1868, Lame Bull 1855, etc.)
- Congressional records regarding the 1877 seizure of the Black Hills
- Contemporary newspaper accounts (though these often reflect the biases of their time)

ON WITNESSING AND REMEMBERING

This novel's central theme is the importance of witnessing and remembering historical truth, particularly when that truth is uncomfortable or challenges dominant narratives.

Elias Harlan begins to understand that his role is not to be a savior or an ally in the modern sense, but simply to see clearly and record honestly what is happening. He cannot stop the dispossession he witnesses, but he can refuse to participate in the lies that justify it.

Similarly, the Lakota elder Tȟatȟáŋka Wašté teaches his grandson that memory itself is resistance. When governments and dominant cultures try to erase or rewrite history, the act of remembering and teaching becomes an act of survival.

Both characters understand, in their different ways, what Mountain Chief articulates: "Unless someone remembers. Unless someone tells the truth."

This is particularly relevant today, as debates continue about how American history should be taught and remembered. The events described in this novel, the broken treaties, the massacres, the starvation, the theft of land, are documented historical facts. They are not comfortable facts. They challenge narratives of American exceptionalism and westward expansion as inevitable progress.

But they are true.

And they matter.

The descendants of the people who experienced these events are still here. The Blackfeet Nation exists. The Lakota nations exist. The impacts of these historical traumas continue to reverberate in contemporary Native communities in the form of poverty, health disparities, cultural loss, and ongoing struggles for sovereignty and treaty rights.

Remembering is not about assigning guilt or shame to people alive today for actions taken by their ancestors. It is about understanding how the past shapes the present, acknowledging historical truth, and making informed choices about the future.

As Elias writes in his simple journal entries: facts, dates, and what actually happened. Not editorials. Not justifications. Just truth.

That is the work of witnessing.

That is the work this novel attempts to honor.

ACKNOWLEDGMENTS OF LIMITATION

I am a white author writing about Native American experiences and histories. While I have tried to approach this work with respect, research, and humility, I acknowledge that I am writing from outside these communities and cultures.

Native peoples' own stories, told in their own voices, are essential and irreplaceable. This novel is not and cannot be a substitute for those voices. It is one white character's journey toward understanding the historical realities of dispossession and his role as witness to those events.

I encourage readers to seek out books, films, art, and scholarship created by Native authors and artists, whose perspectives and stories are central to understanding these histories and their contemporary legacies.

Any errors in this novel, historical, cultural, or linguistic, are mine alone. I welcome correction and continued learning.

A NOTE ON NAMES

The Blackfeet (Siksikaitsitapi) names used in this novel:

- **Makóyi** (Wolf) - the war chief who captures Elias
- **Nitááhkii** (Lone Fighter or Lone Chief) - Makóyi's nephew
- **Ksisstaki** (Beaver Woman) - the girl who gives Elias the wolf carving and the pup

The Lakota names used in Chapter 40:

- **Tȟatȟáŋka Wašté** (Good Buffalo) - the elder
- **Tȟašúŋke Kokípapi** (His Horse Is Feared) - the grandson
- **Paha Sapa** (Black Hills) - the sacred hills

These names were chosen with care and research into Blackfeet and Lakota languages and naming traditions. Both peoples have rich traditions of meaningful names that often reference animals, natural phenomena, personal characteristics, or significant events. Names carry cultural and spiritual weight that cannot be fully captured by simple translation.

However, I acknowledge my limitations in using languages that are not my own. The Blackfeet language (Siksikaitsitapi) and the Lakota language are complex, sacred, and belong to their respective peoples. Their use here is meant as a sign of respect, not appropriation.

The Blackfeet characters in this novel are fictional, but they are meant to represent the real Blackfeet people who lived through the Starvation Winter and the broader dispossession of their lands. The Lakota family in Chapter 40 is similarly fictional, though their experiences are based on documented historical realities of reservation life in the 1880s. Their names honor the real people whose stories deserve to be remembered and told honestly.

IN CLOSING

This novel is dedicated to the proposition that remembering matters. That truth matters. That the voices of those who have been silenced or erased deserve to be heard and honored.

The story of the American West is not a simple tale of progress and expansion. It is a complex, often brutal story of conquest, resistance, survival, and ongoing struggle.

The people who lived through the events described in this novel were real. Their descendants are real. Their stories deserve to be told honestly.

This is my attempt, imperfect as it is, to contribute to that work of honest remembering.

William Mann 2026

www.ingramcontent.com/pod-product-compliance
Lightning Source LLC
Chambersburg PA
CBHW031117160726
47991CB00004B/1420

9 7 9 8 9 9 9 5 8 0 4 7 0 3